Jack Vance

Strange People,
Queer Notions

Jack Vance

Strange People, Queer Notions

John Hollbrok Vance

Spatterlight
P R E S S
340 S. Lemon Ave #1916
Walnut, CA 91789

www.jackvance.com

Jack Vance

Strange People,
Queer Notions

Chapter I

THE STAINED MARBLE GLITTERED like dirty glass and did nothing to make me feel any cooler. I rubbed a little sepia onto the page, stepped back to examine the effect and bumped into an elegantly dressed man making for the open bar at the side of the square.

"*Scusi*," I said automatically, but the man did not nod and continue on his way. He stood there for a moment and stared at me with a peculiar expression, then shook his head as if to erase an improbable thought from his mind. For a moment longer he peered at me intently, then said warmly, "American, are you? What part of the States are you from?"

"Oregon. How about you?"

"All over, dear fellow. Citizen of the world now, more or less. It's damned hot out here." He glanced at my sketches. "Why don't you pack up for a few minutes and have a drink with me?"

Rome in the summer can be hotter than Hades and I didn't need much convincing. "My passport says Clarence Musgrave. You're...?"

"Just call me Kex; all my friends do. There are painters on every corner around here," he said, examining my sketch, "but you're very good, you know."

"You might get an argument from the other fellows."

As we walked over to the bar, Kex ruminated a moment, then said, "I suppose you make a career of painting?"

"Not exactly."

"You're not going to follow it, eh?"

"I'll follow anything that brings me a square meal."

Kex said in a fatherly voice, "Let me give you some advice I've paid dear to get, Clarence —"

"Most people call me Chuck."

"— and that is: don't let a God-given gift waste away!"

There was to be no sale of sepia sketches. I said in a voice tinged with regret, "I don't want to waste away either. There's no money in painting; even less in sketching in sepia."

Kex laughed wryly, with an expression rather like a dog panting on a hot day. "Let me buy you a drink." He signaled the bartender, turned back to me. "It won't be news to you that the artist lives a hard life... In a manner of speaking, at one time —" he paused, then shook his head sadly. "Well, that's all in the past. A person like yourself, now, with talent — real talent — he can make a living on what he produces..."

Here I had to disagree. "I'm not that much of a fanatic. A few months from now I'm going home to Oregon, get me a job in the timber."

"But," cried Kex, "all this study, this training?"

"I trained to play football once. Then all of a sudden —" I snapped my fingers "— it's over. That was waste. This art is different. I'll daub around — my friends will think I know what I'm doing because I studied in Europe, which is hog-wash of course."

Kex laughed his dog-tongue laugh. I watched him out of the corner of my eye. He touched his neat white mustache. "You've got an odd philosophy. I wouldn't call it cynicism..."

"I call it existalism." If I wanted to sell Kex a picture, I had to sell him the romance that went with it.

He pushed up his brows. "Existentialism? You don't seem —"

"No, not existentialism; that's European and old-fashioned. I'm an American. Existalism is my own brand of realism. It simply means existing as long as possible, as well as possible."

Kex frowned thoughtfully. "Well, of course —"

"It doesn't seem too unique, does it?"

"Well, no."

"That's part of the philosophy. It's a terrible strain being unique. Doesn't leave any time for fun."

Kex drank a bit of wine. "But these unique people — I call them neurotics — don't you think they produce the great masterpieces of art?"

"I don't know. Maybe they'd turn out more masterpieces if they weren't neurotics. On the other hand, maybe that's what's wrong with my painting; I'm too normal."

"Nonsense," said Kex, recovering control of the conversation. "There's nothing wrong with your painting. I call it damned good stuff. In fact, I think I could arrange a commission for you on the strength of what I've seen." He paused, then went on meditatively. "I think it should pay fairly well."

I sat up straighter on the bar stool. "A commission?"

Kex watched me with placid eyes. "Yes. I think that's what you'd call it."

"How much and what doing?"

"Well —" he hesitated "— it's a commercial job."

"I'm not proud."

"You'd be hired by the day."

"How much?"

He hesitated. "Let's say — ten thousand lire plus expenses."

"That sounds interesting."

Kex smoothed his mustache. "What I want may seem rather odd to you."

"As long as it's not odd enough to get me in jail."

"Do you know Naples at all?"

"No, I've never been south of Rome."

"Then you wouldn't know Positano. It's on the coast below Naples — in fact between Sorrento and Amalfi, a lovely place. One of the beauty-spots of the world…Quite a little foreign colony living there — artists, writers, so forth."

I waited.

"I keep a flat in Positano, on a year-round basis. Very comfortable place; whenever I want to rest and relax, I drop down for a month or so." He took a quick sip of his wine. "Now here's the deal. You listen and tell me what you think of it. I do a bit of private publishing — a hobby of mine. Fine art, curiosa, advanced stuff a commercial business wouldn't dare to touch. I don't worry about profit and loss — don't have to. I publish what I like just so long as it's high-class stuff. You understand?" He fixed me with a clear and candid gaze.

"Naturally," I said.

"For some time now," said Kex, "I've wanted to put out a Positano portfolio. Black and white sketches: the old buildings, the beach, the boats, the church, the Moorish ruins, the local types, and so forth."

"Out of curiosity — why pick on me? I'm a man of talent, of course — but there are old-timers around town — Tambucchi — Ramus —"

Kex made a wise gesture. "To be utterly frank, an established artist would hold me up. I get by cheaper with one of the younger men."

I nodded doubtfully. It seemed strange, but not too strange. Peculiar but not grotesque.

Kex said confidently, "In a word, I want you to go down to Positano and make me a set of representative studies — charcoal would be best, I think. You can live in my flat and charge your groceries to my account at the store."

I suppose this is where the first small quiver occurred, the first slight jar. I said in a puzzled voice, "Let me get this straight. You want me to move into your flat at this Positano place. I make charcoal sketches, you pay me ten thousand lire a day and buy the groceries."

"Yes," said Kex. "That's about it."

"Hm…Suppose I turn out only one sketch a week?"

"I think you can do better than that."

"I think so myself…Suppose I'm there a month and get drunk and tear up everything I've done?"

Kex looked at me waggishly. "I know human nature, and I don't think you're that sort of chap."

"I'm not so sure."

"I guess we'll have to take each other on trust," said Kex.

"You can take me on trust if you like, but I'd like to see the color of your money."

"Reasonable enough." Patiently he pulled out a money-clip connected to the inside of his pocket by a golden chain. He counted out eleven long pink ten-thousand lire notes. "A ten-day advance plus expenses down. I'll expect you," he added severely, "to furnish your own materials."

"If it's a joke," I said, "it's a very good joke."

Kex looked at me reproachfully. "When will you start?"

"Anytime."

"Tomorrow morning then. I suppose you drive your own car?"

"I'm afraid not."

"Well, you can take the bus. Beastly, of course, but it gets you there."

"I'm not fastidious. If I was, I'd be home in Portland."

Kex toyed with his wine. "I'll be down in three or four days to see how you're coming along. Now —" he hesitated an instant "— here's what I want you to do. Don't work too hard the first day or so. Tramp around town, explore the cliffs, the beaches. Talk to people, but don't mention your work. If anyone asks, say you're a friend of mine, using my flat. Right?"

"If that's the way you want it."

"Another thing," said Kex, "for reasons of my own I have mail coming to the post office under the name of James Hilfstone. I might not get down to Positano for a week and it's important that I receive this mail. I'd like you to check into the post office every day and ask for any mail addressed to James Hilfstone."

I turned the idea over. "Well, I'll ask. But suppose they won't give it to me?"

Kex showed signs of impatience. "Just ask, that's all you can do. Tell them your name is James Hilfstone, if you like. They'll never know the difference. In fact, while you're at Positano, you might just use the name James Hilfstone; you'll simplify things a good deal." He gave me a quick look from the corner of his eye.

"It might be better if things weren't too simple."

"What do you mean?" asked Kex, rather sharply.

I looked at him in surprise. "Nothing at all."

He slowly relaxed. "It's a small matter, of course… Have another beer?"

"No, thanks. I've got a few errands; also, I've got to pack. Incidentally, how do I find your flat when I get to Positano?"

"It's the Casa Umberto." He reached into his breast pocket, pulled out a notebook, removed a folded scrap, scribbled 'Casa Umberto' on the back of it. "Ask anywhere; everybody knows me."

Rather abruptly he rose to his feet, held out his hand. "In three or four days I'll be down. Goodbye till then, and enjoy yourself."

I watched him leave, bouncing and buoyant, well pleased with himself. I looked back at the paper. 'Casa Umberto, Positano'. He wrote a decorative undisciplined hand, rather like Kex himself.

I unfolded the paper — a printed laundry form. On the half folded under was a list of names:

1. Munton
2. Blaine
3. Leibnitz
4. Oleg Vroznek
5. Piombino
6. Pamela, Hester
7. Margaret
8. Alma
9. Hortense
10. Dannister

It looked like Kex was throwing a party. There were five masculine names, five female names, and 'Dannister' who might be either.

CHAPTER II

THE ITALIAN TOURIST BUREAU maintains an information office in the Union Station. Glass windows protect six arrogant young clerks from the vulgar public. The clerks resent answering questions. "Why do they go if they don't know how to get there?" they ask each other with expressive gestures. And, "Have you ever heard the like? This old woman wants a rapid express to Bari at five in the morning." They laugh together. "Put her aboard the local; she's in no hurry...Rafaello, a man at your window!" "Let him wait; just another foolishness; I'm sick of it all. He'll get tired and leave, and it's time for my cigarette."

A pretty girl gets more attention; they flock and flutter and go to painstaking detail, while I wait in growing fury at a forgotten mouth-hole. At last I try the door; by a ridiculous oversight, it happens to be open. I stick my head in. "Anybody here working; or is it your lunch hour?"

They all look at me, contemptuous and angry; I have no right to bother them. One steps over to shut the door. I don't move. He pushes at the door with insistent pressure, glaring at me waspishly. I don't move. "What train do I take to Positano, below Naples?"

He says, "This door must be closed; ask your questions, please, at the window."

"Which window?"

He points.

"I've been waiting there ten minutes."

He says, "There is no train to Positano," as if this will solve the entire situation and I will go away. They are thinking, "Boorish American; how like them all!"

I ask, "How do I get to Positano, then?"

Rafaello, ineffably weary, rises from a far desk, stubs out his cigarette, motions me to the window, goes to stand at his post.

By this time two nuns are waiting. With poorly disguised pleasure, the corners of their mouths twitching, the five others watch while Rafaello, speaking in Italian, solves their interminable problems, and I stand fuming.

I decide I can't beat them; they are too secure inside their glass fort, the door to which has been ostentatiously locked.

Finally the nuns go off toward the queue at the first-class window. I say with careful calmness, "I want to go to Positano, near Sorrento. How do I get there?" But the look I burn into his eyes says, "I'd like to punch you in the nose."

He looks back as if to say, "I detest the sight of you; come at me if you dare." Aloud he is punctilious. "There is no train service direct to Sorrento."

"Then how do I get there?"

He sees he is in for it, shrugs, pulls out his indexes, timetables, references. His five colleagues observe that he has been trapped; they drift over to commiserate and puff their vanity at Rafaello's expense. I hear six conflicting opinions, which at long last are reconciled. I am to entrain for Naples, change to an inter-urban electric car for Sorrento, change again at Sorrento to the Positano bus.

I am lucky enough to catch a train which leaves almost immediately. On the way down I consider my job. One moment it seems legitimate enough; the next, I think there's something fishy going on. I had made one or two inquiries about Kex the night before. Maglione, the doorman at the Jikky gives Kex a good reputation. "A very liberal American gentleman." Leonardo, barman at the Artists and Models Club, hints that Kex is heterosexual — meaning afflicted with many sexes. This is just a hint, however, and Leonardo is large with his hints. Bill Perch, of the *Daily American* is more explicit. "Kex? Gay as a big red barrel-organ."

So far as I could calculate, Kex's private vices did not rub off on his money. The first supposition, that Kex had worked up a mad passion for my body, I discarded. The approach was too impractical. It was not impossible that Kex wanted exactly what he was paying for... It would be foolish to neglect the obvious.

I arrived at Naples, fought off a dozen porters trying to grab my baggage, stared down a number of sharpshooters in tight black suits who looked as if they wanted to pick my pocket, found my way to the electric inter-urban station, fought off more porters, pimps, beggars, guides to Pompeii, took a third-class ticket to Sorrento.

The train started off, threaded the back-streets, circled the bay, with Vesuvius looming to the left. At Castellamare the train took to tunnels, darting in and out of brief sunlit spaces, rattling for the most part through the dark. Half an hour later we came to the end of the line at Sorrento, with the sun just setting into the bay.

At an *espresso* bar I drank a thimbleful of bitter Italian coffee and almost missed the Amalfi bus. Climbing aboard at the last minute, I dropped into a seat which everyone else had rejected, beside a fat old woman with a black coat and mustache to match. She sniffed and grumbled and hitched herself to the window. I rested a buttock on eight inches of what remained and looked out at the scenery. We rode up the hill between dank stone walls, with orange trees angling over like beach-umbrellas. Here on the north slope it was already night, and the passengers spoke in night-time voices. Then we nosed out over the ridge. The sky broke out like an explosion, all the scenery in the world lay below: a hundred miles of Mediterranean, with mountains waist-deep in water dwindling in ranks down the south. The road became a precarious ledge halfway up a cliff, and the bus kited around turns with no decent regard for gravity. I sat holding to the guard-rail; the other passengers were fatalists. The fat woman relaxed and squashed over an additional four inches.

Gradually I loosened my hold and began to listen to the conversation of the people behind me: a spindle-shanked man in a roan suit, and a used-looking blonde. The man was American; he was analyzing the love-life of his acquaintances in a knowing voice. I listened with rather more than half an ear; it was hard to do otherwise. He mentioned a woman called Hortense. "Nothing wrong with her," he said bluffly. "Nympho is a word without meaning. She's just what I'd call a completely normal unmarried woman."

Hortense. I pricked up my ears. A rather odd name; it was down on Kex's list. I turned my head so I could hear even better.

The blonde made a sour remark which failed to carry over the grind of the motor.

"What of it?" argued the man. "Every damn one of 'em wants to marry her and she just won't have any."

Murmurs from the woman.

"Sure," said the man, "that's why we get along so good. I don't give a damn, she don't give a damn. I appreciate a woman like that: sleep with her one night, kick her in the rump the next, and she takes it all as it comes."

"Ha!" laughed the woman scornfully. She shifted in her seat, raised her voice. "You wouldn't kick Hortense and get away with it. She's got a terrible temper; I know."

The man said with a kind of meek complacence, "I got some scabs."

They fell silent. The bus rolled on, blowing its horn at every bend.

An irritating sound: *sneep — sneep... sneep — sneep*. Night darkened mountains and sea. The fat woman beside me had started to doze and was spreading inexorably across the seat like a glacier. I feared that the seams of her black dress might burst, and then there would be a horrible catastrophe, with fat woman flowing out over the edge of the seat, down the aisle, interfering with the driver. But somehow the dress held. Precarious — but it held. She started to snore softly.

Twenty minutes passed. Headlights picked up a figure on the road ahead. The bus stopped, the door opened, a slender dark-blonde girl climbed aboard, crowded into a spot on the rear bench between a pair of laborers. The bus conductor came back to collect her fare; they spoke together in Italian.

The conversation on the seat behind me started up again, but the man had lowered his voice. They were talking about the blonde girl, and now I wanted to hear, as she had rather an appealing look to her. I caught a word or two over the grind of the bus: "— money — peace and quiet — dangerous damn business —" The conversation dwindled, died. The bus squeezed around hairpin corners, bugling with hypnotic persistence. *Sneep — sneep... Sneep — sneep — sneep*.

A spatter of lights showed on the mountainside far ahead. The bus cut in a deep ravine and the lights vanished. The full moon rose and threw a lover's trail across the water; the fat woman had sagged until she was wider than she was high. She gave a sudden snort, constricted herself upright. She shot me a beady glance, knotted her fingers securely through the strings of her purse.

We rounded another bluff, and Positano lay before us: an enormous rocky amphitheater full of dark air and moonlight, crusted with dim white houses, spangled with lights. Maybe Kex was right, maybe Positano deserved to be made known to the world. However, I told myself, you couldn't paint this or sketch it, any more than you could paint a good sunset. Beauty of space and light is different from beauty of mingled pigments; each is foreign to the other. But thinking of the ten thousand lire a day I decided it was worth a try. I'd start with small bits and pieces, and build on up.

The bus halted beside a small wine shop; we seemed a long way out of town; it was evidently a way-station. Two or three passengers got out, among them the blonde girl. She walked around the outside of the bus, glanced up through the window into my face. She stopped in her tracks, staring.

The bus started ahead. The girl stood in the roadway, looking after the tail-light. It was almost as if she were stricken — astounded. I had another of the uneasy intimations that things were not altogether as they seemed.

CHAPTER III

BACK AND FORTH DOWN the hillside went the bus, past black walls and houses, olive trees and unexpected gulfs, horn bleating, brakes groaning, to stop at last in a small piazza at the bottom of the grade.

I dislodged my suitcase from the overhead rack, climbed out the front door, followed by the lanky man in the russet suit and his female friend. He appeared to notice me for the first time, and paused to make an interested inspection. The woman tugged petulantly at his arm — a bleached and pouchy creature in her late thirties; for charity's sake call her an ex-chorus girl.

He disengaged his arm. "Howdy; didn't notice you on the bus." He held out his hand, a lank parcel of bones wrapped in sallow skin. "My name's Buster Blaine. You look to be American, from that shirt."

Blaine. Blaine? Another name from Kex's list; number two if I remembered correctly. We shook hands. "My name's Chuck Musgrave."

He looked me over with curiosity even more open than my own. The light from the post office window illuminated his eyes — they were an extraordinary clear hazel, large, impersonal, mild — a faun's eyes. "Figuring to stay in Positano a while, Chuck?"

"I guess so. Two or three weeks, maybe."

"You'll like it here; we've got a friendly kind of crowd around, now that tourist season's over. Margaret, meet Chuck. Chuck, Margaret. Countess Margaret d'Egliari, to be technical."

I said, "How do you do," without surprise. I have toyed with the idea of becoming a noble myself: Count Clarence di Musgrave.

She nodded rather distantly, "How do you do." It occurred to me that Margaret was another name on the list. List of what? Probably nothing important.

Blaine asked, "Where you staying, Chuck?"

I looked up the hillside. "Casa Umberto, if I can find it. The flat belongs to a friend."

"Casa Umberto?" Blaine ruminated. "Who's the friend? I probably know him."

"His name is Kex."

"Well, well." The russet eyebrows rose, the big hazel eyes studied my face. "Friend of Kex, eh?" And Margaret looked at me with new calculation.

"Something wrong?"

"No, no," said Blaine. "Good heavens no. Here in Positano," he said in a large voice, "we mind our own business…Make a virtue of it."

Margaret giggled unpleasantly. "Yeah? Who?"

Blaine reconsidered. "I guess I said something foolish."

"You sure did, Brother Blaine."

"Well, we just don't care," said Blaine. "That's more like it. We all got our own conduct to worry about."

Margaret took his arm. "Come on, come on. I'm dying for a drink."

"Just a minute, honey. Let me show Chuck where to go. I take it you've never been here before, hey Chuck?"

"That's right."

"Known Kex a long time?"

"Only a couple days."

"Quite a guy, Kex." He shook his head in rueful amusement. "Er, what's cooking? Anything special?"

"Cooking?"

Blaine winked knowingly. Even Countess Margaret d'Egliari was attentive. "Kex has probably put you wise."

"I don't get it."

Blaine shoved his lank hands into the pockets of his roan trousers, squinted in mild puzzlement. "Hm," said Blaine starting all over again. "Old Kex, bless him, put it this way. He's got the damnedest faculty for stirring up devilment, more than any man I've ever seen, and by God, that's going far."

"Well," I said carefully, "you know Kex a lot better than I do."

"I get along good with Kex," said Blaine hurriedly. "But that's not to say he hasn't his little peculiarities. Don't we all, hey Marge? I tell him to his face he's a god-damned liar, a bamboozler, and not to count me in on any of his deals. It tickles him; we get along fine as wine; but he never stops trying."

I wanted to hear more about Kex. "Does he —"

Countess Margaret said crossly, "Damn it, Buster, are you going to keep me here in the cold all night?"

"Hold on just a sec," said Blaine hastily. "I got to show Chuck where Kex lives; it's right up here, Chuck. See that second streetlight? Right opposite is a little store. That's Signora Umberto and she'll have your key."

"Thanks a lot."

"Don't mention it; glad to help. Be seeing you." He and Countess Margaret started down an alley toward the beach; I picked up my bags, climbed the hill: a steep pull.

The shop was a little hole in the wall, full of big cabbages, lettuce, oranges, apples, onions, jars of olives and anchovies, tubs of millet, corn, rice, beans, shelves with dark glossy bottles of wine, racks of spaghetti, macaroni, agnelotti, vermicelli, gnocchi, lasagne, etc. Behind the counter stood a round-faced young man with hair like black excelsior. His mouth widened into a glistening automatic smile as I stepped through the door. I asked him if he spoke English.

"Un po', un po'."

"I want the key to Kex's flat. I'm moving in."

He called over his shoulder; a hard-faced little woman with skinned-back white hair pushed through a limp curtain.

"Signora Umberto?"

"Yes, that's me. What you like?"

"Kex told me to see you for the key to his flat."

"Oh." She looked me up and down with a curl to her lip. "You friend of Kex, eh?"

"Yes," I said patiently.

"He give you note? Letter?" She held out her hand.

"No. He said to see you, that you'd let me in. He'll be here in three or four days."

"Hmph." She flashed me another sharp look. "I guess it's all right." She reached under the counter, brought forth two keys — one the size of a monkey-wrench, the other normal. "Come on."

We crossed the street. She went to a door in the wall, inserted the normal key in a new brass lock, swung the door open, reached inside, touched a switch. Glow filled an arched white tunnel of a staircase.

Signora Umberto went first, hopping down like an old cat with sore feet. We came out on a terrace. To the right was a pale plaster wall, a row of pale green century plants in pottery crocks. To the left was moonlit space and the roofs of Positano: cubes and planes and shapes in a thousand tones of black and gray and silver, with here and there a wan yellow light.

Signora Umberto was working her monkey-wrench key at the door, muttering under her breath. The door opened; she entered, turned on a light. I followed her inside, looked around. Whatever I had expected, this was a surprise. The room was full of the richest color, the most languid comfort. The floor was coarse terrazzo, jade-green marble flakes in a pale green matrix, spread with a gold and rose oriental rug. The walls were pale green, the domed ceiling was white plaster. Two low divans, upholstered in green satin, flanked a black brick fireplace. Three large abstract oils, companion-pieces, in the same shades of black, white, yellow, and rose hung on the walls. Below were low cases full of expensive-looking books. Niches at each side of the fireplace held a huge gilt candelabra with thick green candles. Light came from floor-lamps turned against the ceiling.

Signora Umberto glanced sidewise as if daring me not to show enthusiasm, and ready to scorn me if I did. Signora Umberto disapproved of me. I put on the most supercilious expression I could find, set down my suitcase, pushed open a door. Bedroom. I walked through, opened another door. Bathroom in green tile, with two or three fancy European appliances. I returned to the living room.

Signora Umberto stood where I had left her, trying to press her arms into her sides, trying not to breathe the air.

A dining room with a dark carved table and tall-backed chairs overlooked the terrace. Beyond was an anticlimax of a kitchen, like all Italian kitchens, occupying an area of four square feet. The sink was a hole that might have held a gallon of water, the stove was a three-burner framework hitched up to a tube of gas.

Signora Umberto was looking in after me. "You want a cook? Good maid, do the work?"

"How much?"

"Three thousand lire a week; you feed her, you understand. She's a good girl."

"Too much, too much! I pay her two thousand."

"All right," said Signora Umberto carelessly, by which I knew that a thousand was the going rate. "She's good girl. She come tomorrow morning, cook your breakfast. She's my daughter. I get you groceries from the shop."

"Everything goes on Kex's bill," I said.

She gave me a spiteful glance. "You no pay?"

"No. I no pay."

"Humph." She flounced out of the room; I was alone in the apartment. I carried my suitcase into the bedroom, came back out, sat on one of the green satin divans. The room was chilly. Under the odor of incense and fabric, it smelled of damp plaster. I lit a cigarette, pulled out Kex's laundry list, studied the names on the back.

1. Munton
2. Blaine
3. Leibnitz
4. Oleg Vroznek
5. Piombino
6. Pamela, Hester
7. Margaret
8. Alma
9. Hortense
10. Dannister

Blaine, No. 2; Margaret, No. 7. For the idlest motives in the world I put a pencil check after each of these. Who would I meet next? It was like an elimination game. Positano was more interesting than I had expected. I wondered which, if any, of these names belonged to the blonde girl. Alma? Unlikely; Almas are all brunettes. Hortense?

The girl looked too shy and young to be a well-known nympho. Of course — one never knows. I put the list away, watched the smoke curl up into the air. I was tired after traveling — a pleasant kind of fatigue; I felt no inclination to rest. I looked at my watch; quarter to eight. It would be wise to saunter down to the beach.

I put out the cigarette, washed in cold water, decided I was hungry. The solution to this predicament lay in a visit to Signora Umberto's shop.

CHAPTER IV

I CLIMBED THE ARCHED white staircase. It stirred an association I could not lay my mind to. White soft plaster, rounded over on top, glowing in the reflected light. A story? A poem? *The Chambered Nautilus*? *A Cask of Amontillado*? ... I gave it up.

I crossed the street, entered the store. The round-faced young man with steel-wool hair made with the teeth.

"Bread," I said. "*Pane.*"

"Bread." He pulled a crusty loaf from a bin.

"Butter." He reached up on a shelf, gave me a round roll.

"Cheese...This." I tapped against a glass pane of the delicatessen department.

"*Questo?*"

"No, *questo*. Here. This stuff."

A tall brisk woman in a brown tweed coat came into the shop. She wore round rimless glasses on a long freckled nose. Smooth sand-colored hair parted in the middle, was roped into a bun. No nonsense, said her expression.

"A can of sardines." I pointed. "*Questo.*"

The woman looked at me sideways, her eyes lit up, her glasses gleamed. "Why, you're American, aren't you?"

"And you're English."

She bridled in coy astonishment. "Can you tell so easily? Usually I'm taken for American, German, Swiss, Swedish — anything but English."

"Until you speak."

"Yes, it's my voice that gives me away. You're new here, aren't you?" She looked at my groceries. "Are you staying in Positano?"

"Yes, I suppose so. For a few weeks."

"Wonderful!" She put real enthusiasm into her voice; then, looking back to my groceries, made a swift swoop, picked up the itemized bill the round-faced young man had made out. "I'll warn you, you've got to watch these shopkeepers, they'll take you to your last farthing if you don't check them up." She read. "Humph — just look. '*Pane* — sixty-five.' Never more than fifty. '*Burro* — a hundred and ten.' That's ninety-lire butter. '*Formaggio.*' " She put the cheese on the scale. "Not quite a hundred grams — you see, he's under-weighted you, and over-charged you at the same time."

The round-faced clerk's grin trembled a bit.

"They're the most crooked characters in the world. 'Sardines'. Well that's right — because the price is written on them. Luigi," she held out her hand, "pencil."

Luigi gave her a yellow stub. She crossed out numbers briskly, wrote in new ones, added to a second sum. "There — just on that little bit, he'd done you for over fifty lire." She shook her finger at Luigi, whose smile had gone glassy. "You're a bad boy, Luigi!"

"Thanks very much," I said.

She shook her head complacently. "It's nothing. I get so angry over this petty cheating; I'd like to shake someone till his teeth rattled." And she turned her spectacles at Luigi, who shuffled his feet.

"Er, you live here yourself?"

"Oh yes. My sister and I come every year."

I knew one thing for certain: this wasn't Hortense. Pamela? Hester?

"It's cheap and we're known," she went on. "Regular old Positanesi by now... Of course, it does get a little stale year after year. We'd so enjoy visiting the States, but regulations, you know, make it out of the question." She took an impulsive little step toward the door. "Why don't you come up and have a glass of wine with us? My sister doesn't get out much and always likes to know what's going on."

"Why, yes," I said. "Sure."

"Just half a sec, while I buy eggs for breakfast... *Sei uova*," she said to Luigi very distinctly. "I don't trade here much," she told me over her shoulder, "because Luigi and the Signora are such crooks."

I saw the gray curtain quiver where Signora Umberto stood listening.

"Of course it's handy to our flat…My name is Pamela Ryen, incidentally. R-Y-E-N — *not* Irish."

Ah-ha, I thought. Number seven? Or number eight? I'd check her off at the earliest opportunity. I introduced myself; we went amicably up the hill. I found it hard to say much; Pamela flowed like a freshet. I learned that the British travel restrictions were a terrible trial, that Positano was the friendliest place in Italy "— everybody speaks English here, it's almost like home," that Americans were much more interesting than Englishmen "— they're so much easier to know, much less stiff, really."

The sister Hester was sluggish and pasty, like a sick lizard, with blank eyes and stringy brown hair. "Hester's an artist," declared Pamela, "she does the nicest water-colors; you must see them."

Hester had the grace to say, "Some other time, Pam; you're much too enthusiastic, and I think that Mr. Musgrave wants his wine."

Pamela gave a lady-like little bleat and hurried off to the kitchen. Their flat was dingy and dreary, with chalky blue color-wash powdering off the walls.

Pamela pushed her head in from the kitchen. "Perhaps you'd like tea, Mr. Musgrave?"

"If it's no trouble, I'll have tea, and I'll eat my bread and cheese at the same time."

So we drank tea from green and white pottery, and I ate bread and cheese. Hester sat placidly; Pamela chattered and gossiped; propounded, challenged, exposed; argued, defied, explained.

I learned that they traveled mostly for Hester's health; Hester found England depressing. Pamela liked Spain; Hester liked Italy, "— but we both like Positano. It's completely relaxing; not a breath of the outer world ever bothers us here — until summertime, when, of course, it positively seethes with trippers, and then like anywhere else it's insufferable. The beach — a mass of baking flesh."

"Revolting," murmured Hester.

"And what do you do, Mr. Musgrave?" asked Pamela. "Everybody in Positano does something or other; I think it's marvelous the talent we've concentrated here. I write myself, and, as you know, Hester paints. Positano actually is quite an artistic center — although I must say —" Pamela paused thoughtfully. Hester, reading her mind, nodded vigorously. "In any event," Pamela went on, "Mrs. Revost does wonderful work with ceramics, and Paul Prie and Franz Leibnitz are really world-famous painters."

Leibnitz; number three on the list. But no Paul Prie. I mentioned that I had already met Buster Blaine and a Countess Margaret d'Egliari. What did they do?

Hester sniffed; Pamela remarked carelessly, "I really couldn't say about Countess d'Egliari; I know very little to her credit and only rumors to her discredit. And Buster Blaine — well, he's a writer. Detective-fiction I think — you know, those stories of hard-boiled American policemen and third-degrees and things of that sort." She sat briskly up in her seat. "Hester, do you feel up to it? Suppose we take Mr. Musgrave down to the beach and perhaps we'll see some of our friends? Oleg is always around. Oleg," she said to me, "is one of our nicest Positanesi, and he's really got a wonderful brain, a true intellectual. He's Polish, I think; a refugee from the Communists, but he refuses to be drawn about it. Well, Hester, what do you think? Shall we go?"

Hester heaved herself to her feet; Pamela flung herself into her tweed coat, and without further ceremony we set off downhill.

In front of Kex's door, I said, "Just a shake while I drop my groceries, and I'll be right with you." When I rejoined Pamela and Hester, they were muttering with their heads together; they turned, watched me cross the street. "All set."

Hester looked straight ahead; Pamela's voice was a trifle distant. "Is this where you live, Mr. Musgrave?"

"Temporarily. It's not my flat; it belongs to a friend of mine, he's letting me use it. Kex — do you know him?"

"By sight," said Pamela. "By sight only." Hester said nothing. Pamela took a deep sigh, and rather lamely began to talk. "Naturally, there are many people here we don't know —"

"Nor want to know," inserted Hester.

"— and in a place like this where there's nothing else to do but shred each other's reputation —"

"Or give good cause."

"— anyway," Pamela concluded, "I suppose that it's really up to none of us to judge."

"Let he who is without sin," I said, "cast the first stone."

"Well, yes, I suppose so," said Pamela. She paused doubtfully. "We do hear some strange talk, of course. I understand," and she fastened her brilliant eyeglasses upon me, "that the apartment is modelled after the former King of Egypt's bedroom suite."

"What's the former King of Egypt's bedroom suite like?"

Both Hester and Pamela acknowledged that they had no exact conception. "But isn't it — well, super-luxurious? You know, almost Hollywood?"

"Kex likes to be comfortable," I admitted. "But there's no portable Turkish bath or automatic finger-nail files."

"Well, well," said Pamela thoughtfully. She shot me one of her glittering side-glances. "I must say you don't seem the kind of man to really *relish* that sybaritical nonsense."

I couldn't decide on the spur of the moment whether that was good or bad, and let the matter slide. We were walking down the little passage which Blaine and the Countess had taken. Presently we came to a church with an imposing facade, and a square. Up from all sides led steps.

"The steps of Positano," said Pamela in a reverent voice. "There's a quaint little folk-song, *The Little Steps*, and I believe it's known everywhere in the world." She began to hum. "Dum-de-dum-de-da-da-dum — almost a tarantella. Do you like folk-songs, Mr. Musgrave?"

"No. I'm not much of an addict. I don't object particularly, unless they're too cute, then I rebel."

"I think we learn a great deal of history through folk-songs," said Hester. "They teach us about the way people *felt*."

"*Funiculi Funicula*," cried Pamela, "you know that one, of course. It was first sung in Naples when a little funicular railway was opened, right there on the Via Roma, so quaint. You've been in Naples, Mr. Musgrave?"

"Just passed through."

"And you didn't care for it?"

"It's a depressing kind of place," I said mildly. "If you don't keep one hand on your wallet, and the other on your — well, whatever it is — they've got 'em both."

"They're very poor, of course," said Pamela defensively.

"Yes, I could see that. I think they wanted me to leave in the same state."

We traversed a covered way lined with shops and came out on the esplanade. Ahead was surf, to either side rose massive mountains with the lights of town reaching only a third of the way to the dark ridges.

"Over here," said Pamela, "the Vistamare; it's where everybody goes. It's quite gay Saturday nights; they have music and dancing and really quite a time. We don't come down very often." Regret came into her voice.

"We can't afford it," said Hester firmly.

"When I publish my novel we'll come down every night," said Pamela brightly. "Until then, dear, we'll be satisfied with crumbs. And I think we're every whit as happy. You know very well that anything but the very best champagne makes you ill."

"Yes, that's quite true. Of course, since dear daddy died we haven't seen much good wine."

"No, England isn't what it used to be. But we'll be great again; mark my words, when the world sees the need for good English common sense...But then Mr. Musgrave is American, and we mustn't talk politics..."

We climbed a flight of steps, passed under an arch and through a glass door into the Vistamare Hotel and Ristorante.

CHAPTER V

THE BAR WAS TO THE LEFT; tables filled the area to the right. A fire burnt in a big fireplace, arched like an old-fashioned baker's oven. A wide door led into another room, rather less well-appointed, for overflow and local trade. By one side of the fire two men and two women played a tense and unfriendly game of bridge; at the other an elegant arrogant party of five lounged and chattered in Italian. Buster Blaine sat at the bar, his long shanks angled over a stool. Beside him, but not quite with him — the difference of a subtle inch or two — sat Countess Margaret, and a sullen dark woman with big golden bangles on her ears, both in the same attitudes, heads down, elbows on the bar, leaning forward, almost huddled.

Pamela marched to a table, briskly shuffled chairs; we all sat down. Blaine waved a negligent hand; Countess Margaret turned a fishy eye over her shoulder; the dark woman scowled; the bridge game ignored us; the five aristocrats turned us brief haughty glances, like spoiled cats.

"— *vino rosso* is fairly good," Pamela was saying, "Gragnano, they call it. Of course Lachrima Christi is the most famous local wine; but the Sorrentini is very good, don't you think, Hester? And of course the Valtepucello…"

"I think I'll have the pink tonight, something light for the upset tummy."

"Of course… Arturo," she beckoned a young waiter in a white coat, "two *vin rosé* here."

"Make it three." I looked around the room again. Through the arch five or six young Italians played some kind of vehement game, snapping down cards as if they were killing snakes.

Pamela held out her hands toward the fireplace. "I do so love a really cooking blaze; it's absolutely necessary here in Italy."

"Not a really good climate," Hester agreed.

"In the northern countries houses are built to be warm, and there's always heating; here in so-called sunny Italy the cold blows down and chills a person to the marrow, and there's never anything but those silly little charcoal pans."

"I don't think they're healthy myself," said Hester, "they give off a gas."

Arturo brought the wine. Pamela leaned forward, said in a low voice, "That dark pale man — at the bridge table — that's Oleg Vroznek, really a wonderful mind; it's honestly refreshing to talk with him."

Check No. 4 on the list. Oleg Vroznek was slight, with owlish eyes, a heavy forehead, wax-paper skin, sparse black hair. He wore a shapeless black suit, a pale green shirt, a rusty brown tie, and so could hardly avoid looking grubby.

"He's a Pole," whispered Pamela. "The things he can tell you about the Communists; they're completely sickening!"

"What does he do for a living?"

Pamela shook her head thoughtfully; firelight danced on her spectacles. "I think he's writing a novel based on his experiences. And perhaps he has a small income; some of the refugees were lucky enough to have bank accounts abroad, or jewels, or one or two really good paintings... Incidentally —" she paused uncertainly, then gathered words "— incidentally, don't mention your friend Kex; I think that the two are a little on the outs."

"What happened?"

Pamela looked at Hester, who primly sipped her wine. "Well, I can't say quite for sure. We hear a rumor or two through our landlady. The local Italians know everything that goes on, you can't turn around without word reaching everyone in Positano."

"The grapevine," said Hester. "I think that's the American slang."

I gave up. "Who are the others?"

"That little red-headed man is one of our painters, Leibnitz. Doesn't look much like a painter, does he?"

"No. More like an ex-jockey, or a vaudeville comedian."

"The woman to the right is Mercedes something-or-other; one never knows women's last names." Mercedes was a nervous little black chicken of a woman, close to middle-age.

"The other is Mrs. Revost, who manages a marvelous little shop up the lane. Ceramics and enamel-ware that she does herself, believe it or not. During the tourist season she has a very good thing of it." Both Pamela and Hester looked wistful.

Hester said in a brave voice, "She wants me to let her have a few water-colors to put out."

"I wish I were talented," said Pamela. "Really clever…"

Mrs. Revost was about thirty-five, tall, shapely, if rather gaunt. She had a breathless hollow-cheeked face, moved her hands in nervous jerks.

At the other table one of the expensive-looking women rose to her feet. There was a bout of hand-kissing and punctilio; she waved a languid hand and departed.

"And who are those people?"

Pamela turned the table a cool glance. "We don't see much of them; they're the Count and Countess Paladini, and the Marquis Fidoglio. They own a hotel at Praiano, I think. Rather loud people really — showy, like all these Italians."

Blaine stepped down from the stool and crossed the floor, all knees and elbows. "Hi," he said. "Mind if I sit down a minute?"

"Help yourself." At the bar Countess Margaret and the sullen dark-haired woman were crouched even lower. Blaine followed my eye. "They're getting drunk and they're getting mean. There'll be a riot when they start out of here. The Countess has the foolish notion I'm free and easy about paying her liquor bill and she's been ordering French cognac: Hennessy, mind you."

"T'st-t'st," said Pamela.

"Alma's got better sense. She's drinking the local rot-gut. I've given Giovanni strict orders to put my drinks on my bill and give them their own checks; there'll be a howl you can hear halfway up the mountain."

Alma: another name off the list — a rather handsome woman with a low sharp head, short tangled black hair. She wore a rumpled green slack suit, and was pouring liquor into herself the way a motorist out of gas in Death Valley pours in his emergency five gallons.

Blaine said, "Well, Chuck, I see you've made a couple friends," and added mournfully, "I wish I was young again."

"You're as young as you feel," said Pamela.

"I'm quite a colt by that score," said Blaine, "until I start fighting hangovers." He grumbled, "I wish I had brains enough to lay off this Italian cognac."

"How is your writing coming along?" asked Pamela, as one crafts-man to another. "I haven't put my hand to paper since Friday morning, dreadfully lazy."

There were ten minutes of shop-talk; Hester and I sat back. Pamela confessed that she could never get the dialogue right; it always sounded so stagy.

Blaine told her she didn't get drunk often enough; whenever he himself was really rotten he heard voices dictating entire stories, which he was quick to transcribe before the glow wore off. "That's why my bar bill here is so high. If I had anybody besides myself to swindle, I'd charge my liquor to the expense account."

Pamela laughed incredulously. "Not really!"

"Sure. I can even pick and choose, like tuning in on radio programs."

"Not *really*?" gasped Hester.

Blaine nodded solemnly. "When I get drunk on this red wine I write in a real tough style, whore-houses, gang murders, old women being raped, bullets through the belly.

"On a cognac drunk, if it's Italian, I write true confession stuff. Good French liquor works me up those psychological thrillers where the punch comes not from who gets laid and who gets killed; but exactly how and where and why it happens.

"Scotch — ah!" He rolled up his big yellow eyes. "I go out of this world; I turn loose. I write literature, William Faulkner stuff."

He turned to the bar. "Hey toots. Alma. Come on over. Join the party."

The two women muttered together. I thought they'd completely ig-nore him. Then they slid off their stools, came a little unsteadily across the floor. Blaine gallantly swung chairs into place. Count and Countess Paladini, the Marquis Fidoglio and the unnamed woman glanced over with nonchalant hauteur.

"I'm freezing to death," said Alma. She looked me over with hard cold eyes. She looked disturbingly like a snake — small, flat, sharp head with the brown expressionless eyes. She shifted in her seat toward Blaine; I did not interest her: too neutral, too careful. She rubbed her hands along her arms. "Can't they ever heat up this barn?"

Pamela and Hester had gone a little stiff and distant. They had not bargained for Countess Margaret and Alma. Blaine began arguing with Countess Margaret about the weather. Pamela chattered brightly to me about the local Italians. "They're honest after their own fashion; but how they'll do you if they get a chance. You've got to count every lire..." I noticed that one of the young men at the card game in the back room was Luigi from Signora Umberto's.

As I watched, another young Italian wandered in. This one was a different type: slender, with close auburn curls, a face from a Renaissance bronze. He wore tight lavender-gray trousers, a yellow shirt, white shoes — a peculiar costume. He stood over the card game with none of the others giving him any attention.

Luigi glanced up at him, made a flippant remark. The newcomer leaned forward questioningly. Luigi spoke again, the others laughed. The newcomer straightened up as if his feelings were hurt; his eyes swung around the room, flickered over me.

Countess Margaret leaned suddenly toward me, said in a harsh throaty voice, "You spotted him quick; you guys are sure fast that way."

Startled, all I could do was stare at her. Blonde hair hung over her pouchy face; her eyes, pale baby-blue, were stupid, glittering with hate. Why was she picking on me? I was unable to see how I had provoked her; I hoped she was not planning a drunken scene. I looked around the group, and was annoyed to find that they were watching, not the Countess, but me. Blaine was dispassionate; Alma contemptuous; Pamela and Hester embarrassed and uncomfortable. Indefinably they all stood behind the Countess; I was the outsider, the encroacher. I said, "What goes on? Somebody let me in on the gag."

Alma said in a silky voice, "I suppose you wouldn't know, but Chi-Chi is Kex's — special friend."

"Oh, I see...Well, if it's anybody's damn business — which it isn't — I'm not down here as Kex's special friend."

Countess Margaret sniffed. "I don't care a peep whose friend you are. I just can't stand you fruit-cakes."

Blaine intervened hotly. "He's not, Marge; didn't you hear him? I ask you, does Chuck look queer?"

They all looked at me. "Of course not," declared Blaine. He told me in the manner of a confidential aside, "Marge can't stand a homo, not since her old man ran off with a talented Bulgarian."

"I was just as talented," grumbled the Countess Margaret.

"Couldn't have been," said Blaine, "otherwise you'd still have your old man. Proof of the pudding."

Alma looked at me with sly trouble-making snake-eyes. "If he's not queer, how come he's staying in Kex's flat?"

"Damned if I know," said Blaine. "I guess that's his own affair." They all looked at me once more.

I was angry now; I wanted to shock them. I spoke on a perverse, rather childish impulse. "As a matter of fact I've come down here to be James Hilfstone."

"Who?" asked Hester, leaning forward as if she were hard of hearing. "Who?"

"James Hilfstone," I said. I saw that faces at the bridge table had turned. "Whoever he is."

"I don't care what your name is," mumbled the Countess. "I still can't stand a queer; they make me sick. That's why Positano makes me sick. They hang around here like flies."

"Every man to his own taste," said Blaine. "That's what the world needs, tolerance for the other guy. Now I don't go around reading out of the Bible, telling everybody what they ought to do."

"Well," said Pamela, "to a certain extent, perhaps you're right… But still there are certain times when our duty is clear-cut —"

"How do I know it's so clear-cut? I look at you and your sister. I say to myself, those two ladies need a man apiece; why don't they talk to some of these hard-up local boys, who'd be glad for the shack-up?"

"Really," said Hester mildly. Pamela drew in two or three deep breaths.

"But you see," Blaine went on, "I don't say anything of the sort. I don't know for sure whether it's really the right thing; maybe it's not quite what they're accustomed to, so I keep my mouth shut."

Alma smiled at him in a sleepy secret way. "What would you tell me, Buster?"

"Baby, you wouldn't want me to say. Not here."

There was noise outside, a quick pound of running footsteps. They stopped. Through the glass panels of the door I caught the glimmer of a tan sweater, a white shirt, light blond hair.

Pamela and Hester had finished their wine. They sat quietly, each with a hand on her glass, toying with the round shape, staring into the reflection of the fire.

Arturo came over. "Anything, ladies, gentlemen?"

"Get me a brandy and soda," said Countess Margaret. "You know what I drink."

"Yes, Madame."

"Me too," said Alma.

Blaine said, quizzically, "You two girls must have come into an inheritance."

Alma smiled sleepily, looked at her fingernails. Countess Margaret raised her head sharply. "Why —" she checked herself, bit her lip. Then: "The last time a gentleman invited me to a bar —"

"The last time a lady dragged me into a bar," said Blaine, "she stood the drinks, then I bought her a couple rounds in my flat afterward."

"Seduction in the Blaine manner," said Alma. "Smooth as silk."

"Hell, ladies, let's not kid ourselves, this is a competitive world; we got to look out for ourselves. Anyway I don't call it seduction; I never seduced anybody in my life. I might have re-duced, and maybe in-duced, but I never se-duced. I leave that for the college crowd. I'm just a man that knows his own value; I just call a spade a spade. And when I say that I'll buy any of you ladies here a drink or two out of a full bottle of Courvoisier I got in my flat, I mean just that; if you happen to stay awhile that's nobody's business but our own." And he sat back blandly expectant.

Pamela thoughtfully chewed her lip. Hester twisted her empty wine glass. They looked up together, met each other's eye. Pamela said, "I suppose we'd better be on our way, Hester."

"Yes, I suppose we must."

Both sat hesitantly a moment, as if reluctant to let go of their glasses. Then Pamela motioned to Arturo: "*Conto.*"

As they walked out the door, I saw again the tan sweater, the white shirt, a face with yellow hair looking through the glass pane in the door.

He was looking at me; now he thrust open the door, swaggered in — a tall young man, brown as a stoneware teapot, with a thick crew-cut thatch of yellow hair. He stood looking at me with a peculiar expression — stony blind rage. I turned to Blaine. "Who the devil is that?"

"That's Freddy," said Blaine noncommittally. Freddy took long strides across the room, stood looking down at me.

"Come outside," he said in a husky voice. "I want to talk to you."

"Talk to me? What for?"

"I'll tell you outside."

"I don't know you from Adam's off ox."

He clenched his fist; his mouth was white and working; he almost looked as if he would burst into tears. Blaine said, "What the devil's got into you, Freddy?"

Freddy said in a quivering voice, "This dirty bastard here —" he focused his eyes on me, the eyes widened. "Who the devil are you?" The chap was clearly beside himself.

"I guess I'm a dirty bastard."

Alma said in her most syrupy voice, "This is James Hilfstone — he says."

Freddy jerked back, stared down at me in revulsion. "By God, how you have the gall to sit there —"

"Take it easy, Freddy," said Blaine.

"Leave him alone," said Countess Margaret. "If he wants to hit a queer, it's his own business."

Freddy backed away. "If I had a gun I'd shoot you." He wound up, threw a tremendous round-house in my general direction. I moved away, picked up a chair, held it lion-tamer fashion. "Someone get this maniac off of me."

Arturo caught him by one elbow, Giovanni by the other; tenderly they eased him out the door.

I put the chair down. The bridge game rather regretfully resumed play, the four aristocrats relaxed, made remarks to each other. My hands were shaking; I felt an unpleasant tenseness in my stomach. I asked Blaine, "Has he gone for his gun?"

Blaine pursed his lips. "I don't know where he'd get one."

"Good!" I settled myself. "Is he always like that?"

"Well, no. You understand, he's a little odd. Not bad, that is, really *bad*. But he's not what you'd call a deep thinker. A little easy-going. Simple. But I've never seem him vicious before."

"Poof." Alma lit a cigarette. She was very disappointed; the sulky look was returning to her face. "He got into a fight with that Dino over his sister."

"Well, that's normal, with Dino's reputation; damn gigolo and freak to boot."

Countess Margaret sniffed. "He wouldn't have made a pass if she hadn't given him the green light."

Blaine shrugged. "Maybe yes, maybe no. I'm telling you just because a chap takes after a fellow who's making passes at his sister doesn't mean he's vicious."

"I never made a pass at his sister," I said. "I don't even know his sister."

"Well, don't," said Blaine. "It's a darn funny bunch; they don't tie up with anybody."

"The whole damn bunch is nuts," said Countess Margaret.

Blaine said, "After all, which of us isn't nuts in some way or other? If we weren't, we wouldn't be holed up here in Positano."

"Gad!" Alma spat out the word like a hot marble. "How I hate this place, this —" she lapsed into obscenity "— rotten stinking Positano. Fruits and queens, winos, crooks, bum artists, hack writers —"

"My dear woman," said Blaine.

"— punks, fags, snowballs, phonies —"

"Alcoholics," suggested Blaine.

"What of it?" she flashed. "Gotta do something to hold on to your mind. Name somebody around here who's got a better vice."

Blaine made a droll face at me.

"Don't sneer," cried Alma. "You'd sleep with your grandmother."

"Hell," said Blaine, "I'd sleep with a pig if there was nothing better. And I'd feel I was doing the pig a favor. Hey, Chuck?"

"I'm still wondering why that Freddy wanted to go for me."

"Got you mixed up with somebody else, no doubt."

"James Hilfstone," said Alma maliciously.

"But who the hell is James Hilfstone?" I asked.

There was a pause. "You got me," said Buster Blaine. "Never met the gent." He looked at me with his head cocked sidewise, a plaintive expression on his face. "I'd like to get this straightened out — not that it makes much difference. Is your name Musgrave or is it Hilfstone?"

"Well, to string along with the joke — it's Musgrave."

"He's being cagey," snapped Countess Margaret.

Alma yawned. "What difference does it make?" She looked craftily at Blaine. "Are you going to buy me a drink?"

"Not here I ain't."

She put her hands on the table, looked levelly at Blaine, and the gold bangles in her ears bobbed and swung. "My God, it's got to a sorry state when I have to wrestle you off an hour to get a drink."

"You'll be a lot sorrier," said Blaine, "when I start giving you drinks out of charity."

Alma turned away, her head hunched forward. "Are you coming?"

"Right behind you."

Countess Margaret watched them go. Her face was doughy, her skin creased and blotched as a dirty handkerchief. "Slut," she said without enthusiasm. She looked across the table, considered me. She looked at her glass.

I rose to my feet. "I think I'll be going too. Goodnight."

"Goodnight."

I walked outside through the glass-paned door, wandered down the esplanade. It was that hour when morning is not even a thought, when night can only go on becoming later and later. The town was like an upturned crypt, with houses pale as old bones. The moon had gone beyond the hill, the surf rumbled and groaned along the beach, and all the wan houses ranked on tiptoe up the hillside stared over the water in amazement and awe, as if they saw things I could not even imagine.

I climbed steps and walked through dark alleys, climbed more steps, always steps, came out into the road. A parapet overlooked town and sea. I paused a moment to catch my breath. The Vistamare still showed one or two lights; elsewhere the town was dark, except for a few forlorn street lamps. All the local inhabitants — the fishermen, storekeepers, farmers, laborers — lay in the warm stupor of sleep. Only the aristocrats, the uneasy foreigners yet twisted and turned, or sat awake, staring into their highballs.

Kex had ordered me to make sketches of the local types, the Italians; I thought it would be rather more significant to sketch the strangers. I pictured Blaine's long face and long shanks done in long strokes of charcoal; Alma's sharp sullen head, turned sidewise up from a highball with her sharp teeth showing; Oleg...I could form no clear image of Oleg. The blonde girl on the bus — I could not remember her too well either, except that she was rather pretty in an unorthodox way, and moved as if on a series of nervous impulses. But I'd like to sketch her too...

I turned up the road. Ahead of me a pale shadow moved. I had been aware of it; subconsciously. I knew that up the road was a dim shape.

Now I saw it. And now it was gone — past the door leading down to Kex's flat.

I walked slowly up the hill. No pale shape now. Imagination. I opened the door, flicked the switch. The light came on — but very dim. Much dimmer than I had remembered. The staircase was full of shadow. I hesitated, rather frightened. Strange. Perhaps I had been mistaken. I started down the steps. Something narrow bit at my instep. I stumbled, sprawled; the toe of my other foot caught; under me was nothing. The stair became a chute. Concrete angles pounded my shoulders, head, knees, elbows; there was a whirl of shadows and shapes. Up was down and down was up, with pain jarring everywhere. I hit on the back of my shoulders with my head and neck under, and continued over in a limp somersault.

I lay quietly; I was still conscious — or was I? I could not move or see; I felt nothing but the quiet of lying still.

Creak-pad...Creak-pad...Creak-pad...

But I could hear. I heard the sly *creak-pad* of steps. I tried then to rise up on an elbow; *creak-pad, creak-pad, creak-pad*: three quick steps — then sudden blows, kicks. At first calm, measured, faster and heavier as spite took hold. He aimed for my shoulders, my head, my ribs. I faced the wall; he couldn't find my crotch. I tried to move, to curl up. The kicker was panting, from excitement, from exertion. I made a feeble attempt to turn over, I suppose with some instinctive attempt to see who stood over me.

He backed away, turned, ran up the stairs. If he had planned to kill me, he had done something less than a good job. I made it to my hands and knees, fell flat; I glimpsed something sand-colored disappearing through the top door.

CHAPTER VI

AFTER FIVE MINUTES REST, I crawled to my feet, tottered into the room. I was aching from head to foot; but no bones seemed seriously broken.

I switched on the light, dropped upon the divan. Who was it, who was it? Who had been able to work up such a case of rancor in the few hours since I had arrived? Naturally, I thought of Freddy. I gingerly raised my wrist, looked at my watch. The crystal was scarred and scratched; the time was one-thirty.

Groaning and wincing, I pulled off my clothes. My elbows both ached vilely; every breath hurt my ribs. Oh Freddy, I thought, if it's you, you'll pay — half-wit or not...

I stumbled into the bedroom and, ignoring a spasm of fastidiousness, climbed into bed. I lay sweltering with ache, and began to suspect that bones were broken after all. Perhaps I'd better send for the doctor. But who would I send? Suppose I had a busted kidney or fractured liver, or whatever is meant by internal injuries...But the pain seemed concentrated, like marrow, in my bones; I told myself I wouldn't die. I wanted some aspirin, or alcohol, or almost anything.

I became angrier, so angry I began to twist back and forth in the bed and hurt myself. Kex! At the bottom it was Kex who was responsible for my bruises and aches. Kex! I asked myself bitterly, would Kex pay my doctor bills? Would Kex buy me a casket if I got killed? My rage spent itself. I lay calm, except for the throbbing in my bones. Well, anyway, that was that. I was playing no more of Kex's games, pulling no more of his chestnuts out of the fire.

I fell into a restless sleep.

Discreet rattling from the kitchen disturbed me, then the rasp of a hand-mill grinding coffee finished the job. I deduced that my cook was at work.

I raised my wrist to check the time. Pain stabbed my shoulder. Bruises, aches, pains — everywhere. How? Why? I remembered and hissed between my teeth... A nightmare, the kind of nightmare that leaves bruises.

A tapping sounded at the door. A plump squirrel-cheeked woman peered curiously through. "You like breakfast?"

I eased myself up on one elbow, felt my face. Swollen, spongy as new bread. "Just some coffee," I mumbled. "Black, no sugar, not too strong."

"Looks like you have accident."

"I fell down the stairs."

"Oh! That's bad! You fall down, eh? Too much vino maybe?"

"Right. Too much vino."

She chuckled comfortably, wise in the ways of men, and backed away from the door. Three minutes later she brought in a mug of coffee, and stood in the doorway watching me drink.

"You stay here long?"

"I don't know."

"This nice flat, eh? Just like America."

"Very nice."

"You friend of Kex, eh?" And she tilted her head a little sidewise.

"No... Not especially."

She laughed uproariously, shaking and twisting as if someone were tickling her. "You good boy, eh?"

I made no answer and she did not seem to require any.

"What you like for lunch?"

"Anything."

"You like nice veal cutlet?"

"Sounds good."

"I get a piece of pork. You like him the way I cook."

I lay back, closed my eyes. I opened them a moment later to find her six feet away, leaning forward interestedly. "You got it bad," she said admiringly.

I held out the cup. "Any more outside?"

She brought me a refill, and as before stood in the doorway watching me drink and chattering. Her name, I found, was Ignazia. She had been born in New York and brought back to Italy when she was twelve. Her husband was a master fisherman and brought her the best fish in Positano cheap. "He's dumb," she said. "In New York they call him a dumb wop. Never been out of Positano in his life. Can't talk American, can't hardly talk good Italian."

I gave her the empty cup, settled into the bed.

"You don't want nothing? No bacon, eggs?"

"Not now. I'm going to lie here and try to sleep." I closed my eyes.

Thirty seconds later I opened them to find Ignazia two feet away, peering into my face. She said, "I get you hot rag, take down the bumps." Without waiting for yes or no, she bustled into the kitchen and a few minutes later was scalding my face with hot compresses.

Sleep seemed to be out of the question. As soon as the compress water cooled I struggled out of bed, got into a bathrobe belonging to Kex and limped out on the terrace. Ignazia pulled a deck chair into the sunlight; I settled myself with a groan or two.

Ignazia returned inside, washed the coffee pot and cup, then coming out on the terrace announced that she was leaving, that she'd be back at twelve to cook lunch.

I had been doing some thinking. I said, "Just a moment," and limped inside. With black ink I blocked out a sign on a sheet from my sketch pad:

NOTICE!!

To whom it may concern.
My name is Clarence Musgrave.
I am not and do not know James Hilfstone.
Take your persecutions elsewhere.

"Take this up," I said to Ignazia. "Pin it on the front door."

"Okay." She held the sign off, read it aloud with gusto. "What's that mean?"

"I wish I knew." A poor kind of wisecrack, but I was up to nothing better. She nodded as if I'd said something clever and departed. I returned to my seat in the sunlight, hoping to bake the soreness out of my muscles.

The sun sailed up into a pure blue sky. The sea shimmered and spar-kled. I thought, this is what they mean when they speak of wintering in Italy. Then scuds of clouds came over the mountain. Five minutes later the sky was like the inside of a featherbed. I cursed and waited ten min-utes, but the clouds came even thicker; I gave up and limped inside.

Ignazia had laid a fire; I bent over the fireplace like an old man with rheumatism, put a match to the paper, then settled back on the divan.

The divan was very soft. The room was ripe as musk. I rose to my feet and went to the bookcases. A nude boy, in bronze, with elongated limbs and a dismal El Greco face stared at me. I turned him so that nakedness compelled a little less attention, and bent to glance along the books. Like everything else belonging to Kex, they were obviously expensive, richly bound in leather or heavy cloth. The titles were not at all familiar: *Pavilion of Delight, Angel in Hell, Erotic Encyclopedia, Suramâit, Flowers of Passion, The Loves of Danae.* "My bloody sacred aunt!" I said to myself, and read on. *Five Little Virgins and How They Grew, Ten Nights in Tangiers, The Portal of Ecstasy, King Granion's Treasure, Secrets of a Girl's School.* I came to a foreign section. *L'Amour Sacré et Profane, Erotique Chinoise, Fleurette et Flamond, Fantasmo, Aphrodite.* I picked up a large flat volume entitled *Les Sylphides.* Beautiful naked girls, some very young. Pornography, but ice-cream deluxe, connoisseurs stuff. The girls were as fresh as May, with that look of wanton innocence most profoundly disturbing.

I sampled here and there. *The Way of the Gods* — weird indeed. *Chounzy* — little negro boys and girls, photographed in Haiti. *Arcana Erotica, The Mount of Venus, McMurdo's Manual, Rife Goes to a Drag Party.* Enough was enough.

I heard footsteps and hastily shelved the book. Ignazia was return-ing early. But these were hesitant steps, nothing like Ignazia's resolute tread.

A figure in gray passed the window; I leaned forward incredulously. There was a tap at the door. I rubbed my face. I was tousled, red-eyed, swollen, bruised, unshaven.

I went to the door, opened it. The blonde girl stood in front of me. Her face was very pale, her lips were clenched and white.

"Hello," I said dubiously.

"Hello." She looked warily over her shoulder, as if she had no wish to be seen. "Can I come in?" Her voice was under rigid control. Whatever she had come to do, she had keyed herself up to almost the snapping point.

I looked her over. She carried no purse or bag. I reached out, patted her pockets. She drew back, staring a question.

"Come on in," I said. "I don't know what you want, but the sooner we get this annoyance cleared up the better."

She came hesitantly inside. I shut the door; she looked around as if she wanted to run. "Take a seat."

She looked swiftly around the room. Whatever she thought of the décor, no hint appeared in her face. It was a pretty face, if an unorthodox kind of prettiness. Her hair was a short pale gold tangle, close to her head. Her eyes were long, narrow, her mouth was a generous slash across rather thin cheeks. She looked hardly twenty, and carried herself with a girl's nervousness.

I went to the fire, she followed and settled herself slowly on the divan, her eyes never leaving my face. "What can I do for you?" I asked.

Her words came in a rush. "You can tell me why you came here!"

"That's easy," I said. "First. I am not James Hilfstone —"

"I know that; I can see you're not."

"— second, I'm not queer. Those seem to be the bases on which everybody gets mad at me."

"What are you doing here?" Her voice rose a little, as if her control were close to its end.

I seated myself on the divan opposite from her. "I'm here because —" I had to laugh "— because I was hired to."

Her hands — thin, tanned hands — opened and closed. "But who hired you?"

"Don't you know who owns this flat?"

"No... I was walking past, I saw your sign. I knew it was you. I came down —" she hesitated "— to find out —"

"Go ahead. I'm just as curious as you are. To find out what?"

She licked her lips, looked into the fire. "It's a long story. But we — my family — have had trouble with James Hilfstone. It seems a very peculiar coincidence that you should be so much like him and going around claiming you're not him, unless you're trying to make trouble too."

"It's not a coincidence, and I'm not trying to make trouble. But someone is."

"Who?"

"Kex."

"Kex? Isn't he the American, about fifty with the mustache and white hair?"

"Yes, that's Kex."

"But why should he want to make trouble for us? We don't even know him."

"Maybe he's just a born trouble-maker."

She looked across at me with an uncertain suspicious expression. "But what are you doing here?"

I told her. She did not seem reassured. She chewed her lip, her eyes became large and thoughtful. "But what made you put out that sign?"

I felt my face, touched the bruises. "See these?"

"What?"

"Bruises, swellings. I don't look this way normally."

"Oh."

"I got these last night. At the Vistamare some young maniac named Freddy tried to beat me up. They threw him out so he came up here, fixed up a little surprise for me — a string across the passage. I came home, tripped over the string, fell downstairs. He came down and kicked me while I was still out."

"Freddy did that?" She stared at me in wonder. *"Freddy?"*

"Well — I suppose so. I don't know who else it could be." I thought a moment. "I couldn't swear that it was Freddy. I caught a glimpse of his sweater, that's all. I couldn't see anything for certain; I thought I was dead."

"What time was all this?" Her voice was scornful.

"About twenty after one."

"Then it wasn't Freddy. Because Freddy was home at half-past twelve."

"But is Freddy your —"

"He's my brother."

"Oh…Well, if it wasn't Freddy, who was it?"

"I'm sure I don't know."

"Incidentally, what is your name?"

"Betty Dannister."

She looked up from the fire. "You seem surprised."

"I shouldn't be. Er, who is Hortense?"

"I think it might be the woman who has the gift shop, the pottery place."

"Oh, her." The tall hollow-cheeked woman playing bridge. Mrs. Revost.

Betty sniffed. "If you knew her, why did you ask?"

"I didn't know her by name."

"You seem intent on making a mystery of everything."

"It's really not so much of a mystery. I heard somebody say something about a woman named Hortense, and I wondered who she was. Tell me about yourself. Do you live here permanently?"

She looked steadily into the fire. "Yes."

"You're American, aren't you?"

"My father is American, my mother is English. I went to school in Switzerland."

"But why are you living here? I should think you'd go crazy."

She looked into the fire several seconds. Then she said in a colorless voice, "I don't have any other place to go. My mother isn't well, and Freddy needs looking after. And, anyway, we're very happy here; it's a lovely place to live."

"Rather quiet."

"Yes. There's not much to do."

I put a few more sticks of wood on the fire. "This James Hilfstone — what kind of chap is he?"

"I don't want to talk about him."

"But, damn it, I want to know who it is I'm supposed to be impersonating."

She looked at me with a tinge of scorn in her eyes. "You can always leave."

"Yes. I can always leave. But as long as I stay here and do charcoal sketches of Positano I make ten thousand lire a day. That's good money for an art student. I'm not posing as anybody. Quite the reverse. If anybody wants to think I'm somebody else, that's their lookout. And also, I'd like to find out who jumped me last night."

"You might get hurt again."

"I'd get in one or two licks of my own first. Does this Hilfstone man live around here?"

"I don't think so. The last I heard he was in England."

"Does anyone else around here know him?"

"I don't know. I wouldn't think so ... It frightens me ..."

"Why should it frighten you?"

"I think that something terrible is going to happen."

"But why?"

She gave me a long slow look. "Why should you care?"

I put on a foolish grin. "You'd think I was crazy if I told you."

She moved uncomfortably. "I don't know what you're talking about."

"How old are you, Betty?"

"Nineteen."

"Do you have any boy friends?"

"No."

"Doesn't it get lonesome?"

She stirred. "I never think about it ... I think I'd better go."

"No — don't go yet."

She looked puzzled. "Why not?"

"Oh," I made a vague motion, "I like your company."

She turned and looked into the fire.

I said, "Maybe someone else around here is mad at Hilfstone?"

She was attentive again. "Why do you say that?"

"Because of last night. I can't think of any other reason ..." I remembered Countess Margaret. "There's one woman that doesn't like me; she thinks I'm queer. It seems her husband deserted her for a pansy."

"Who's that?" Betty frowned.

"Countess Margaret d'Egliari. The blonde American woman that looks like she's made of putty."

"Oh, her." Betty laughed hollowly. "Horrible creature, she tried to seduce poor Freddy — I can't imagine her laying a trap for you."

"I can't either. Besides she was at the Vistamare when I left. It wasn't the Countess — but I've got half an idea ..."

She rose to her feet. "I've got to go."

"Stay and have lunch with me."

She looked around the room. "I don't think I'd better…This is an overpowering room."

"I don't like it either."

"Then why do you stay?"

"Money, my dear girl, money."

"People seem to think of nothing else."

"Have you ever worked for a living?"

"No."

"Your father has lots of money?"

"Yes. I suppose so."

"Then you're hardly an authority on poverty and avarice."

She laughed. "I suppose not. But I'd trade all the money and security and everything for —" she stopped. I was learning to anticipate this hesitation in her; it came whenever she wandered a hair's-breadth from generalities into personal matters. "For what?" I prompted patiently.

"Oh — I'm not sure, really." She started for the door.

"When can I see you again?" I asked.

She stopped, looked at me. "Why do you want to see me again?"

"Because you're pretty and attractive and pleasant."

She shuddered and went to the door.

"Is that bad?" I asked.

"No. Except — I'm not built that way."

"You're built very well."

"I — don't like you," she said evasively. "You look too much like Hilfstone."

"Do I — *really*?"

She considered, as if compelled to do me justice. "No, you really don't. Not when I see you up close. From a distance it's startling. But up close you're a different person entirely."

She opened the door. "Incidentally — don't mention to anyone I've been here, will you please?"

"No. There's no reason why I should."

"Especially not Freddy."

"I don't imagine I'll do much chatting with Freddy. But why especially not Freddy?"

"Oh, just because."

"I won't tell anyone. But when can I see you again?"

"I don't know. I'm going to be very busy…"

"Can I come around to your house?"

"*No!*"

"Very well. Excuse me for not seeing you up the stairs."

"That's all right. Goodbye."

"Goodbye." I watched the slim figure cross the terrace, start up the steps; then I returned inside, shut the door. Ignazia was due in half an hour, and I decided that I was hungry.

CHAPTER VII

IGNAZIA WAS LATE. I became very restless. I stepped out on the terrace, to find wet black clouds rolling low overhead. I went back in, stood with my back to the fire.

I sat on the divan but my joints ached worse than ever. I considered lying down, but felt too restless. I went to the bookcase, read some more titles: *Bordello Days, The Escapades of Harry Thaw, The Golden Phalanx, The Odalisque, Witchcraft: Black, Red and Purple, Patchouli Pajama, The Necronomicon*, by the mad Arab Abdul Alhazred. On the bottom shelves were lavish editions of the classics: *The Golden Asse of Apuleius*, Petronius, Rabelais, Chaucer, Boccaccio. Then, beside these as an anticlimax—it was certainly one of Kex's sly jokes—were a dozen paper-bound comic-strip parodies: *Maggie and Jiggs, Tillie the Toiler, Li'l Abner and Daisy Mae.* Kex had the most catholic of tastes in his pornography.

I looked at a few pictures, but presently the fundamental vapidity of the books began to tire me. Sex is something a sensible man doesn't want to read about, any more than a hungry man likes a cookbook. The stimulation might do everything for Kex; it was wasted on me; it was bringing coals to Newcastle. And I thought of Betty Dannister, who interested me very much. Why not call on her? This was the twentieth century. Was it because I looked like Hilfstone? I speculated for a few minutes, decided not. She had been so emphatic, so alarmed, that any such explanation fell flat.

Of course I knew nothing of Hilfstone, or of his connection with the Dannisters. Some kind of mystery existed, but for the life of me I could not conjecture why I, who admittedly was *not* Hilfstone, but only an innocent adjunct to Kex's flat, should be treated like Hilf-stone.

Ignazia came bumping down the steps. She came in without knock-ing, stood stock-still in the doorway grinning at me. "Well, how you feel?"

"Good."

"You hungry?"

"Very hungry."

"Good. I got nice piece pig. You like broccoli?"

"I like anything but oysters and brains."

"This ain't brains; this is broccoli. See?" She flourished a huge bun-dle of greens. "Ten lire the bunch. Cheap, eh? In New York that costs thirty cents. Here ten lire. Now I cook."

I watched her get to work. She almost filled the kitchen. "Ignazia — you know Mr. James Hilfstone?"

"No. Never."

"You know all of Kex's friends?"

"Sure, them darn finocchi. No good for nothing." She cocked me a sly side-glance. "I forgot; you one of Kex's friends."

"No — not me. I hardly know him."

"Ah." She nodded; her squirrel cheeks bounced. "I tell the old lady — that's my mother, the Signora — I tell her you not fruit-cake like Kex. She say, what for you here? I say —"

"Ignazia, do you know the Dannisters?"

"Dannister, eh? He got the house over the hill, on the next beach. Big house, lotsa rooms, lotsa money. He's a very important man."

"He lives here all year?"

"Sure. He's got a nice place. Motorboat, big car, everything the best."

"He come into town very much?"

"Don't see him much. They don't have Positano help. They got Ger-man woman, can't talk Italian."

"How about Freddy?"

"Oh, that one." She shook her head. "He's crazy, drives the car like he's gonna kill himself."

"And the girl, Betty?"

"She's strange. Not crazy like Freddy; she's crazy different. She don't stay home, she don't come to town, she walks all over the hills. That's bad. Some of these men, they get fresh. Italian girls they know better, they stay home."

"Rather a strange family."

Ignazia nodded tolerantly, implying that strange behavior in foreigners was hardly a matter for surprise. "They got lotsa money. They girl she just come home from school in *Svizzera* — that's the Swiss — now's a good time she should be getting married, but she don't have no men come see her."

"How about Freddy?"

"Poof. Him!" She snapped her fingers in scorn. "He chase all the girls. They don't like him. He's crazy; they scared of him. That's the good girls, that is. The bad girls — they don't talk."

"Kex — does he ever talk about the Dannisters?"

"Kex talks about everything. Kex, he's a funny man, nicest finocchio in Positano, everybody like him — all the Italians; he's a good man, spends lotsa money, gives big tips, don't hold back."

I went to stand in front of the fire, and, in an astonishingly short time, Ignazia served me spaghetti in tomato sauce, a pork chop with broccoli, a lettuce salad, crackers and cheese, with a mild red wine.

"What you like for dinner? You like fish? Chicken?"

"Cook anything you like. Chicken sounds fine."

"Maybe I cook a nice fish."

I stoked the fire, lay down on the divan, and fell asleep. About three o'clock I woke up to find the sun blasting against the windows and into the room. The fire had gone out, my joints were stiff, I had a bad taste in my mouth.

I sat up, rubbed my head, lit a cigarette. Ignazia was gone, but something was simmering on the stove, smelling very good.

After a while, I went out on the terrace, looked up the stairs, pictured myself pitching down. A wonder I hadn't broken my neck. I climbed painfully to the top, scrutinized the place where the trip-string had been tied across. On each side of the staircase a nail had been driven into a handy crack; to the protruding head of each the buff fibers of strong ship-wright's twine were still visible. And once more I boiled with fury; the injustice of it all; me, an innocent art student, meaning harm to no one! On my first night in Positano, I had been ditched, dumped and kicked. I swore that I'd see a satisfactory end to the episode!

The next problem was naming the guilty party. What did I have to work on? Some first-class detective work was essential. I studied the nail heads and wondered what Sherlock Holmes would make of them. They looked like ordinary nails to me; the twine looked like ordinary twine. I examined the knots: ordinary half-hitches. Nothing significant there.

I rose to my feet, scratched my unshaven chin. The door. It was locked, with an expensive modern lock. I had a key, Ignazia had a key. Kex, no doubt, had a key. Or maybe he left his key with Signora Umberto. I did not think either Signora Umberto, Luigi, Ignazia, or Kex had set me a booby-trap. Someone else had a key to the front door; perhaps I could find him by tracking down the key.

What else did I have for a clue? The glimpse of tan sweater — or was it white? The light had been dim…The light! Dim. I hobbled back downstairs, examined the light. Paper had been wrapped around it, a half-sheet of an Italian newspaper.

I examined the newspaper. No subscription address. There would be no way imaginable I could trace the newspaper. It might bear finger-prints, but they would do me no good.

What else? Footprints? Perhaps on my short-ribs, but not much value for identification purposes. I went back up and down the stairs looking for something which an intruder might have dropped. But he was less cooperative than criminals I have read about, and had left me no mementos of his presence.

I returned inside, found some kindling, rebuilt the fire. Sitting on the divan, I reviewed the episode as vividly as possible: the string at my ankle, the hurtling tumble down the steps, lying quiet in a state of daze, the footsteps. Once again I heard the footsteps: *creak-pad, creak-pad, creak-pad*…So I had another clue. Find a man with squeaky shoes. Definitely it was not Freddy. Freddy as I clearly recalled, had worn a pair of brown moccasins with heavy crepe rubber soles.

I continued to think. I remembered that as soon as I had shown signs of life the kicker had taken himself elsewhere. He either feared me or he feared recognition. He might easily have killed me with his trip-rope; why had he not finished the job? I could not have moved to save my life. But instead of smashing my skull, he had kicked me — an act of spite, rather than resolution; weakness, rather than murderous abandon. Another clue.

The portrait of my attacker was assuming shape. I must seek a man in a light shirt or sweater with squeaky shoes and a key to Kex's apartment. A weak man of malice and extravagant reaction...

The day went slowly. Ignazia came in about six-thirty; at seven she served dinner: broth with vermicelli and parsley, four fish, pink as a baby's rattle, fried in full possession of their heads and tails, french-fried potatoes, string beans in garlic oil, white wine, a salad of new lettuce and scallions, little pastries filled with custard, and finally fruit, cheese and coffee.

I went to bed at nine with one of Kex's books, *Sexual Pathology*, by Krafft-Ebbing, pornography solemnly but transparently disguised as science, and spent an hour and a half in a weird purple world.

Next morning I was in fair condition. My bruises had turned mottled yellow; I walked with no more than a slight limp, my ribs ached only dully. I ate a good breakfast of bacon and eggs, and taking charcoal pencil and sketch-book, climbed the stairs to the road, set out for the beach.

The day was blustery. The sky was a big swatch of blue and white gingham, the sun ducking alternately in and out of sight. I walked down old stone steps, past white stucco walls, stained and mottled, and came out on the esplanade. Surf was thundering up the beach; the boats had been well drawn up. I looked along the front of the various wine-shops and restaurants; no one in sight. I bought a newspaper at the news stand. A *Daily Mail* from London, four days old, and took it to the Vistamare terrace where two walls made a sun-trap sheltered from the wind. A young healthy-looking couple I did not recognize were drinking coffee, very absorbed in each other — American honeymooners, perhaps.

I took a seat at a wrought-iron table; Arturo came out. I ordered coffee, and looked over the paper. Five minutes later a man in gray corduroy trousers, a mustard-colored sports coat of English cut appeared: Oleg Vroznek, the refugee Pole.

He hesitated, then diffidently approached my table. "May I?"

"Sure; sit down."

He put both hands on the table, slowly lowered himself into a chair. A pale thin gangling man like a plucked owl, not too old, with solemn unwinking eyes, an air of perpetual inquiry.

"You're the chap staying up at Kex's place, aren't you?" He spoke English very well, with strong varsity intonations.

"Yes. My name is Chuck Musgrave, I'm not James Hilfstone and I'm not fruit."

Oleg peered at me seriously. "My name is Vroznek — Oleg Vroznek. I am not 'fruit' either."

"I think we ought to start a club," I said.

Oleg laughed, a queer almost soundless panting. Arturo came up for his order, and he asked for orange juice.

"I must watch my diet," he told me soberly. "I can't touch fried foods or sweets, tea or coffee, and I limit myself to half a liter of wine a day." He went on to tell me about his ailment, some sort of Polish heartburn, which he was treating after the prescription of a Finnish herbalist now residing in Nice. Then he said abruptly, "I hear you had an accident the other night?"

"Why, yes, so I did … How did you hear of it? I told —"

He grinned, showing a set of beautiful white teeth: too perfect, too white to be true. "Here in Positano you don't need to tell the news; one just knows."

"Perhaps you know what happened, then."

Arturo brought his orange juice; he seized the glass, ducked his head, extended his elbows, sipped. A large production for one small sip. "I heard," he said deliberately, "that you fell downstairs. Here in Positano that sort of accident is usual; one doesn't die of tuberculosis or cancer or pneumonia; one dies of tumbling down two hundred feet of stone steps; it happens often."

I looked up the hillside; the sky had suddenly become clear of clouds, bright as a new blue basin. The houses were hard and sharp in the sunlight, brightly pink, blue, beige, white, blocks and squares, with precise black holes for windows. I measured the length of one flight of steps, tilting my head back to find the top. "I'd hate to be the mailman."

Oleg pointed far, far up the mountain, past Positano, past a dozen olive groves and terraces, past four great crags and a beetling ridge. "See that steeple? That's Montepatuso, a separate little village. No road, nothing but steps. Everything must be carried up the steps. Some of the villagers have never even come down to Positano."

"What do they do for amusement?"

"Ha!" he wagged his finger, "they have their own amusements; they have their church. Church is a great thing in these people's lives."

"Poor devils," I said, "if they invested the money they waste on religion in a few good schools, an agricultural institute, a vocational college, they might be able to come down to Positano once in a while — even get as far as Sorrento."

"Ha, ha!" exclaimed Oleg with pleasure. "My friend, you exhibit the typical American fixation, the pragmatic fallacy, in its most definite form. Forgive me if I talk bluntly."

"Go ahead, talk as blunt as you like."

"We're an older race here in Europe, we have a spiritual tradition that you in the New World have discarded. The church is the dearest thing in the lives of those villagers; if you destroyed it and gave them all bathrooms and American kitchens with refrigerators and big American cars, you'd destroy their life." And, sipping his orange juice, he regarded me solemnly over the lip of the glass.

"Forgive me if I talk bluntly," I said.

"By all means."

"You exhibit the typical European fallacy, the idea that Americans, in avoiding picturesque poverty have thrown away their souls. You're judging us by yourself. You think that we produce kitchens and bathrooms and big cars for their own sake — ends in themselves, articles of conspicuous consumption, as Veblen puts it. That's a mistake; we produce for use. A rich European insists that everyone knows he's rich; his goal is a higher social class. Why else be rich? He's made his wad; he slaps everybody in the face with it. He buys luxuries. Well, in the States, by and large, we don't think that way. We buy refrigerators to keep our meat cold and our vegetables fresh. We like big cars because they're more comfortable. We install good plumbing in our houses because it's comfortable, and because we enjoy keeping clean. We wear sports clothes; if it weren't for a few snobs, the high-fashion shops would starve to death. The haberdashers wring their hands because they can't sell Americans fancy underwear."

Oleg blinked. "If that is the case, why do you put all the chrome on your automobiles: the Dollar Grin?"

I winced; he had hit a sore spot. "Admittedly the front end of an American car looks like it had run into a peddler's wagon and was escaping with the loot."

"Very vulgar. Flashy."

"Almost as flashy as the inside of St. Peters in Rome," I said. "Practically as blatant as Paris gowns, and just about as vulgar as the ornaments on a typical English mantelpiece."

"Well," Oleg made a deprecating gesture, "you're pointing to our middle classes."

"Who do you think the American car is designed for? ... The Caddies, the Packards, the Chryslers and Lincolns — they're all middle-class cars."

"And your upper classes, what of them?"

"Brother Oleg, we don't have any upper classes."

"Ahem," said Oleg. "Here's Munton."

Munton: No. 1 on the list, lead-off man. He came toward the table, tubby and lethargic, with a big bald head, a ginger mustache, skin the color of laundry soap. He wore a suit of heavy brown-gray tweed, a brown shirt, some sort of striped necktie. Oleg introduced us: Munton nodded, did not offer to shake hands, nor did I.

"Sit down, sit down," said Oleg. "I'm having the most interesting discussion with Mr. Musgrave, and I'd like to hear your views."

"Just for a minute, can't stay... Arturo!" Munton made a large peremptory gesture. "Cinzano."

Arturo bowed low, scurried away. Munton darted a glance at me from small sunken lizard eyes. "What's the argument? This is Kex's friend, eh?"

I did not think it worthwhile to explain that my name actually was Musgrave and my sex life followed a pattern that the primmest of Munton's maiden aunts would approve of.

Oleg was saying, "Mr. Musgrave is an American, as you can see. He defends the American outlook on life; I the European."

"Mm." Munton glanced from one of us to the other; his big body perfectly rigid, only his eyes flicking back and forth. "Gives plenty of scope for disagreement, I should say."

"Mr. Musgrave does not believe that the Americans have suffered spiritually from their unprecedented period of prosperity."

"I don't get you." Munton frowned impatiently. "What do you mean 'spiritually'? Blamed if I've ever heard two people agree on the word. Americans got a lot to learn certainly. Unstable on the whole, I'd say. Hollywood stuff, bing-bang-ring-a-ma-jing nigger music. Need steadying, need a strong hand. When they've lost two or three wars, and been through it, they'll be the better for it."

"Hm, interesting," said Oleg thoughtfully. He looked at me, but I was watching five young men on the beach. They wore shorts that were tighter than skin-tight, and were standing in a circle, keeping a soccer ball in the air by the most agile of kicks and buttings with the head. Among them was Chi-Chi, Kex's boy friend, lithe as an eel, hopping, dancing, kicking, butting, full of energy. The ball flew twenty feet over his head; he leapt up for it regardless, landed crouched, ran along the sand toward the terrace. He picked up the ball, raised his head, looked up at me. I met his eyes for a second — a long, long, second. His face was bland, inquiring, interested. I don't know what he saw on mine. He turned away, gave the ball a tremendous kick.

I turned back to the table. I looked at the coffee cup. The coffee was cold, but I sipped it regardless.

Munton looked at his watch. "Mail's late as usual. Expecting a very important letter from my bailiff; sale of blood stock. Keep a model estate in Hampshire." He darted a swift glance at me. "What's the news from Kex? Coming down pretty soon?"

"I don't know for sure."

"Oh. Aren't you down here waiting for him?"

"No."

Munton's face still wore a sly look.

"I'm down here on business of my own," I said, "which is painting; Kex is letting me use his apartment."

Oleg was behaving rather oddly. At the first mention of Kex's name he pulled himself into his chair, sipped his orange juice, looked pensively out across the sea.

"Well, well," said Munton. "Kex is a generous soul for all his eccentricities."

"Such as?"

Munton glanced toward the pensive Oleg, and grinned. "Kex likes his fun, doesn't care too much who resents it. Going to land himself in a fix one of these days." He slapped the table with his hand. "Glad to know you, Musgrave; I must be off." He rose to his feet. "Cheerio."

Oleg said formally, "Cheerio."

Munton stumped across the terrace. Oleg said thoughtfully, "A hard man to talk to, Munton. A peculiar man."

"He pictures himself as the *pukka sahib* type; sporting and military."

Oleg was doubtful. "Yes, perhaps. But I think it's far deeper. I picture Munton as a man who has gone soft inside — soft as an egg." He squinted at his orange juice; it was clear that he relished this type of conversation. "He was interned here during the war, you know — lived on Ischia, had a very good thing of it, I understand." Oleg paused delicately. "Like all of us to a greater or lesser extent, he is at war with himself. He has an estate in England that he always speaks of, but which he never returns to. I believe he can't face austerity. But, as you point out, he dramatizes himself as a hard-shell colonial, British to the core, and the spectacle of this chap so at odds to himself is rather pathetic."

"Well, yes," I said, "when you put it that way, I suppose it is."

"It's a hobby of mine," said Oleg. "I love to study my fellow man, to calculate his viewpoint, the springs of his behavior." He nodded his head. "For instance, what do you make of her?"

Alma was coming rather shakily down one of the alleys which gave upon the esplanade. She wore the same rumpled green slack-suit in which I had first seen her; her face, flat like a lizard's, looked sorry and disarranged. She put her hand out to the wall to steady herself.

"What is your opinion of her?" Oleg repeated.

"Well," I said doubtfully, "I don't know her very intimately. Just a garden-variety drunk, I suppose."

Oleg looked at me as if slightly surprised and disappointed. "She's an alcoholic, certainly. But why? *Why?* That's the element of interest. What's in her mind when she takes her first drink of the day — which I understand, is upon awakening?"

"Oleg, you've got me there. I've no idea what's in her mind. I don't know anything about her, except that she doesn't like me and shacks for a drink."

Oleg made an impatient negative motion. "Superficial. But I do have the advantage of you, as I know something of her background. For instance, would you recognize her as a one-time concert pianist?"

"She looks rather unstable."

"Of course she does. I find her personally quite repellent. Her head — like a python's ready to strike." Oleg became quite excited, opened and closed his long pale hand. "But now she drinks. She dopes, if she can afford the price — why? To forget? No. To remember! A touch of arthritis —" Oleg snapped his fingers "— a career ruined, over. She drinks, in her mind she hears music, applause, triumph…"

"Interesting. How about Blaine?"

"Oh, Blaine, he's a deep one." Oleg pursed his lips. "Blaine has come here either in search of something or to leave something behind. He's profoundly sensitive, and — so I believe — a very kind-hearted man." He shook his head, smiling gently. "Positano is a strange place — perhaps Ulysses came here to eat his lotus; who knows?"

"And Kex?"

The smile vanished instantly; Oleg lowered his eyes. "Kex. Ah, hm." For a moment I thought he would remain silent, but after a sniff or two, a blow of the nose, a sip of his orange juice, he said, "Kex is the embodiment of mischief. I see Kex as one of the minor imps, an elemental — something both more and less than a man. He never ages, he never has been young. He has the soul of a goat, an ass, a buffoon, a harlequin. Kex —" Oleg shook his head. "He is cruel, or better, callous, with the cruelty and callousness of a student dissecting a tadpole. Kex is generous, but only in that it buys him novelty… But then, I bore you, and indeed, Kex is not one of my favorite persons. In fact, I think that he is three thousand years past his time; he was intended by fate for a pre-Mycenaean, a satyr."

"And the Dannister kids — do you know them?"

"Only by sight. I have never spoken to either one of them. The girl — a charming sprite. There's a great deal of Botticelli in her face. She walks and walks; there's a weight on her soul, but it can't be her own weight; she's too young to have lived her own tragedies—they'll come later."

"Oleg, you're a pessimist."

He peered at me. "Ha, my friend, my American friend, you expect always the happy ending—your national folk-tale. No, no—I don't find it reprehensible; it's better to expect happiness than to crouch your neck for the sorrow. But we of Europe—Europe, the small peninsula off vast Mongolian Asia—we know better. Excuse me, my mail. I live here at the Vistamare, you know."

Arturo handed him three letters, two in white envelopes addressed by hand, the third in a blue envelope addressed by typewriter. This last he hesitated over, then opened. He read the letter at arm's length, his face tilted far-sightedly back, his eyebrows raised. He finished, he moved not a muscle, but sat holding the letter. Then deliberately he raised his eyes, gave me a peculiar cold look.

"Excuse me," he said, and taking his letters he left the table, crossed the terrace and disappeared into the Vistamare.

I looked after him with some puzzlement, trying to identify the exact quality of the look he had given me. Accusation? Bitterness? Or merely abstraction?

I called Arturo, paid for the coffee, and decided to wander home for lunch.

I stepped down from the terrace, and came face to face with Alma, who was on her way up. Her face was mottled like a pinto pony: red, pink, white, crusts of tan and peeling skin. Her hair was tangled and unkempt. She looked a witch and smelled like a vat of sour mash.

"Hello," I said and started to slip past her.

In a thick voice she said, "Hello yourself, you son of a bitch." She swung her scrawny arm up, slapped my face.

I jumped back, astounded. Tears were pouring down her cheeks. "Go ahead and slug me, you filthy heel, go ahead…"

I turned away, walked fast up the hill toward the apartment.

CHAPTER VIII

I HAD A TYPICALLY ITALIAN lunch, *lasagne alla romana*: layers of flat pasta, ground meat, cheese, hard-boiled egg, the whole baked in a buttery tomato sauce.

"Ignazia," I said, "offhand I'd call you a damn good cook!"

Ignazia stood grinning in the doorway. "You like, eh?"

"I like. If you weren't a married woman I'd take you back to the States with me."

She put her hands on her hips, guffawed. "Marriage, that don't mean nothing. I go whether the old man like it or not. He's no good for much; catch fish — what's that? Nothing. Any damn fool pull out the fish. Takes brains to be a good cook. Wait, I show you." She turned away, opened a closet I had not noticed before, a dark recess behind a panel, very secret. She reached in, rummaged, came up with a dusty bottle of wine. "This good wine — Frosinone. Kex, he got all kinds of wine."

"Open it, by all means," I said. No question but what I deserved a bonus for my aches and pains.

We shared the bottle and I went out to sit on the terrace, which was now baking in sunlight. It seemed a good time to review the situation. Clearly, in hiring out to Kex, I had taken on more than I bargained for. If I had any wits about me — so I told myself — I would clear out. Naturally, I intended nothing of the sort. I liked my daily ten thousand lire; I enjoyed Ignazia's cooking, and Kex's private hoard of wine. I was beginning to wonder how the affair would turn out.

Why had Alma slapped me? Why had Oleg turned me that queer cold look? I remember reading once upon a time a story called *The*

Mysterious Card. I forget the author; it might have been Richard Harding Davis. The hero received a card in the mail bearing some words of French. He could speak no French himself, and whoever he asked to translate nearly fell over in disgust and fury. His wife left him; his best friend turned against him. I felt as if I were carrying around, in the shape of my face, some version of *The Mysterious Card*; everyone who saw it wanted to punch it.

Well, well, I thought, blinking up into the sunlight, it looked like interesting times ahead.

I rose to my feet, stretched, decided to carry out Kex's instructions and explore the town. I climbed the stairs, looked up and down the road with something close to caution, and started off in the direction of Amalfi. On the steps up to the Ryens' flat I paused; perhaps Pamela and Hester might want to come for a stroll, during which I'd be sure to hear a good deal of gossip.

I climbed the steps to the door, where I became conscious of high-pitched voices within. I could not discern the words, but I heard Pamela's furious barking and a shrill wailing sound from Hester. I raised my hand to knock, then hesitated. Within, Hester broke into loud sobbing, while Pamela cried out. "Never, never, never! I don't care —"

I retreated down the steps, and feeling haunted, started south along the road.

Positano vanished behind a monstrous buttress of limestone. The crags towered overhead; below was the calm Mediterranean. Cactus, century plant, wild rosemary, broom, a magnificent bush with star-shaped clusters of green leaves grew among the rocks.

Fifteen minutes brought me to a gorge running back into the mountains. Cliffs cupped in a cubic mile of sunlight, hazy air; tiny acreages of olive trees clung to terraces fantastically perched like eagles' nests. The road crossed the gorge by a stone bridge; I stood by the balustrade, flipping stones off into space. A peaceful beautiful spot.

Two peasant girls came past, carrying bundles of brush. A little Fiat coupe about the size of a wheelbarrow came buzzing along the road, a bumble-bee on roller skates. It disappeared; there was utter quiet except for the sound of distant surf.

I leaned against the balustrade for half an hour, then turned and walked moodily back toward Positano. The world seemed full of trouble and grief.

I passed by the Ryens' flat, hesitated at my own stairs, weighing the beach against the apartment. I decided against the beach. The balcony overlooked material for a dozen charcoal sketches, of which I'd perform one or two in case Kex got technical…

A short man, about forty-five, with a big lumpy nose, sparse black hair stood negligently near Signora Umberto's shop. He was wearing a crisp light gray suit, smoking a big cigar, and seemed to be interested in the flight of a distant seagull. As I unlocked the door he came forward. I watched him warily from the corner of my eye. He seemed a particularly discordant note against the landscape, like a policeman in a bar. Not that the man resembled a policeman; quite the reverse.

He stopped about four feet away, looked me over with cool interest, just short of dislike. "You're Musgrave — that right?"

"Couldn't be righter."

"I suppose you've got me tabbed by now."

"I don't think so."

He surveyed me intently through his cigar smoke. "I'm Piombino."

"Ah, Piombino." No. 5 on the list. He saw the flicker of interest, nodded slowly, as if I'd verified one of his suppositions.

"I thought I'd save you the trouble looking me up," said Piombino.

Riddles, mystification. I said to Piombino, "That's very nice of you." If I played cagy, a few facts might pop out. I might learn what piece I represented in Kex's game of human chess. So far, I seemed to be one of the more exposed pawns. "How did you know I wanted to see you?"

He waved his cigar at the door. "Shall we step down, out of the dusty road, perhaps?"

"By all means. Don't break your neck on the steps."

He gave me a sharp glance as if I had said something meaningful, then marched stiffly ahead down the steps.

I moved out a couple deck-chairs. "How's this?"

"Suits me fine. I'm an easy man to please." He took his seat, blew out a screen of cigar smoke, watched me from the other side. "Well — what's the story? Let's get it over with."

"I don't have any story. You came here to see me."

He narrowed his eyes. "You play it close to your chest, don't you? Who sent you? Joe Rocco?"

"Never heard of him." I leaned back, beginning to enjoy the interview. This was like a scene out of a movie.

Piombino's mouth twitched. "If you'd let me in on your girlish secrets we'd get along quicker."

"Do you know Kex?" I asked thoughtfully.

"I know who he is. Why?"

"This is his flat here. I'm his guest, so to speak."

"So he's in the rackets; so what?"

"How do you figure he's in the rackets?"

"Well, blow me, you're hanging out here, ain't you? Ain't that a tie-up?"

"It is, unless you're wrong about me."

He blew out an impatient plume of smoke. His hand was shaking and the knuckles showed white around his cigar. Piombino was becoming edgy. "Let's cut the comedy. Joe Rocco wants something he ain't entitled to. He might have had a kick coming a while back, but the way it works out, he's made a better go than I have. He might just as well write the whole deal off to profit and loss. I don't pack that kinda weight anymore. My expenses have been simply awful; you've no idea."

"All very interesting, but why tell me?"

"I'm laying a groundwork; you've got to understand my position. I don't know how you sniffed me out; I don't care. But it doesn't need to get back to Joe. He's a nice kid, but what he don't know don't hurt him. What do you say to that?"

"It makes no difference to me one way or the other."

"That's the way to talk!" said Piombino with an unconvincing show of joviality. "Hell, you're a long way from home. I'd like to see you get a break." He puffed hard on his cigar, shot an abrupt question. "How much you making on this deal? Flat figure or percentage?"

"I'm hired by the day, to be perfectly truthful."

He grimaced. "Some of you guys don't care what you do for a living. Mmph — ten years ago I could play kinda hard myself, but my nerves gave out; I can't take it anymore. I'm keeping clean as a whistle. It's all out-go, no income. I'm willing to make a little adjustment, just you and me, but Joe is out of luck. A business agreement, you understand? You go back, you haven't seen me, I've cleared out for the four winds and the seven seas. Get me? You never caught up with me. I was last seen bound for Central Africa."

I reached for my cigarettes; Piombino made a convulsive movement. I looked at him with mild curiosity, lit up. "Just who," I asked, "do you think I am?" I meant the question literally; Piombino took it as a rhetorical remark, signifying indignant rebellion.

He said in a syrup-smooth voice, "I pick you for a smart cookie, trying to get along." He rose to his feet, changed his mind, sat down again. I decided to end the masquerade; there was no information to be had from Piombino.

"Friend," I said, "you're wrong. I'm not the man you think I am."

Poor Piombino misunderstood me again, and now thought that I had been toying with him, that I was in reality a faithful henchman to Joe Rocco, or whatever the name was. His lips pulled in and out; his forehead shone. "Wait till tomorrow. I'm no cheap-skate. Then you take a blow. Tell Joe or Manny or whoever that Piombino's gone native; he's not to be found. That's the best way; then there's no trouble, and life's lovely everywhere."

"I'd like to live a lovely life, but Kex keeps putting burrs under my saddle."

"What's Kex got to do with this?"

"That's what I'm trying to find out."

"Forget Kex," said Piombino querulously. "Now it's all settled. You've never seen me. Right?"

"All right, I've never seen you. Anything else?"

"No, that's good." He blew out a great breath. "Fine. I thought we was going to have troubles for a bit."

"One thing isn't clear. How did you hear about me?"

"This is just between us?" he asked wistfully.

"Just between us."

He reached in his pocket, brought out a blue envelope, passed it across. It had been postmarked at Rome. The address read: Mr. Larry Piombino, Hotel Luxa, Positano. I pulled out the enclosure, a single sheet of gray paper, with a typewritten message.

Dear Larry:

This is to warn you. A character named Musgrave has
just flown in from the States. He is with it. I can't say
too much, but you will understand what I mean. J. R. is
looking for you. He means trouble.

K. D. Vedalia

I re-read the note. "Who is Vedalia?"

"Old friend of mine," whispered Piombino, perhaps in reaction
from strain. "Last I heard he was in Los Angeles. God only knows how
he flushed me out."

"Piombino, this letter is a gag." I handed it back.

"Gag? What do you mean 'gag'? You name's Musgrave, ain't it?"

"I've gone to great pains to make that clear."

He inspected me craftily. "What's all this Hilfstone question?"

"Somebody got it into their head my name was Hilfstone —"

"He's hot, eh?"

"— and I had to set them right."

"Funny things happen around this place."

"Kex gets all the laughs."

"Silly old queer." He jumped to his feet abruptly. "I think I'll be
going. Everything's straight now. You ain't seen me, right? I flew the
coop. Right?"

"Anything you like."

He hesitated. "You make it sound too easy." He nervously puffed on
his cigar. "If you got something up your sleeve, you better forget it. I'm
a good-hearted old bastard until I'm pushed. Then I get mad. Don't get
any ideas."

"Brother Piombino," I said wearily, "if I've told you once I've told
you ten times the whole thing's a gag."

He nodded vigorously. "That's fine; that's the right way to look at
it. You won't be seeing me. I'll send you over a little packet tomorrow."

"What do you mean 'packet'?"

He waved his cigar. "You leave that to me. I got to do some checking.
All I can say is that it'll be fair. I'm gonna take a trip to get some air, and
I want to have things on a friendly basis before I leave."

"We'll never be any friendlier; but I tell you you're barking up the wrong tree."

"Let's not go into all this again, shall we not?"

"Okay, brother Piombino. If you want to go leaving packets here and there as if you were playing Drop the Handkerchief, it's your funeral."

He swallowed some smoke. "Don't say that word; I'm superstitious as hell."

"Just as you say."

"Well — so long. Everything's copasetic; right?"

"Right."

He waved his cigar, disappeared up the stairs. I heard the street door slam shut.

I wondered if Oleg's letter in the blue envelope had been post-marked Rome.

I wondered if Alma had received a letter in a blue envelope.

I wondered how many more blue envelopes had gone into circulation.

I wondered if someone receiving a letter in a blue envelope might be less reasonable than Piombino.

Chapter IX

It was now three-thirty. I went inside, puzzled out the latch to Kex's secret wine closet, removed a dirty bottle of Vicente Gomez sherry.

I pulled the cork, took bottle, glass, and a jar of olives out on the terrace, where I sat sipping and spitting olive pits over the balustrade. A thought came to chill me like a cold current of air. It was not a new thought; I had skirted near it once or twice before. I sat up straighter in the chair, looked over my shoulder. I might well be in danger of my life, very real danger... Piombino might have brought a gun with him instead of hints at a packet. What would I have done then? It had the ring of authenticity, this letter. The author — presumably Kex — knew the convincing details. I was lucky Piombino considered himself a peaceful man.

But Piombino was only one out of many. If I understood his hints correctly he meant to pay me to double-cross my presumable employer, one Joe Rocco. I could with very little effort look upon this money as a windfall, bounty from the heavens. I considered the ethics of the situation... Blackmail by proxy? Passive extortion?... Probably. People so inclined have high death-rates, especially in neurotic places like Positano... I would send the money back with a polite note.

What would Piombino do then?

Suppose he acted on the assumption that I refused to double-cross Joe Rocco, that I was hot on his track? It might be both simpler and safer if I took Piombino's money and kept my mouth shut. And then suppose a real emissary from Joe Rocco arrived on the scene? I jumped to my feet, drank the sherry in my glass, climbed the stairs, headed for the beach.

I took a slightly different route and found myself passing Mrs. Hortense Revost's ceramic shop. I paused, looked in the window. On display were a wine jug shaped like a gourd with six little tumblers, all glazed violet gunmetal, with vague greenish-white streaks. In the background was a large green-black plate, with three antelope in blue and white chasing each other around a circle.

I raised my eyes, looked inside. Shelves bore a hundred other articles; behind a counter Hortense herself at work, bent industriously over a table.

On an impulse I entered the shop, curious to observe her reactions, and thus test my theory concerning the blue envelopes. The shop was a pleasant little white-washed cave, decorated only by its own ware. Shelves to right and left glowed in off-whites, copper greens, iron yellows and russets, cobalt blues, manganese purple-blacks and gunmetals. Highlights glinted back and forth from gloss to gloss; the matt glazes shone with silky richness. The very shadows on the whitewash, the myriad parabolas, ovals, crescents projected by the sidelong light, gave off subtle color.

Behind the counter was a throwing wheel, clay-bins, drying shelves full of raw ware, and a decorating table, where Hortense now sat among trays of color.

She looked up as I entered; her eyes met mine, dropped in what seemed demure confusion. She very gently put down her brush, rose to her feet. She was probably pushing forty, but somehow conveyed a sense of youthful zest. At twenty she must have been terrific; she wasn't bad now: tall, almost lanky, but well-articulated, graceful, like a dancer. Her features were hard, fine, and gave an impression of interesting irregularity, although nothing seemed misplaced or exaggerated. Her face was perhaps too long, her eyes too close, her nose too thin and high-bridged, but these were minor matters. Her mouth, a little parted, gave her a look of breathless fervor that during the last twenty-five years must have brought men battling for her favors. If I could believe what I had heard of Blaine's conversation on the bus, Hortense was not one to put up a prolonged resistance.

She spoke in a light effortless voice, "Hello, did you want anything special?"

I said, "No. Don't let me disturb you; I'm just looking around."

"Please do." She stood by the counter, giving me a careful detailed appraisement — a kind of speculative summing-up — that made me intensely aware of being a man. I put my hands in my pockets, looked around the shelves.

"Do you turn all these out yourself?"

"Oh no, not everything. I can't compete with the Vietri potteries on things like this —" she pointed to a stack of plates, decorated with fish "— or these, with the dogs and birds. I do all these single pieces, all these wine sets."

I picked up a gray, white, and green coffee mug, with a clever handle that looped effortlessly around the forefinger. "It must be a lot of fun, making things like this. I've always had a notion to try it."

"I enjoy it very much," she said. And after a minute she added, "I saw you the other night in the Vistamare, didn't I?"

"You couldn't have avoided it, after young Freddy tried to make hash out of me."

She laughed. "Freddy's really very sweet. He gets extravagant ideas, and then he's like a knight in white armor... Are you staying long in Positano?"

"I don't know. It has its attractions." I was looking at her with what I suppose was a meaningful look; it was as hard to avoid flirting with Hortense as it was to carry an ice cream cone without giving it a lick. She seemed to expect it, like it. Her breath came a little shorter; she leaned forward, eyes sparkling. I caught a trace of fresh perfume.

"Sometimes it's very dull."

"I haven't found it dull."

She laughed. "If you'd been here as long as I have, you might think differently... You're American, aren't you?"

"Isn't it obvious?" I looked down at my clothes: slacks, sport-shirt, moccasins.

Her voice changed by the slightest shade. "You don't look much like a detective."

"A detective?" I was startled. This was what she had been leading up to.

"Yes. Aren't you?"

"No."

"That's too bad. I wouldn't mind if you were. I like detectives. Some of my happiest hours have been spent with detectives. I like the American kind best. The English are always so careful and precise and funny, like absurd little boys at a game. The French, of course, are unspeakable. The Italians, worse."

"Where did you get the idea I was a detective?"

"Oh —" she shrugged "— news gets around very quickly."

"What am I supposed to be detecting?"

I very clearly felt wariness, ice-cold calculation behind her flippant manner. "Don't you know?"

"I can guess."

"Well?"

"It was in a blue envelope, wasn't it?"

She said nothing.

"And I'm supposed to be detecting you."

She opened her eyes wider, narrowed them quickly, swayed a little bit. "If you are, I don't know what you could be detecting for."

"Well, forget it. I'm not a detective. I'm not a gangster. I'm not a queer and my name is Chuck Musgrave." My recital was growing like the chorus to *Old MacDonald Had a Farm*.

"What are you, then?"

"I generally call myself an art student to avoid long-winded explanations."

"Oh?" Her voice was quietly skeptical.

I grinned sourly. "The letter in the blue envelope made a convincing kind of a case, didn't it?"

She blinked, her mouth closed, she looked mulish. "How do you know I got a letter in a blue envelope?"

"I don't know for sure. I'm just guessing. But whatever it says it's probably all malarky — at least that part that concerns me."

"Suppose —" her voice was mild "— suppose it said to watch out for a young good-looking detective posing as an art student?"

"I'd say that someone was playing a very involved game at your expense. Also mine. I'm being paid, but not enough; I'm going to ask for a raise."

She was quite bewildered; she looked toward her handbag with a worried frown. "If you're not a detective," she said in a husky abstracted undertone, "that makes it worse…"

A long shadow filled the door; Buster Blaine stood with one big hand on the door lintel, leaning forward. "Hello, Hortense."

"Hello, Buster," in a toneless voice.

"Hi there, Chuck."

"Hello, Buster."

He let himself swing forward, so that he looked like an ungainly doll about ready to cave in. He squinted at me. "How's the world treating you?"

"About as usual."

"Come on up to my flat and have a drink."

"Sure." I looked at Hortense. "Goodbye."

"Goodbye."

We walked down toward the esplanade. "Nice girl, Hortense," said Blaine carelessly. "She's got a nice little place there."

"How does she do it? She's American, isn't she?"

"Originally German. Her husband was a big-time general in the Wehrmacht — von Revost."

"Von Revost. A war-criminal, wasn't he?"

"That's what they called him; that's what they put him away for." We moved to the wall to let a line of ragged urchins stream past us, a sack of sand on the head of each.

"She left him long before the war; that's to her credit," said Blaine. "She wouldn't put up with it."

"Then what?"

"Damned if I know. England, the States, then here. I guess she got lonesome for the old country. But she won't go back to Germany."

"She turns out some nice stuff."

"She's a hard worker; won't sponge off nobody like the other floozies around here. She's a damned nice girl. Miserably lonesome, I should say."

"I'd think she'd leave Positano then."

"No, she's got herself established; she's got friends here; she's got her little shop, she's part of something."

We walked across the concrete flags, dodging more urchins, circled fishermen in blue denims and black mustaches mending nets, climbed a flight of steps, entered an alley smelling rather poorly. "Drains," said Blaine. "Sometimes it's as sweet as a rose in here; again —" he pointed to a medium-sized boy wetting against the wall, watching the world pass by with a limpid and unconcerned gaze, "— that doesn't help much either. Oh well, this is Italy."

He pushed open a door, ushered me with an exaggeratedly polite gesture into his lodgings. He had a long narrow room with white-washed walls, domed over like a Quonset hut, with a balcony overlooking the beach. At one end was a low bed, covered now with a spread curiously like a Navaho rug; at the other was a big round table, supporting a bottle of brandy, half-full, an untidy ash-tray, a portable typewriter, a book or two. Against the wall was a rickety case containing a dozen pocket-book mysteries, a human skull crusted with splotches of black and red mold, a carton of cheap Italian cigarettes. A tweed deer-stalker cap hung on a peg; in a corner stood a banjo.

"Sit down," said Blaine. "Find a seat; place is a mess, natcherly. I gotta get myself a good woman."

I pulled a chair alongside the table; Blaine brought over assorted bottles and glasses, making quite a rite of it. "How do you like it? Straight, plain water, mineral water?"

"Mineral water."

He mixed a couple of drinks. "Here's to crime."

We drank. "Ah," said Blaine. "Nothing like it, first drink of the middle afternoon."

"When do you work?"

He looked with hesitancy toward his typewriter. "Two or three times a week I lock the door and pitch like hell, and then relax till the next spasm."

"Do you write under your own name?"

"No." And he said, "How you getting on?"

"Fine. Everybody seems friendly, except the guy that —"

His face was as wooden as a cigar store Indian's, but I felt him quicken to interest. I still had no wish to talk about my adventure on the stairs, although by now I was pretty sure of the guilty party.

"Getting back to Hortense," I said. "How does she stay in business? Isn't there a law against foreigners owning businesses? How does she get away with it?"

Blaine contracted half his face in a slow lewd wink. "Easy. All she needs is an obliging Italian to front for her, pay the rent, fill out the forms, bluff the carabinieri. Hortense never lacks that kind of help."

"She's got a guilty conscience," I said. "She thinks I'm a detective."

"Funny how ideas get around." He looked at me under drooping lids. "I don't suppose you claim that honor, by any chance?" He took a casual swallow from his glass, but over the rim his eyes were fixed like limpets to my face.

"Blaine," I said thoughtfully, "you write murder stories; presumably you write about detectives. Do I resemble your idea of a detective?"

"The detectives I write about," said Blaine, "don't resemble anything on or off this earth." He swirled the brandy ruminatively around his glass. "You don't *look* like a detective. But that —" he aimed a long yellow big-knuckled finger at me "— that might be your stock in trade — that kind of look that makes people relax and blurt out all their sins. And they never know how misguided they've been until they're standing in the dock watching you whisper advice to the D.A."

I laughed sourly. "If I were proving I was a detective, I'd show you a badge. But I can't prove I'm not by *not* showing a badge. What's the difference anyway? Everybody thinks I'm something besides what I am. I might as well relax."

Blaine poured us both a two-finger refill. "It's a funny deal. The truth is —" he paused while he poured the mixer "— you're getting a funny kind of rep around here. Just like you say, nobody knows whether you're fish or fowl. For instance," and he turned his most ingenuous look at me, "who is this Hilfstone guy?"

"I don't know," I said shortly. And then, because I was annoyed, "What did you do with the letter that came in the blue envelope?"

Blaine reacted even more vigorously than had Hortense; he jerked as if I had held out a lighted cannon-cracker. "Ho, ho," said Blaine in a subdued voice, "what's going on? I thought I was playing you along calm and pretty. I don't get it. How —" he paused uncomfortably.

"How do I know? Deduction, my friend. Understand, I don't have any idea what's in the letter; I imagine it warns you the jig is up, that Musgrave has come to Positano to catch you red-handed."

"Well, yes," said Blaine weakly. "That's about it. Well, what are you up to?"

It was almost too much. "My God, man, I'm an innocent bystander. The man for you to worry about is Kex!"

"Well, I've naturally had that idea. I'm not worried about Kex. He's harmless in himself. It's just what he does that scares me. He starts things going that he can't stop. He calls them jokes. He's an elaborate son of a bitch, Kex is. He might think it hilarious to put us all into jail. Not that I'm worrying about anything like that, you understand," he added hastily.

"Naturally not," I said with a poker face.

Blaine looked at me quizzically, and lit a cigarette. "How come you knew about a letter in a blue envelope?"

"I guessed."

Blaine took a slow drink. "Pretty sharp guessing."

I reached in my pocket, found my wallet, fished out Kex's laundry list. "If Kex is joking, these are the people that are supposed to laugh. Two of them for sure got letters in blue envelopes. Your name is on the list too."

Blaine took the list, read off the names: "Munton, Blaine, Leibnitz, Piombino, Vroznek, Hortense, Alma, Margaret, Pamela and Hester Ryen, Dannister. Hm. Makes a nice bunch. A well-assorted congenial selection." He made a saturnine grimace, shook his head. "Imagine that gang cast up on a desert island." He turned the page over. "Kex's laundry. The Dirty Shirt List." He whistled through his teeth. "And just once more — where do you fit in?"

"Well, it was like this." And then, caught by a twinge, I halted. Kex had instructed me to say nothing of my work; so long as I was accepting his money I was theoretically obliged to obey his orders. However, he had not instructed me to pose as a detective. If he had, my fee would have been even higher than the figure I was planning to hit him up for.

Blaine watched my struggles of conscience with undisguised interest; the cigarette in his mouth, smoke oozing from his nostrils.

I said, "What I told you is the truth. I'm an art student. Kex is letting me use his flat — presumably so that Freddy and all the other Dannis-ters would think I was Hilfstone, and go into a flip. He sent out letters in blue envelopes to everybody on this list, so that everybody thinks I'm whatever they're the most scared of…The last, about the letters, is sheer supposition."

"Hm…Off-hand I'd say you had a ticklish job. Suppose somebody on that list was real desperate, and got the wind up bad? There's some excitable people around here."

"You're not telling me anything I don't know. Freddy tried to beat me up. Alma slapped my face."

"She did?" asked Blaine with amused admiration. "Why, that alco-holic little fireball!"

"Anyway, I'm trying to breeze it around that I'm *not* a detective, *not* a queer, *not* James Hilfstone, *not* God-knows-what-all."

"I can see your point," said Blaine. "Here, have another shot."

For in my agitation I had drained the glass. We sat in silence a moment. Then I said, "You don't seem too upset about your blue enve-lope."

He shrugged his high shoulders fatalistically. "It's just Kex; there's no sense getting upset at Kex. It's just his nature to be the way he is; I don't let it bother me, although I guess I'm in the minority. Oleg hates his guts. With good reason, I must say." He shifted his position, draping across the chair loose as a rope ladder. "Kex is a funny guy, no denying it. We all have our cross to bear. Kex's is boredom. He's too full of Old Nick just to sit and stare into space; not brainy enough to go in for something real deep. So he messes around in all kinds of mischief. He's got the mind of a moth, he tastes, and sips, and flutters on."

"How does he keep out of trouble?"

"Darned if I know. So far he's beat it out. It can't last forever. Some-thing tells me this is the time. Oleg would probably have knifed him last year if he had the chance. Kex pulled a really raw deal — hired a pretty young girl from Naples to come down here and seduce Oleg. The girls around here won't look at him, don't like him; old Oleg gets pretty hard-up. So naturally he falls all over himself when this lovely thing gives him the eye. For a week they chase each other back and forth up the beach, the girl keeping just two inches ahead. Oleg, the poor fish, is about nuts; his tongue is hanging out. He goes overboard for the girl, wants to marry her. She finally lets him have it; the next day she folds her tent and blows back to Naples. The truth is she can't see Oleg for sour owl-spit; she just worked a week according to Kex's recipe. Oleg somehow traces her to Naples and runs her to earth, where she's entertaining six or eight American gobs every night. She laughs at him, tells him the whole story."

"My God," I said. "That's not much of a joke."

"No," said Blaine, "it wasn't. It was what you might call a tragedy. To add insult to injury, the girl has given him a dose. He has to go to the hospital to get a cure."

I shook my head. "I don't think I'd have taken it. I think I'd have blown my cork, killed a few people, starting with Kex."

Blaine took a long drink. "I think Oleg had just about that in mind. Kex, who had been sitting on the Vistamare terrace all this time, twirling his mustache and playing grab with Chi-Chi, took it into his mind to visit Egypt. He's a pal of Farouk's, who was then on the throne, and so off he goes. Oleg simmers down, but naturally he still can't stand the sight of Kex."

"I'm surprised he came back to Positano."

"It took guts. Oleg's got guts, and he's like the others around here — square pegs, trying to find a place to light in a world of round holes." He took up the Dirty Shirt List. "This is Kex all over. Always something new — a kid with a new toy. Kex is a square peg just like everybody else; Positano is his spiritual haven. He gets bored and leaves but he always comes back with a new way to raise hell. One time he brought hashish in from Egypt. We all ate hashish like it was candy for a week. The next time he brings a hypnotist down from Rome. We're all hypnotizing each other until Countess Margaret throws a wing-ding and Paul Prie shoots a gun at Leibnitz, and a chap named Maybanks thinks he's a cat and jumps onto the top of the house and the family inside howls bloody murder. Kex doesn't want to be annoyed with everybody's headaches, and goes to Deauville." Blaine paused to refresh himself with a pull at his glass and another cigarette.

"There's supposed to be an eighteenth century caravel full of gold, sunk right off that island out there. Kex hires a barge and a diving suit and goes down looking for treasure. The funny thing is — it could only happen to Kex — he finds half a dozen ingots. The Italian government confiscated them, but Kex had more fun than rats in a hat."

Blaine sighed. "Kex and his deals — ether parties. I went blind for six hours. Had to crawl along the street feeling out ahead like an inchworm. Blind as a bat — sober too. And then he's thrown drags up at his flat. I went to one of them, had to dress as a woman. I'll never try that again … Another time he decided to experiment on Cary Johnson, nearly killed him. First Kex hopped him up on marijuana, talked him into eating benzedrine, gave him a big sniff of cocaine, and topped it off with peyote mash. Talk about a bang! You never saw anything like it. The guy started walking up walls, trying to pull open his chest so he could listen to his heart tick. He wound up screaming for three hours and fighting off horrible monsters. When he came to he said he saw things he couldn't bear to think about, in five brand new colors. About two weeks later he tried to crash a bank in Sorrento and got put away."

"What I don't understand is how Kex hasn't been put away."

"Pull. Kex knows everybody, and most everybody likes him that doesn't know him too well. He's a likeable guy — modest, mild, grabs all the checks. There's no malice in him; he just likes to see things hum, likes to try out new sensations, likes to laugh."

I picked up the Dirty Shirt List. "So far I don't see anything funny in this."

"No telling what Kex's got going." He took the list, looked down the names. "It's kind of a funny selection. For instance, he's got Munton but not Kavenaw, Munton's sidekick. He's got Leibnitz, the German artist, but not Paul Prie, the Frenchman. He's got me but not Maybanks. And why he includes Pam and Hester, poor little sparrows, and Dannister beats me all to hell. I can't figure it."

"Maybe he only picked the ones that would jump."

Blaine raised his eyebrows, frowned at the list. "Why Munton? The soul of British rectitude. The Ryens — innocent as a maiden's dream. And me —" his lower jaw dropped a little; his voice took on a faintly hollow note "— there's nothing on my conscience except a couple books from the Chicago Public Library."

He read down the list: "Piombino — used to be a big dope baron;

they shot him back to Italy along with Luciano... Alma... Hortense... Margaret. I can't figure what he's got on the girls. The Ryens." He clicked his tongue. "Dannister. That's where Kex is going to run into a mess, fooling around with Dannister. He's not the fooling kind."

"What could he get on Dannister?"

Blaine shook his head. "Beats me. They're a funny bunch. The girl's a cute piece; Freddy's a pup, not dry behind the ears. The old man looks like a proud Castilian aristocrat — austere kind of bloke. I've never seen the lady, Mrs. Dannister." He paused, then continued ruminatively. "Lots of funny rumors about the Dannisters, different one every week."

"Such as?"

"Oh, fantastic things: the girl went to Switzerland not for finishing-school, but to give birth... Mrs. Dannister is crazy... They kidnap and torture children... Dannister killed a French duke in a duel and now he's afraid to show his face outside of Positano." He saw my face, laughed. "It's these local inhabitants. About their only amusement is the antics of the foreigners. And no story loses anything in the telling. You ought to hear what they say about me." He wagged his head in melancholy resignation. "You know what they call me?"

"No."

"'The goat on stilts'. That's a fact; ain't it the limit? 'The goat on stilts'!"

There was a knock at the door, a quiet little *rat-tat-tat*. Blaine folded himself together, rose to his feet, crossed the room, opened the door. A small boy handed him a note, said something in Italian. Blaine responded, shut the door, ambled back to where I was sitting.

He hesitated for as long as it takes a watch to tick twice, then handed me the note. "It's for you," he said dolefully.

I looked at the superscription: Signor C. Musgrave, Casa Umberto, written in a neat lean hand. Blaine sat watching me from the corner of his eye. I hesitated a moment. "How the devil did the boy know where to find me?"

"Someone saw you come in; you can't get away from people here."

Slowly I tore open the envelope. It was signed: Alfred Dannister. I read the note:

Dear Mr. Musgrave:

Certain disturbing information has reached me which makes conversation between us imperative. I suggest that you call at my home tonight at nine p.m. If either time or place is inconvenient, kindly let me know and I will arrange accordingly. In the absence of such notification I will expect you at nine.

Sincerely yours,
Alfred Dannister

I folded the note, thoughtfully replaced it in the envelope, tucked it in my pocket. Blaine followed my every movement; I could see he was almost beside himself with curiosity.

"Nothing important," I said off-handedly. I pushed back the chair, rose to my feet. To my surprise the floor was swaying like the deck of a boat; Blaine had fed me an unsuspected quantity of brandy. I steadied myself against the table.

"Going?" said Blaine.

"Yes...I think I'll run up to the apartment for a bath and a shave."

"Er, anything I can do for you?" Blaine had his eyes fixed to the pocket where I had put the note.

"No, not a thing. Thanks for the brandy."

He came to the door, looked after me wistfully.

I climbed the steps to the road, started up the hill. In the street in front of Kex's flat was a long low convertible, a magnificent metallic green-gray job. Kex had arrived in Positano.

I knew it even more definitely when I saw that my sign had been pulled off the door — pulled with a petulance that left little tabs of paper hanging to the corner tacks.

I took a deep breath; blew the brandy fumes from my lips. I had things to say to Kex. Kex no doubt had things to say to me. There might be quite a to-do.

CHAPTER X

I LET MYSELF IN, descended the pale tunnel, deliberately, step by step.

The sun had dropped behind the hill; the terrace was awash with cool gloom. The door into the flat stood ajar. I pushed it open, stepped in, with a rather tight feeling at the pit of my stomach. It was as if I were afraid of Kex.

He sat at the dining room table, wearing a crisp pale yellow turtle-neck sweater and natty blue slacks. His white plume of hair was brushed till it almost snapped with sparks; his mustache was brisk and jaunty. A flask of Chianti was by his right elbow, a plate of crusty bread to his left, a big wooden bowl half full of lettuce, radishes, onions, in front of him. He ate with his fingers, picking out pieces of salad, dipping into dressing, popping the bits into his pink mouth.

Ignazia, with a sullen look on her face, stood in the kitchen, watching a kettle.

Kex waved cheerily at me. "Ah, there you are."

"Here I am."

"Sit down; have some salad?" He started to make a gesture toward Ignazia with an air of alert and solicitous hospitality.

"No, thanks." I took a chair opposite, sat watching him. "I always lunch late," said Kex. "A very light lunch, usually a salad." He took a gulp of wine. "And how do you like Positano? Does it bear out my statements?"

Apparently Kex still intended to maintain his pose of the dilettante publisher, with me the hireling artist. "Very interesting place. Interesting people."

He nodded. "Both the local inhabitants and the foreign colony. A variegated group, but very friendly and whole-hearted."

"I suppose you could say that," I replied, thinking of Alma and Countess Margaret and Freddy. And Chi-Chi.

"How's the work coming?" He took a mouthful of lettuce and watched me with an expression of benign inquiry.

I hitched my chair forward. "It depends on what you mean by work."

Kex raised his eyebrows. "Why, the sketching, of course."

"Oh, the sketching. I don't know whether I can afford to stay with it."

"My word," said Kex in mild surprise. "Why not?"

"I seem to be running into opposition. People don't like me around here. A woman slapped my face today. The first night I was here somebody tripped me downstairs."

Kex shook his head in astonishment. "Ignazia told me you had an accident — but I can't believe it was intentional!"

"He didn't come down and kick me afterwards by accident."

"Fantastic!"

"I thought that somebody must be working under a misapprehension — so I put up that sign. I see you've pulled it down."

Kex frowned judiciously. "I must say I didn't quite approve of that sign. Likely to put queer notions into people's heads. Never was a place like Positano for rumor; if you recall, we agreed to be, well, discreet about your purpose here."

"I couldn't have been more discreet," I said, "and I got trapped the first night I arrived. Naturally, I can't have that. In fact the first chance I get I plan some small retaliation in kind."

"Ah," said Kex, "you know who's responsible?"

"Yes, I think so."

"A terrible thing, a terrible thing," said Kex, eyeing me cautiously.

"I've started to think that the most discreet thing for me to do would be to leave Positano."

"No, no!" cried Kex, aghast.

I shrugged. "If you want more courage, it's going to cost you more money."

Kex glanced toward Ignazia, who was pouring hot water into a teapot. "I must say I don't like being held up."

"You're not being held up. I was paid to make charcoal sketches, not to serve as a human punching-bag."

Kex ate the last of his salad. "The tea, Ignazia, then you can go."

Ignazia put cups, lemon, sugar and a teapot on the table, and departed with the suggestion of a flounce.

Kex said ruminatively, "This is really rather far-fetched."

I grinned. "No one knows it better than I do."

"Don't you think you're being — well, just a little unfair?"

"Unfair? How do you mean? I'll make charcoal sketches for you any place in Italy, any place in the world, for ten thousand lire a day. But to let people slap me, kick me, beat me up, shoot me, the price skyrockets. Let's not kid each other. Whatever you've brought me down here for, it's not art."

"Hardly that," said Kex cautiously. "I wouldn't go so far as to say that."

"You're not saying it. I'm saying it."

He poured tea with studious concentration. "What do you suggest that your status should be, if not an artist? In other words —"

"I understand you. You want to know how far I'll collaborate with you?"

Kex blinked and frowned. "I must say I don't like either your tone or your implications."

I saw I had taken the wrong approach; under no conditions would Kex allow himself to call a spade a spade. "Put it this way. I'll stay here in Positano. I'll even make charcoal sketches if you like. But I won't pose as anyone other than myself, by either act of commission or omission..."

"Well, well," mused Kex. "Assuming that I agreed to these conditions, what do you think your salary should be?"

"I want a thousand dollars a week, in advance, plus expenses."

"*What?*" roared Kex. His eyebrows threatened to meet his hair.

I sipped my tea, while he simmered down, giving off angry seething sounds in the process. "My God, man, are you insane! For a thousand a week I can hire all Positano and half of Sorrento! What kind of weakminded yokel do you take me for?"

I grinned. "All you need to do is to say no."

"Of course I say no."

"Very well. I'm starting back to Rome right now."

Kex balled his fists — pink ineffectual little knobs. "Don't you think you're being ridiculously unfair?"

"Not in the slightest. A thousand a week isn't a lot of money if I get killed."

Kex looked genuinely startled. "Killed? Who's talking about getting killed? This is Positano, in a civilized country, not Chicago."

"Civilized people can get just as irritated as any other kind."

"But that's the most arrant nonsense," spluttered Kex. "I'll admit that I — well hired you because you resembled a friend of mine —"

"Hilfstone."

"Yes, Hilfstone. And I thought I might play a little joke on some friends here in Positano — but you've got completely the wrong slant on things. Killing! Ridiculous!" No question but what Kex was utterly sincere. "People don't kill people over jokes!"

"A lot depends on the joke. Personally, I don't intend to take a chance. I have an idea that you've already spent quite a bit of money on this 'joke' — and I don't see why I shouldn't cash in with the others."

"But — a thousand a week! That's as much as my —" his voice trailed off.

I reiterated patiently, "If I stay alive it's good pay. If I get killed, it's nothing. I'm willing to take the chance — for a thousand a week."

Kex rubbed his chin, looked off through the window where a few yellow lights penetrated the stone and twilight complexities of the gorge. "If I paid you this fantastic sum, you'd have to do exactly as I tell you. Exactly."

"And make sure of getting bumped off? No thanks."

Kex said crossly, "I think you're belaboring your point. There's absolutely no chance of any such event."

"Maybe not. But I'm going to pretend that there is. I won't agree to anything but maintaining residence here in Positano for as long as I'm being paid." This was an easy concession; I had decided to remain whether I was paid or not, mainly because of a girl with a mop of dark blonde curls.

Kex chewed up toward his mustache. "I had no idea when I hired you that you'd try these extortion tricks on me."

"Call it extortion, if you like. If you'd told me the truth when you hired me, this situation would never have arisen."

"I'll pay you fifty dollars a day."

"No."

Kex chewed at his mustache. "I don't have that kind of money with me."

"Write me out a bill of sale for your car. I'll accept that for two weeks work."

"I should think you would!" cried Kex in outrage. "That's a five thousand dollar Chrysler!"

"But don't forget it's used. I'll make it three weeks work."

Kex laughed in bitter amusement. "I've never seen such supreme gall, such — such —"

"Let's do it this way. You write me out a bill of sale, dated today, for services received. I'll write another one to you, dated a week from now, selling the car back to you for 1,000 dollars, but it'll be void without my receipt for 1,000 dollars."

Kex wore an expression, grim, rueful, amused. "By hook or crook you'll swindle me out of my car, eh?"

"No. I'm just trying to protect both of us."

"I'll protect myself, if you don't mind...I'll write you a check."

"You might stop it before I could put it through."

Kex put on an injured expression. "Do I seem the kind of chap to do a thing like that?"

"I'm not quite sure what kind of chap you are."

"Very well then..." Kex seized a sheet of paper from a notebook, dated it, wrote. "There, does that suit you?"

I read carefully. "I think that covers most of the angles."

"Now," said Kex, "let's have that return bill of sale."

I borrowed a sheet from Kex's notebook, wrote. "There you are, nice and legal, Philadelphia-style... And now, may I have the car keys?"

"The car keys?" said Kex quizzically. "And suppose I want to use my car?"

"It's my car now, till I get that thousand."

"It's no such thing," said Kex stiffly. "You'll get your money as fast as I can cash a check. In the meantime I don't allow anyone to drive my car."

"I don't want to drive the blasted car; I want something to look at! Just in case you decide to go away suddenly, say to Egypt, I want to be sure I don't have to file suit with nothing but that IOU for evidence. In other words, I'm just trying to build an ironclad protection against any and all kinds of sharpshooting. If I have custody of the car *and* this IOU, you won't fly the coop."

Kex became suddenly and suspiciously jovial. "Very well, I'm satisfied. You certainly couldn't steal the car, and it's insured." He tossed a leather packet of keys on the table. "The world being as it is, I suppose we all have to be careful. But now that I'm paying you this outrageous sum, you'll have to cooperate with me, and —"

"I'll cooperate by staying in and around Positano for as many weeks as you pay me for. I'm not posing as James Hilfstone, I'm not pretending to be a detective, and in addition —"

There was a knock on the door. Kex and I sat looking at each other a startled instant, then I got up.

A small boy with curly black hair and beautiful olive-gray eyes held a fat yellow envelope up to me. I took it, looked at the superscription: 'To C. Musgrave', written scratchily in black ink.

I gave the boy twenty lire and ripped open the envelope. Through the gap flickered the green, white and black of the most beautiful artwork in the world — U.S. twenty dollar bills, a wad three-quarters of an inch thick.

"Who is it?" called Kex. "What's he want?"

Without any definite idea of what I would do if I caught the boy I ran out on the terrace after him. At the top of the steps the door slammed shut. I tucked the envelope in my pocket, returned into the flat. "Who was it?" asked Kex once again.

"A note for me." Piombino had not been fooling. It put me in an uncomfortable position; it weighed in my pocket like a brick.

Kex swung around on his heel, strode into his living room. He lit the fire, sat primly upon one of the green satin divans. He turned to me. "One thing I want clearly understood —"

I shook my head. "You're paying me for one thing, one thing only — to stay in Positano. Remember that — you're paying for no more than my physical presence here. If I get killed you've hired me dirt cheap."

Kex stared at me a second as if a new set of concepts had occurred to him. "Well — yes," he said, "that's quite all right."

"Tonight," I said, "I'm visiting the Dannisters. I plan to make it clear — if it isn't clear already — that I am not Hilfstone, don't know him, never heard of him until you mentioned his name."

"But —"

"And then Freddy can beat you up instead of me the next time he feels inclined."

Kex's handsome face puckered. "I really don't think it would be wise to —" he hesitated.

"To what?"

"Well, nothing at all, actually… May I ask what time is your appointment?"

"I'm starting now."

"I must say I don't think it's advisable."

"Why not?"

Kex scratched his clean white plume. "Well, you've mentioned the word danger; I think that if there's any chance whatever of physical danger it's at Dannister's."

"May I ask why?"

Kex smiled indulgently. "I detest people who purvey malicious gossip. All I can do is to warn you."

"Thanks."

Kex stared at me thoughtfully. "You don't like me, do you, Chuck?"

I looked him over dispassionately. "I wouldn't go quite so far as to say that. I don't hold with your idea of good clean fun. Beyond that I'm not involved, one way or the other."

"I'm really not such a bad fellow," said Kex bluffly. "When you know me better you'll see that for yourself."

"Incidentally, what are the sleeping arrangements around here now?"

"Oh." Kex looked blank a moment. "I'll have Ignazia make you a bed on one of the divans. Tomorrow you can move down to the Vistamare or the Garibaldi. I think you'll be more comfortable."

"Fine… Goodnight."

Kex bounced to his feet, once more cherubic and overflowing with bonhomie. "I'll be interested in what happens at the Dannisters', if you have no objection to telling me."

"No. I guess that's included in the thousand. Goodnight."

"Goodnight."

And strangely, when I climbed the white-washed conduit to the street, most of my resentment toward Kex had vanished. Maybe he wasn't such a bad fellow after all. A victim of circumstances, frivolous, selfish, but at heart not such a bad fellow. A big, thoroughly spoiled Persian cat, intent on pampering himself.

When I reached the road I stopped by Kex's car, patted the massive fender — a magnificent twenty feet of intricacy. And now, although I had Kex's keys in my pocket, I raised the hood, removed the rotor from the distributor. Kex might have more than one key.

It was eight o'clock. Time for dinner at one of the beach restaurants, and then to the Dannisters'. I was curiously exalted. Maybe Kex hadn't done me such a bad turn after all. I fell into a sudden fine mood, with the sheer act of living a matter for excitement.

CHAPTER XI

THE SHOPS OF POSITANO were still going full blast; children were playing in the street; the four thousand people who were born, married, buried in Positano pursued their lives, and the foreigners were less than weeds in the garden. Neither really existed for the other; we were two worlds joined at a very few points: at the Vistamare, at Signora Umberto's store, people like Chi-Chi; each provided colorful background for the other.

In front of the cinema a group of young men and girls, rigidly separated, waited for the second show. As I passed conversation dwindled. Forty-five people stared with fascinated concentration, trying to read the secret of my existence. Something savors of black magic in these Italian stares; they absorb, suck up, deriving strength to themselves as a savage drinks courage in a dying warrior's blood. The Italian stares as if he would look into your soul: unabashed, open-mouthed, single-minded.

I ran the gauntlet, sauntered down the hill to the beach.

From the esplanade I could overlook the Vistamare terrace. The tables were full, strange faces for the most part, except Munton, sitting with four people unknown to me.

I ate spaghetti with ham and cheese at the opposite end of the beach. At quarter to nine I started up the hillside. The esplanade left off, the steps began — dank stone steps lit by dim yellow street lamps, few and far apart, leading up at abrupt unexpected angles. These were the dangerous steps, where, according to Oleg, all good Positanesi met their end. I passed passages and tunnels which in the dark looked mysterious and intriguing, but which I knew would only smell of urine.

I plodded on up, stopping now and then to pant. Up, up, back and forth, up a thousand feet along the helter-skelter stone steps. Now they plunged under a house, now they led up a sheer wall of rock with a black gap below, and far across the gorge shone the random lights of the steps and alleys and passages opposite.

I came out on the upper road, set out in the direction of the Dannister house. The road sloped up for a hundred yards, then began dropping in big switchbacks. I thought, there must be an easier way than climbing up, then coasting down.

Five minutes later I met two young peasant women carrying bundles of fodder. I used one of my two Italian phrases. *"Dov'è casa Dannister?"*

Both pointed down the road, both speaking together. Two hundred yards farther I found a wrought-iron gate, to the left on the seaward side. A lantern hung from a springy wrought-iron loop, illuminating a brass plate. An elegant flowing script sprouting ivy leaves read: 'Villa Sirenia', and underneath, in smaller letters, 'Dannister'.

I tried the gate; it was locked. I saw a button, pushed it, waited. Ten seconds passed, then light poured up through the wrought-iron gate; the latch lifted with an electric buzzing.

I pushed through the gate, came out on a cliff-hanging terrace overgrown with rich green plants. Steps led down the hill, marked by lights inside globes fashioned from red, green and yellow bits of glass. The steps zig-zagged back and forth a dozen times, finally led out on another terrace. The house rose ahead.

It was an imposing place, built like a castle, looming over the sea. Dim light shone from three or four windows; the others were dark. A secret house, full of sullen strength. A door stood open; waiting for me in the frame of light was a man I knew to be Alfred Dannister. He was tall, spare, and stood with every muscle and nerve under conscious control. He wore a gray suit of rather old-fashioned cut, and was clearly not a man of easy familiarity.

"Mr. Musgrave?" He did not hold out his hand.

"Yes."

He looked me over, head to foot, a long electric, searching instant. He seemed to relax, or more accurately, gave the slightest perceptible exhalation of breath. "Very decent of you to call; won't you come in?"

I entered a hall, arched like a crypt, and now, in the glow of amber sidelights I saw Dannister in more detail. He was hardly more than forty-five or fifty, but seemed part of an age thirty years gone. His face was marble-calm, with the placid stony beauty of a 1925 matinee idol. He looked vital, intelligent. A rat-catcher mouth gave him grimness. By no means did he seem the man to rot away his life in Positano.

He led me into a large living room panelled in dark wood, hung with good, although conservative, pictures. A deep crimson oriental rug covered the floor; light came from old-fashioned lamps with silk shades. Two rectangular tables, precisely across the room from each other, displayed a large variety of English and American periodicals, arranged in neat and exact formation. Leather chairs faced a fireplace, where logs burned with quiet intensity. We were alone in the room.

I looked around warily. If Kex were to be believed, I was now in a place of danger. I felt no great apprehension. Dannister would hardly lend himself to so plebeian an activity. I looked left and right; where was Betty? The man that married Betty got a rather uncomfortable set of relatives as a tie-in. Freddy, the brash young simpleton; the unyielding father; God knew what else.

Dannister took me to a seat by the fire, went to an antique sideboard. "Do you drink Scotch? With soda?"

"Yes, thanks." I took a glass bubbling and tinkling with ice, and settled into the chair. Dannister was far more formidable than I had expected.

He seated himself, and wasted no time getting into the subject. "Somehow, Musgrave, you've involved yourself in my personal affairs." He sat back, watching me with eyes not in the slightest degree friendly.

"I have done nothing of the sort," I said.

"I find that hard to believe."

"It happens to be the truth."

Dannister smiled faintly. "If you intend blackmail, you're approaching the matter from an oblique angle. I'm puzzled."

I said rather shortly, "Because you're starting out on a set of false premises."

He opened his mouth to speak; I hurried on ahead of him. "I know that your name is Dannister; I know that you don't like a man called

Hilfstone, whom I resemble. That's all I know of you or your personal affairs."

"I'd like to believe you."

"But you don't, obviously."

"Under the circumstances, I don't see any other course open to me."

We sat looking at each other, momentarily at loggerheads. I asked, "What are the circumstances?"

He shook his head, a faint look of amusement on his mouth — a beautiful sensitive mouth; it was not hard to guess where Betty and Freddy got their good looks.

"You say I'm a blackmailer. I say I'm not. Until I actively start blackmailing you — I'm right."

"There are some peculiar coincidences that indicate otherwise."

"Such as what? You hint of circumstances and coincidences, but you bring none of them out into the open."

He shook his head again, with the same expression of sardonic amusement.

"Because I look like your friend Hilfstone?"

"Partly — although Hilfstone is hardly a friend of mine."

"If I look like Hilfstone, it's no fault of mine."

"No, but you bring yourself to Positano, proclaiming that you are *not* Hilfstone. Why would you come here, why would you use the name Hilfstone, if there were not collusion between you? The answer is inescapable."

"I'd hate to have you on a jury trying me for my life."

Dannister's lips twitched. "What other answer is there?"

"The story of what actually happened."

"I'm willing to listen to you."

"I came here because a friend asked me to make charcoal sketches of Positano."

"And who is this friend?"

"Kex. Up to five days ago I had never heard of Positano, then I met Kex and he sent me down here."

"Kex." Dannister looked into the fire. "I don't believe I've ever met him … But your story doesn't dispose of certain other circumstances."

The interview was proving a trial. I had expected Dannister to be like the other Positanesi: effete, vague, a little soft. Dannister was hard and brilliant. "I suppose," I said wearily, "that you got a letter in a blue envelope, denouncing me as a blackmailer."

Dannister looked at me a full five seconds. "What leads you to say that?"

"The other members of the Dirty Shirt Club have got them."

Dannister broke into a short sharp laugh. "I don't pretend to understand you."

"No, it is rather fantastic. Certain other good citizens of Positano have received letters denouncing me; I don't see why you should be neglected."

"Apparently you consider yourself a victim."

"Victim — guinea pig — shill — accomplice — sucker."

Dannister stood up, took a pair of quick steps, stood with his back to the fire. "The more you talk, the more you succeed in bewildering me."

"I'm sorry. But in any event — I'm no blackmailer. You can rest easy on that."

Dannister said thoughtfully, "I'm not afraid of blackmail."

"What are you afraid of then?"

Dannister sipped his Scotch. "Nothing," he said flatly. "I have brought my family here to live a quiet life. If anyone thinks to disturb this quiet life, so much worse for him." And he fixed me with a sudden glare that would have instantly changed my mind, had I intended him a bad turn. "I can't understand why anyone would go to such lengths —"

"You don't know Kex. He would have made a good Nero."

"Kex," said Dannister in a careful voice. "I must make his acquaintance." He looked at me with a trace less hostility. "I hope you understand my position."

"Yes, certainly. I hope you understand mine."

Dannister smiled his faint cold smile. "I apologize for the actions of my son. He is rather abrupt, and I must say at first glance there is a resemblance between you and — and Hilfstone." He opened a drawer in the sideboard, took out a photograph. "That's Hilfstone. Have you ever seen him?"

I inspected the picture with the most intense interest — a small passport-type photo. "This doesn't look like me... He's fifteen years older than I am. His nose is longer, his chin is sharper, he's fatter in the neck."

Dannister was watching me closely. "You're right. Hilfstone resembles you only superficially; although, your profiles are very similar. Still you look enough alike to surprise a casual observer. My son and daughter, for instance, don't know Hilfstone the way I do."

"Who is this Hilfstone, if I may ask? I know it's none of my business but I'd like to know whom I'm impersonating."

Dannister looked into the fire. "Hilfstone is an embezzler, a forger, a wastrel. Hilfstone has the morals of a jackal. When I heard of your presence in Positano, I was sure that somewhere in the background was Hilfstone." His voice became lower. "I thought I had seen the last of Hilfstone. But I see now that by some means or another he has found me again."

"Not necessarily," I said without conviction.

Dannister shrugged; for an instant the control of his face relaxed; he looked weary to the very bone.

He turned away from the fire. "More whiskey?"

I accepted a refill. He replenished his own glass, returned to his chair. "May I ask what are your present plans? How long do you plan to stay in Positano?"

"I don't know, at least a week." I hesitated a second, then said, "To tell the truth, I've become interested in what's going on."

Dannister said, "Don't you think you're — well, rather putting your head in the lion's mouth? Suppose, instead of asking you over to speak to you, I went out with my gun and shot you? I assure you, I'm quite capable of it."

"In that case, I'd have made a bad bargain with Kex."

"Kex seems to be at the bottom of the entire business."

"I would say so."

"What on earth does he have in mind? Money?"

"No. According to local theories, Kex is bored."

"Incredible."

"Not when you know Kex. He's capable of almost anything."

"And how did you meet Kex?"

Before I could answer, a door opened and Freddy swung into the room. He was wearing tan shorts, white sneakers, a faded red sweat-shirt. He carried three small pink fish on a line. "Look," he cried, "look at these!" He swung the fish back and forth, beaming at them in tri-umph. His glance moved from Dannister to me; his grin was wiped off as if by a sponge, and I thought he would swing the fish at my face.

"You — you —" words failed him. He turned to Dannister. "This is the man I was telling you about. Look, he had the nerve to come here to —"

"Freddy," said Dannister quietly.

Freddy fell silent. The arm holding the fish slowly subsided.

"You had better go upstairs until I am finished talking to Mr. Mus-grave."

Freddy's mouth sagged. He glanced toward the ceiling. "I don't want to go up there; I don't want to be bothered with those —"

"Freddy!" Dannister's voice stung.

"I want to clean these fish. I want to —"

"Upstairs!"

Freddy turned on his heel, stalked sulkily out into the hall.

Dannister said in an unruffled voice, "Freddy is at the age when dis-cipline is most necessary and, likewise, the hardest to accept."

I made a dubious sound. Freddy looked to be about twenty-one, seven years younger than I was. I felt no need of discipline when I was twenty-one, although, nevertheless I got it, army-style.

But then, I, Clarence Musgrave, and he, Freddy Dannister, were two different cups of tea. There was no question but what my host had his problems.

He gave his attention back to me. "Who else has received these let-ters?"

I gave him the names on the Dirty Shirt List.

Dannister sat in a brown study for perhaps a minute. Then he said, "If I were you, I would leave Positano tonight; I would go without a second thought."

"Undoubtedly you are right," I said. "But I'm not going to do so."

"May I ask why not?"

I was not too easy in my mind about the ethical doctrine involved in taking Kex's money to stay in Positano. At the moment when I had been grinding it out of him, it seemed like the smart angle to play; now I began to have qualms. "For one thing," I said, and with complete honesty, "I've become interested in this affair. Secondly, I've become interested in one or two of the people involved — one of which, to be completely candid, is your daughter." Perhaps I was carried away by the impulse of the moment. I knew as soon as I had spoken that I should have kept my mouth shut. Dannister sat like a wax dummy, staring at me with obvious astonishment, even shock.

His voice came to him, husky, dry with an emotion I could not name. "Does Betty know this interest?"

"I don't know."

"I don't think she will be flattered. I suggest that you do not presume upon chance acquaintanceship — especially under circumstances as ambiguous as those of the present."

I straightened in my chair, the skin tight at my cheeks. Dannister was showing a pig-headed obduracy toward me, an irritating skepticism. I said, "I've explained my part in this affair; apparently you don't believe me."

The cold smile trembled on Dannister's face. "You overstate my position. I am reserving judgment. The information I have received is quite circumstantial. I would be foolish to ignore it entirely."

"But use your head! If I planned blackmail, would I come here and confide to you — this interest I mentioned?"

"At this stage," said Dannister, "nothing would put a strain on my imagination."

"I'll go with you on that point."

"The blackmail is a minor issue in any event. There are other reasons which lead me to discourage you."

I opened my mouth to remark that Betty should be allowed to make a few of her own decisions, either pro or con, but I never got the words out. From upstairs came a chorus of faint squealing cries, such as small children make if suddenly startled or terrified.

Dannister jumped from his chair, hissing, "Freddy, Freddy, Freddy!" between his teeth, and ran out of the room. A door at the far end of the room opened, Betty slipped through. She gave me a quick enigmatic glance, ran after her father.

I rose to my feet, listened to their footsteps thudding up the stairs. A door opened, shut; then there was almost complete silence.

I now did something of which I am not particularly proud, but still not mortally ashamed. I went to the sideboard where Dannister had taken the photograph of Hilfstone, pulled open the drawer. As I had half-hoped, half-expected, a blue envelope lay in plain sight. It was neatly cut across the top. With trembling fingers I drew out the letter, unfolded it.

The letterhead listed the names of Bray, Medlary, Caldecott, Chivers and Bray, solicitors of Grays Inn, London. The letter was datelined at Rome, and formally addressed to Alfred Dannister, Esq., at Villa Sirenia, Positano, Italy.

> *Dear Sir:* (ran the body of the letter)
>
> *Reluctantly I take this means of reporting a rumor which, having been heard in London, I took the liberty of corroborating in Rome.*
>
> *Briefly, James Powan Hilfstone has learned your present residence. He has been seen in the company of one Clarence Musgrave, an American, terming himself an art student, but actually a professional squire of gullible elderly women, and bearing a remarkable resemblance to Hilfstone.*
>
> *I fear blackmail is in the wind, concerning a matter of which I shall not take note here. My informant reports that Musgrave apparently is to be the edge of application, Hilfstone being disinclined to take a blackmailer's risk.*
>
> *Please call on me if my fears prove justified.*
>
>

> *Very sincerely yours,*
>
> *Bradshaw Bodley Caldecott*
>

I held the letter in a hand cold as ice. My heart was thumping like a burned-out bearing. I thought I had reached a fair estimate of Kex's villainy; that no act of his could shock me further. I had been wrong. I was burning with fury. 'One Clarence Musgrave — professional squire of gullible elderly women!' Even though I had known in a general way what the letter had contained, the actual text filled me with cold rage. At that moment I could have killed Kex.

I heard steps on the stairs; I came to, remembered where I was. Hastily I folded the letter, pushed it into the envelope, dropped it in the drawer. I had time for one fleeting glimpse at a second photograph. It showed me wearing a tennis sweater, standing alongside Betty, who wore a peculiarly short skirt. Strange! Numbly I realized that the man must be Hilfstone of fifteen or twenty years ago, and the woman Betty's mother.

I shut the drawer, sprang to my seat, just as Betty herself came into the room. She came hesitantly across to where I was sitting. I jumped to my feet. The sight of her face was starting to send tight little thrills along my diaphragm.

This feeling, added to my fury at Kex, put me in quite an extravagant state. I said, "Betty!" in a voice that sounded strange and distant.

She stopped six feet away from me, looked at me with eyes full of trouble and inquiry. "Why did you say a thing like that to father? About me?"

"Did he tell you?"

"No. I was listening. I heard every word. He'll think I encouraged you."

"What if you did? There's nothing wrong."

Her eyes glistened damply. "Yes, there is."

"I don't understand why."

"There's many things you don't understand; and that you never will understand, and you'll have to believe me!"

I had wanted Betty to speak for herself; she was doing so, but I was still dissatisfied. "I want to see you, Betty, and talk with you — not here, somewhere else. Tomorrow. How about it?"

"No!"

"Don't you like me?"

"No. Even if I did — I just couldn't!"

"Why not? Why can't you? I'm not what —" I caught my tongue. "Don't believe whatever that letter said about me."

"Oh I don't. It's not that." She turned a startled look over her shoulder, a motion full of fright and guilt. "My father mustn't see me talking to you; he'll think —" her voice died.

"When can I see you?"

She made as if to leave. "I've got to go before —"

"Tomorrow."

"No, I can't!" Breathlessly, "I can't!"

"Then I'll come here; I'll wait till I see you; I'll climb the fence."

"No! Oh, please, you don't know."

Footsteps, slow, deliberate, sounded on the steps.

"When can I see you?"

"I — I'll go walking tomorrow."

"What time?"

"I leave here at nine — half-past nine."

The footsteps were halfway to the landing. I stepped forward; Betty swayed back in alarm. I caught her hard; she gasped in terror, but she met my face — a swift fleeting kiss, hot and sweet as burning caramel. She ran to the far door, disappeared.

Seething like a tea-kettle, shaky and all a-crawl inside, I leaned back against the mantle.

The gaunt form of Alfred Dannister appeared in the door. He was carrying the three pink fish which Freddy had taken upstairs with him. He swept the room with his eyes, then came deliberately into the room. He laid the fish on the nearest table, across a magazine, went to the sideboard. My own glass was still half-full. He poured himself a half-inch of whiskey, added a squirt of soda.

He turned toward me with an air of measured deliberation. "I think we have covered the points at issue."

"We don't seem to have come to any meeting of the minds; you still consider me a crook."

He shook his head. "On second consideration, I do not. I think you are a dupe, a headstrong young man with wisdom still ahead of you."

I was intrigued. "What's changed your mind?"

"You made the point yourself, in connection with my daughter."

"Oh."

"You were right, let us say, for the wrong reasons."

I made no effort to understand him. "Well, if you're satisfied, I'm satisfied."

CHAPTER XII

I WALKED ALONG THE ROAD, in and out of the shadow of the cliff. The moon glittered like a silver teapot; the sea was calm, dark and hard; clouds piled around the horizon like whipped cream on a cup of Roman coffee: an extravagant outlook. I was in an extravagant state to match, with emotions churning around my brain like colored rags in a washing machine.

I thought of Kex; I could hardly keep my feet on the ground for fury. A 'professional squire' I was — of 'gullible elderly women': demonstrable libel. I would sue Kex for a million dollars.

I thought of Dannister and his more than strange conduct; I almost came to a halt for perplexity... I thought back over the evening at Villa Sirenia, it seemed as dramatically mysterious as a stage set, with all those who lived there fulfilling dramatic parts.

I thought of Betty — I had been saving her for the last — and my head went light and my skin tingled; I had felt the same way after my first date, and had thought myself long through with such adolescent pangs.

I considered Betty's face — a strange face, as if an argument had raged in the institution which designs new faces: whether to give her classic beauty, gypsy pungence or a fey Celtic flower-look. Certainly a nice compromise had been arranged.

I thought of Kex again, and once more became furious; and went through the entire cycle, the various emotions coming across my mind like hot flashes, and so preoccupied, walked far up around the gorge, with the town fragile and frozen far below, and then coming back along the other at the south verge of town, I met the main road, started down and found myself in front of Pamela and Hester Ryen's apartment. Their window was a blank citron-colored square.

I came to a halt. If they had received one of Kex's letters they might well be in a state of anxiety — which perhaps had contributed to the angry voices I had heard earlier in the day. I thought blithely, I could talk to them and set their minds at ease; indeed it was my duty to relieve them if it were in any way possible. I climbed the steps, knocked on the door.

There was silence inside, the empty feeling of a house from which the owners have stepped out for a moment. I knocked again; and now came a step inside, slow, heavy, a portentous step.

A dead drab voice — Hester's voice said, "Who is it?" It was flat and lack-luster as if she were talking from a numb sleep.

"It's Chuck Musgrave."

I waited. She made no answer. The door lay between us; I could not imagine her face. After a moment I said again, "It's me — Chuck Musgrave. I want to talk to you."

"Go away," she said, very quietly — almost a whisper.

I said, "There's been a mistake; I want to talk to you."

Silence from inside. I could imagine her standing rigidly, her head bent a little forward.

"Where's Pamela?" I called. "Let me talk to Pamela."

After a moment I turned down the steps, continued along the road, feeling rather dampened.

And there was the door down to Kex's flat. Kex — cherub-faced devil, perverted child. And the rage came almost to swamp me; I could feel it in my mouth, it hurt the pit of my stomach. Down the pale staircase was Kex, a white-eyed insect in a snail-shell.

I stood looking at the door, sweating with the intensity of feeling. A faint sound came up from below — the vibration of voices, the soft sound of a door shutting.

I put the key in the bright bronze lock, opened the door. At the bottom of the steps was Chi-Chi, his foot on the bottom tread.

He looked up; I looked down. His chiselled mouth drooped, his fine eyebrows rose. He slowly started up the stairs, then with a return of nonchalance, came a little faster. His footsteps sounded: *creak-pad, creak-pad.* I grinned, remembering footsteps that sounded *creak-pad* coming down the stairs.

He noticed my expression, lowered his eyes, hesitated; then, putting on a look of debonair assurance came trotting up toward me.

I stood in the center of the passage; as he came up to me he had to halt. I looked deep into his eyes for an instant, then punched, smash on his nose. It crushed with a sensation like stepping on a hard-boiled egg; Chi-Chi fell over backwards. I swung around in a follow-through; Chi-Chi rumbled and thrashed down the stairs.

This was wonderful; it couldn't have been better. I felt like shouting in exultation! I ran downstairs to find Chi-Chi on his hands and knees, dripping blood and vomiting.

Kex had come out on the terrace, flapping a bathrobe around himself, his eyes like clam-shells, his mouth an astonished pink hole. "What on earth, what on earth —"

I said, "That's the lad that tripped me downstairs the other night; he's just now got paid back in his own coin."

"What's this? What's this?" bleated Kex, looking from me to Chi-Chi and back.

Chi-Chi laid over on his side and began to groan. "Go get a doctor, man!" cried Kex, backing away from the mess. "Do something! Don't just stand there!"

"He's nothing to me. He can bleed to death for all I care."

"That's a damned callous attitude!" said Kex in mounting rage.

"He kicked me fairly callously himself."

"How do you know it was him? It might have been anyone in town."

"No. Not very likely. I've known he did it for a couple of days now. Nobody else had any reason to do me dirt that early in the game. But this thing did."

Chi-Chi was sitting slumped against a wall, holding a handkerchief to his nose, his face gray and creased — a miserable sodden self-pitying lump of flesh.

"Freddy Dannister didn't come up here. He was home in bed. Chi-Chi here assumed I was your new boy-friend and decided to take steps."

"You can't be certain of all this," blurted Kex. "It might have been —"

"No. Not with shoes that squeak in the same key. That's too much of a coincidence."

"This is terrible," said Kex in an abstracted voice. "Chi-Chi, how are you?" And he bent solicitously forward, still not approaching closer than six feet.

Chi-Chi gasped out Italian curses.

"He says you've broken his nose," Kex remarked.

"Too bad."

Kex made a flapping gesture, like a distracted chicken, and ran up the stairs. I went inside and packed my sparse belongings. Outside I heard staccato voices — Ignazia, Signora Umberto, Luigi, Kex. There was five minutes of argument, then Luigi and Signora Umberto helped Chi-Chi up the steps while Ignazia came in for a bucket of water, followed by Kex.

Kex said in a portentous voice, "Under the circumstances I think it might be just as well —" he caught sight of my suitcase and finished lamely "— if you went on down to the Vistamare tonight."

"I think so too; in fact I'm on my way. Incidentally, I hope you aren't squeamish about libel suits."

"Libel?" Kex stared in puzzlement. "What are you talking about?"

"I'm a professional squire of gullible elderly women, am I?"

Kex's jaw relaxed, his mustaches slanted downward. "Did — did Dannister tell you that?"

"He showed me the letter. I'm going to sue you for a hundred thousand dollars — as soon as I've finished working for you."

Kex laughed weakly. "You have an unparalleled sense of humor."

"I hope you're able to laugh while you're signing the check."

"Poof. Nonsense. You can't sue on anything like that."

"I certainly can. And I will. And I'll collect. The 'professional squire' was the straw that broke the camel's back. 'Gangster' and 'detective' — they were bad enough, but I'll include them in our thousand dollar a week deal. 'Professional squire' — that's hitting below the belt."

Kex went to the sideboard, poured himself a drink, with feline niceness of motion. "You've been taking an increasingly aggressive tone with me, Musgrave."

"Don't you think I have good reason?"

Kex gestured easily with his drink. "I agreed to pay you the salary you demanded, fantastic as it was. Surely you intend to give something in return."

"We've already discussed that. I made it plain, I made it emphatic, that for a thousand dollars a week I was contributing my physical presence here in Positano, no more. Libel comes extra."

"May I point out that you can't possibly prove me responsible for this so-called 'libel'?"

"That's what courts are for. Dannister and I talked the whole thing over. He thinks I can collect. So do I."

Kex ran his hand through his crisp white hair, sighed heavily. "That's nonsense and you know it." His voice became angry. "I've had about enough of your lip. Get out of here!" He turned his back on me, strode to the sideboard.

"Am I to consider my employment at an end?" I asked.

Kex struggled with himself. "No," he said reluctantly. "The bargain still holds." He swung around grandly. "When I make a bargain, I stick to it; there's no welching or threatening from my side."

"You haven't been tripped downstairs yet. Also you haven't been libelled. Do you want to settle out of court?"

"For what, in God's name? For what?"

"Libel."

"You've got libel on the brain, Musgrave; you still can't prove I've libelled you."

"I know damn well I can."

"Dannister got an anonymous letter. So what? How does that concern me?"

"It has your fingerprints all over it." This was a shot in the dark; it hit home. Kex blinked, scratched his neck.

"Fingerprints would be smudged," declared Kex without conviction.

"Not a chance. Dannister took pains with the letter. He plans to have a word with you too. I'll ask you again, do you want to settle out of court?"

"Blackmail!" cried Kex, his mustache quivering.

"Blackmail nothing. I'm asking you if you're willing to settle out of court."

Kex patted his mustache back into shape. "Suppose I effected a settlement with you — it would have to cover any and all damages you might consider to have occurred during your stay here."

"Excluding physical disability."

Kex waved his glass airily. "You've been reading too many cheap thrillers. I merely don't want any more threats of libel suits."

"So you're guilty of others?"

Kex grinned. "Perhaps there were a few indiscretions — exaggerations, over-statements."

I considered a second or two. "Fifty thousand dollars should cover everything."

"Fifty thousand dollars!" screamed Kex.

"Think what a court would award me —"

"You're insane!" snorted Kex. "Your reputation has no such value."

"That's for the court to decide."

"I wouldn't think of paying you any such sum."

"How high would you go?" Now we were getting down to brass tacks.

"Oh." Kex chewed on his lip. He snapped, "I had not expected this affair to cost me a fortune."

"It might cost you more than that."

"What do you mean?"

"I wouldn't give a plugged nickel for your life."

"Oh nonsense," spat Kex. "Here —" he handed me a fountain pen and pulled a sheet of paper from a desk "— write: 'In consideration of the sum of one thousand dollars I hereby' —"

I laid down the pen. "One thousand dollars? Come again, Kex."

"I won't go higher, I refuse to be victimized."

"The shoe is on the other foot. I've been victimized and I'm trying to collect."

Kex grumbled, "If I had known you were going to take this attitude I would never have taken you into my confidence."

I said scornfully, "Since when have you taken me into your confidence?"

"In any event," said Kex primly, "I won't pay you any such preposterous sum. Fifteen hundred is my top limit."

"Well, I'll come down a thousand. Make the check out for forty-nine thousand."

"Pooh."

I rose to my feet. "I'll take it to court."

"An Italian court? Do you think you insult an Italian by calling him gigolo? That's how half of them make their livings."

So we argued, back and forth. I could bring him no higher than twenty-five hundred; he could talk me no lower than thirty thousand. "Look," I said finally, in utter disgust, "tear up that bill of sale I wrote you for your car, and I'll call it quits."

"My car!" bleated Kex. "That's the ultimate, the absolute limit in cheek. I've gone to infinite pains to —"

"Also a thousand dollars, so I can afford to buy gas. At a hundred and thirty lire a liter, it's cheaper to ship the car by freight than drive it."

Kex paced up and down, waved his hands like semaphores, expostulating with such vigor that I finally exclaimed, "You write me a check for sixty-five hundred and give me a bill of sale for the car. If and when the check goes through, I'll tear up the bill of sale. If not, I keep the car and you've got to tear up the bill of sale I gave you."

"I don't understand this; it's getting too complex; there's already three or four bills of sale…"

"I understand it," I said. "Take my word for it; you're getting off easy."

Kex, hoarse and red-eyed and a trifle drunk, threw up his arms. "Very well. I'll have to trust you. Write me out a receipt, stating that the amount covers in full all damages sustained through any statement of mine, written or otherwise."

"During the current month."

"Oh, all right. During the current month."

"That means next month, if you write any more letters I can sue you again."

"You haven't sued me at all yet, you've just out-talked me!"

We traded documents with solemnity. I refused a drink, took my suitcase and left.

The terrace was dark where Ignazia had scrubbed away Chi-Chi's blood; the white staircase was pale as eggshell.

Out on the street I stopped by Kex's convertible. What would I do with it if I had it? I couldn't afford to run it, certainly not in Italy, where even the smell of gasoline costs money.

The contingency was unlikely. Assuming that Kex and I both survived the next week or two, I had no reason to think that Kex's check was not as good as gold.

I suddenly decided I was tired — desperately tired. The exhilaration of the morning had worn off; the flux and sweep of events had wrung me dry of response; I was an emotionless husk, a haggard shell of a man.

I stalked downhill through the shadows. The moon had set; Positano was pale as a cemetery.

The Vistamare was the sole oasis of life. Four or five tables were full, mostly with people I did not recognize. Blaine lounged on a bar stool beside Alma and Countess Margaret precisely as on the first night. Oleg Vroznek sat playing a morose game of solitaire; when he looked up, saw me, his eyes hooded over; he bent over his cards.

I was too tired to explain the circumstances to him; I walked past the cashier's desk and told Giovanni, who sat reading a newspaper, that I wanted a room.

Twenty minutes later I had taken a hot shower and was stretched out on cool sheets. I suddenly thought of the money I had received from Piombino, and reaching over to my coat, pulled out the envelope, counted it. Two thousand dollars. I thought wryly that Piombino had assessed me as an easy man to buy — a mere two grand. What to do with it — keep it or send it back? A question of nicest balance. It was not my money, I had not earned it, but strictly speaking, neither had Piombino. I had as much right to it as he had... Added to the sixty-five hundred from Kex it made a good day's work. The payment on an apple orchard in Oregon, a Los Angeles County lemon grove. Drowsily I wondered if Betty would prefer Oregon to California. Tomorrow I would ask. I fell asleep.

During the night I had a chilling dream, very little of which I remember. There was a pale mask of a face and two wispy shapes, fluttering, spiralling upward into the darkness. I mention this dream because the next day when I heard about Pamela and Hester Ryen dying, I thought of it again. It must be coincidence; it has to be. I don't want to think otherwise. If I thought I had powers of divination I'd be afraid to go to sleep.

Chapter XIII

I awoke, showered, shaved and went down to breakfast with a ravenous appetite. Over bacon and eggs and sliced oranges Giovanni brought me the news.

"You knew them very well, those two English ladies?"

"Not very well. What's the trouble?"

"Last night —" he flicked up his hands "— they are dead." He pulled out a chair, seated himself with an expression that conveyed, "Such is what may happen to any of us."

I laid down my knife and fork. "How did they die?"

Giovanni shrugged. "Who is to say? I was not there; certainly it could not have been a pleasant sight."

"I don't mean —" I stopped and started all over again. "What killed them?"

"The pills — a whole bottle of pills for sleeping. They drank it in tea." Giovanni screwed up his face. "Always tea for the English."

I heard my voice coming from a long distance. "Both of them?"

"Both of them," said Giovanni with somber relish. "One, the tall nervous one, she sleeps on the bed; the other, the sick one, she sits in a chair. The mayor has telephoned to Naples for the British Consul."

"But why?"

"No one knows."

"There was no letter, no farewell?"

"Nothing."

I stirred my coffee, seeing the cup with blind eyes. Giovanni jumped up, wandered away; I sat stirring my coffee. I remembered last night; I heard Hester's voice through the panels of the door. Already she sounded dead, already she had passed that final barrier of decision, already she knew that life for her had been left behind. What was going on in her mind when she heard my voice? I must have seemed like the devil himself standing beyond the thin panel of the door. I had an odd vision: myself through Hester's eyes, my face glistening, oily yellow-green with evil, my eyes afire, my mouth wet… A wonder she had not flung the door wide and slashed me with a knife. Perhaps I had it coming. Was I not partly responsible for their deaths? Was I not Kex's paid nightmare? Was I not then a murderer as openly and overtly as Kex himself? I drank some coffee. My throat was numb and constricted; I had difficulty swallowing.

What should I do now? What recompense could I make? Leave Positano, leave Italy, leave Europe? Go back to the States, hide in the remotest badlands, in Idaho, Utah, Arizona? And what would I accomplish then? The damage was done; I had catalyzed Kex's schemes by my sheer presence.

So I sat huddled over my coffee, feeling as miserable and numb as I have ever felt.

Gradually the numbness thawed; counter-arguments began to form; gradually I began to gather some small comfort to myself. The exact degree of my culpability seemed rather hard to define. In fact, I could not see where I had done any wrong except by the mere fact of association with wrongness.

Certainly I had taken Kex's money — but I had done my best to defeat his plans, and this I had done openly, with Kex's knowledge. I told myself with perhaps a shade of sanctimony that I had cheated not even Kex. I had nothing on my conscience. I had agreed to stay in Positano, but would Kex's letters have been less agonizing if I had gone? Things might well have been even worse. In spite of taking Kex's money I found myself unable to see where I had any direct responsibility for the deaths of Pamela and Hester Ryen.

Somewhat cheered, I drank a second cup of coffee, and looked at the time. Nine-fifteen. I studied the face of my watch with a vague tickling at the back of my brain. It seemed that there was something I was neglecting, something important. I reviewed the recent past… Had I arranged to meet Kex? Blaine? I did not think so. Mail, telephone, doctor, dentist… I relaxed and drank a third cup of coffee.

My mind wandered back to Pamela and Hester. It was unimaginable that Pamela, so full of sparkle and talk, could kill herself. The impetus must have come from Hester. This was more comprehensible; I could understand parchment-faced Hester turning away from life like a tired housewife closing the door on an untidy room. But it was all so incomprehensible!

What had they done, two old spinsters, that the threat of exposure could drive them to suicide? I considered a few possibilities, without satisfaction, then looked at my watch. Quarter to ten. Again the vague tickling, the urgency. Who, what — *Betty!*

I jumped out of the chair, was outside in three steps. At nine-thirty Betty was leaving Villa Sirenia; I was to meet her. How could I forget, how could I, how could I?

I ran like a hare across the esplanade, through a startled cluster of urchins playing with round stones, past sardonic fishermen mending nets, nearly upsetting a vague-looking man in a yellow coat carrying a portfolio and paint-box. I ran up the stairs, halted, waited impatiently while four elegant blonde women in slacks, sweaters and jewelry sauntered past me. Then up again, running up the stairs as if I were afraid of missing a train. I passed a boy with a donkey, a girl with a basket of bread on her head, two fat women wheezing and laughing, and all stared after me with amused contempt — another mad foreigner.

Red in the face, and heart pounding, I came out on the upper road. I was thirty minutes late. If she had already gone I would never find her.

I set out along the road and presently came to the wrought-iron gate. The road was empty. I halted — dejection. No Betty. The sun slanted hot and white along the mountainside, the sea rippled in a peacock's tail of catspaw patterns, vivid blue and green.

I saw her, sitting on a low wall, half-hidden by a sprawling century plant. She was wearing blue jeans and a white blouse; her face was pink with self-consciousness for so obviously waiting for me. She slid to the road, half-turned away, not daring to meet my eyes.

I felt unaccountably shy myself. "I'm sorry I kept you waiting."

"It doesn't make any difference." She looked at me, then over her shoulder toward the wrought-iron gate; as if thereby stimulated or impelled, she turned, started quickly off along the road.

I caught up with her. Clearly this was not to be a run-of-the-mill romance. A flash of an idea, a perverse discord crossed my brain: Blaine and his romances with Alma and Countess Margaret.

I found my voice. "Something rather terrible happened last night. I got thinking about it this morning and — well, with one thing and another I was late starting up the hill."

"What happened?" she asked in a colorless voice.

"Did you know the two Englishwomen that lived near me — Pamela and Hester Ryen?"

" 'Did' I know?" She turned her face toward me. I could hardly keep my eyes away from her; I was getting it bad. "I know who they are; I've seen them — a tall quick one like a school teacher, a shorter plump one who looks sick."

"That's right. They're both dead."

"Dead." She spoke the word quietly, thoughtfully. "How?"

"They got one of Kex's letters, last night took sleeping pills."

She said nothing. We went past a wine-shop, a half-dozen curious heads turned to stare after us. From a balcony three women scrutinized us with the keenest absorption, divining our ultimate secrets. No one in Positano wanted to miss any detail, no matter how trivial, in the daily lives of the foreigners.

We were coming into town. I asked, "Where are we going?"

She slowed her step, looked up, around the mountains. "Anywhere, it doesn't matter."

"Where do you usually go?"

"Nowhere specially. Sometimes up to Montepatuso."

"Don't you get tired walking?"

She shrugged. "I don't walk because I like walking. If I had a car I'd drive."

"Why do you go then?"

"Because I don't like to be at home." She turned into a dark staircase leading up through olive groves. "Let's go up here."

Steps zig-zagged up the mountainside, around limestone knobs and turrets, past cavities festooned with stalactites. There was no opportunity for words.

Positano became like an ornate wedding cake, with spun-sugar

houses and churches and hotels. Three times we passed peasants leading tiny donkeys loaded with brush, once a nattily dressed young
Italian, probably a Neapolitan, who eyed Betty as a cat eyes fish.

Where the path angled around a bluff we sat to catch our wind.
Betty said with her eyes out across the sea, "I wish I understood what
was going on around Positano."

I said after a moment, "It reminds me of a greenhouse with a lot of
strange plants — pitcher plants, mistletoe, sea anemones, orchids — when
suddenly a mad gardener sprays everything with growth-hormones and
turns on ultra-violet lights and injects radioactive plant-food into all the
roots —"

"And Kex is the mad gardener."

"Yes. I guess we could call him that. He's also one of the hot-house
plants. It's quite a queer situation."

She looked at me wryly. "I suppose I'm one of the hot-house plants
too."

"No, no —" I started to protest.

"Oh yes I am," she said coolly. "I'm just as strange as anyone else
around here."

"Well, you're strange in a nice way."

"You don't know me very well."

"I want to know you lots better."

Her mouth tightened with just a hint of primness — an unnatural
expression which was quickly relaxed. "I wouldn't trouble if I were
you." She looked steadily out to sea. "In a week or two you'll be leaving
and things will be settling down to normal again."

"I don't know about that."

"About what?" she asked with quick interest.

"About things settling down to normal."

"Oh."

"It seems to me things are just getting under way. To do Kex justice I don't think he suspected that anyone would take him seriously —
enough to kill either themselves or anyone else. He didn't calculate
very well."

"But *why*? Why should he interfere at all?"

"That's something you'll have to ask Kex."

She surveyed me dispassionately. "Why are you staying here?"

I felt suddenly hot and embarrassed. I had it all straight in my own mind, but would she see it the way I did?

"First of all, I'm being paid."

"Money," she said scornfully.

"But I'm not doing anyone any harm; in fact I've tried to reassure everybody who's on Kex's list. I tell myself I'm doing good instead of harm."

She shrugged.

"That's one reason. Another is that I'm interested in what's going on; I don't want to walk out now. The third is — well, frankly, it's you."

"Me." She seemed puzzled.

"Yes. Has it escaped you that I'm very much interested in you?"

"Well — no." She was remembering last night. I was too.

"And you don't seem to dislike me."

"No...But —" she hesitated. Her mouth tightened.

"But what?"

She made no answer.

I grumbled, "All this mystery is preying on my nerves."

She grinned. "Let's go. We're only halfway up."

The slope was easier; the steps were wide slabs of mossy limestone, seemingly as old as the hills. The path roved back and forth through sparse olive groves, terraced bits of soil growing artichokes, lettuce, potatoes. Behind was the sea, calm and blue as the paint on a travel poster.

Betty said, "Up here is the only part of Italy I'd regret leaving."

"You're not thinking of leaving, are you?"

"No."

"Is your father?"

"No."

We were silent another ten minutes, when we came to a village high in the crags, the stone houses crusted on the rock like a peculiar porous lichen. This was Montepatuso.

In a grocery shop I bought a loaf of bread, a cheese shaped like a small smooth gourd — provolone. These we took out on the terrace of a wine-shop overlooking the sea, and here, in the warmth of the sun and the breeze of the sea, we ate our lunch, with four small children watching from a low doorway like mice.

Betty had little to say. I told her one or two things about myself. She listened quietly, but asked no questions and told me nothing in return. I would have suspected either boredom or stupidity had she not been so obviously possessed of neither. I thought she was shy and preoccupied. I thought she was lovely, sensitive, intelligent, with the life in her pent like a head of steam. For a space we sat, neither of us talking, Betty looking out to sea. I sat watching her with the sense of experiencing something transient and fugitive, which I would never know again. I tried to encompass the instant wholly, absorb it, make it part of myself, so that I might have it with me always; that I might, in effect, halt time.

Marvelous, I thought. A week ago Betty had not existed for me. Now here she was more important every second. The situation was so intense as to be unreal, like a picture seen through a crystal lens. The sunlight was richer, the air clearer, the flux of time slower, more distinct.

"Betty," I said, "I'm going back home before long."

She turned her head, looked at me thoughtfully. "How long?"

"As soon as I see how this mess clears up."

She sat still considering me without too lively an interest. This was a different Betty from the agitated girl of last night. This Betty seemed to have settled doubts within herself; it was a Betty whom I felt I could deal with less confidently.

Nevertheless: "When I go, I want you to come with me."

She smiled. "No."

"That's what I thought you'd say. I want to know why."

"There's lots of reasons," she said quite flippantly.

"I'm listening."

"I can't leave my father and mother."

"Girls have been leaving fathers and mothers for quite a while now."

"Mine are different."

"They're human, aren't they? They seem to have enough money."

She went on as if she had not heard me. "Or perhaps it's me who's different; I think that's it."

"Not in one or two of the most important ways."

"How?"

"Well," I swirled the wine in my glass, watched it critically, "last night I kissed you and you seemed to like it."

"I'm not so sure about that. I was rather excited. Actually, I don't think I care much for men. I like — women."

I stared at her with a heavy sinking feeling. She laughed. "Don't look so shocked. That's hardly a novelty around here."

"But I am shocked. If you mean what I think you mean."

"I suppose it's the same thing. But I'm not sure. I'm really all confused."

I said dryly, "I should think you *would* be."

"I don't seem to like women very much either. But I haven't tried very hard. The woman in the pottery shop has been flirting with me; she seems rather nice." And she watched me sidelong to see how I was taking all this. I felt sick to my stomach; I felt as if I had a sash weight for a liver.

I said as carelessly as I could, "Hortense? I thought Hortense was normal. In fact, super-normal."

"She seems to be everything. She's slept with Freddy."

I sat back in the chair, considering this strange pitiless creature in front of me. I said at last, "You can't be serious."

She shrugged. "Why not? A person has to be something."

"Why not be normal? Even get married. That's what I was hinting about."

She shook her head stonily, definitely. She was drawing farther away from me every minute. "I don't want to be normal." She looked at me a little wildly. "I'm *not* normal."

I was puzzled. "What on earth's wrong with being normal? Some of my best friends are normal."

She laughed, half-bitter, half-defiant. "If you're normal you have — babies."

"Yes, at times. What about it? They're messy little horrors, so what? You don't need to have them until you feel like it."

She looked at me uncomprehendingly, as if I were talking gibberish. "How can you help having babies if you're normal?"

A peculiar suspicion was growing in my mind, stranger and stranger. "You don't know how not to have babies?"

"No." She was interested.

"There's lots of ways. Some work, some don't." I felt like smiting my forehead with my hand; a fantastic incongruity that could happen nowhere else but Positano. A sophistication that contemplated homosexuality with carelessness, an innocence which knew nothing of contraception. I told her about three or four different methods. "They're even teaching the women of India the rhythm method. What did you learn in your Swiss finishing school, for heavens sake?"

"Nothing of that sort."

"But haven't you ever had any boy-friends?"

"No." She looked scared. "No. Never."

"You've got one now. Me."

She looked thoughtful. "No."

"Can't you ever say 'yes'?"

"No, no. And after today I can't see you again."

"But why not? Betty, you've got to tell me — because maybe I can help. I want to help. Won't you tell me?"

She shook her head, looking at her fingers. I reached out, took her hand. "You must be awfully lonesome, holding all this to yourself."

She said nothing.

"How does this chap Hilfstone enter into the picture?"

"He doesn't, directly. He's just a nuisance."

"Your father acts as if he's more than a nuisance." I thought of Kex's letter to the Dannisters. "Incidentally, did you see the letter your father got yesterday?"

"How did you know he got a letter?"

"Everybody on Kex's list got letters, all denouncing me. The Ryens got one; last night they killed themselves."

"Someone should kill Kex."

I shrugged. "Sooner or later he's going to get it. But what I wanted to say — don't believe anything you might read about me — because it's a lie."

She said nothing.

"Betty."

"What?"

"When I leave — will you come with me?"

Her mouth jerked up at the corners, her eyebrows arched, her face became a sad droll mask. "No, I told you I couldn't."

"Do you want to?"

She hesitated. "No. I can't. Can't — can't — can't. You won't understand me." She rose abruptly to her feet. "Perhaps," she said with European formality, "we should be going."

I paid for the wine; the four children with eyes like watchful mice faded back into the shadow.

We walked through the village; I reached out, took Betty's hand, and thus we walked, each with his own thoughts, on a narrow path leading along the mountainside.

After a while I said, "Betty, when you first saw me did you ever imagine things would be like this?"

She made a wry sound between her teeth. "I've never been so unhappy before in my life."

I stopped, pulled her around so that we were face to face. "But it's more than that, isn't it?"

She stirred fretfully; she would not let herself answer.

"Isn't it?"

"I don't know. Perhaps."

I bent forward to kiss her again; then, at the stony blind look in her eyes, stopped short.

But now as we continued around the path I felt a different spirit in her, quieter, more submissive, more yielding, as if inflexibility were very tiring.

We climbed down another monumental flight of steps and finally came out on the road to Amalfi. As we walked back toward Positano, the deaths of Pamela and Hester which I had put to the back of my mind, together with my own equivocal position, began to loom, and crowd aside the more intimate problem of Betty. The closer we came, the more worried I became. The air was too heavy, there was too much emotion lying around loose. Something was going to pop. What and in which direction I had not the slightest idea. But the closer we came the more reluctant were my feet.

It was almost as if I were afraid. In fact, I was afraid.

At the outskirts of town, where the road separated into a high road and a low road, Betty came to a stop. I turned, facing her.

"I'll go on around the top," she said in a hurried voice. "Please don't come any farther."

"When will I see you again?"

"I don't know. I don't think we'd better."

"I'm bored with asking why not — so I won't."

She smiled a ghost of a smile. "If you knew, you'd understand — and you'd be grateful to me."

"You're not at all my idea of a mystery woman."

"Goodbye, Chuck."

"Wait." She stopped. "When will I see you?"

"But I said —"

I made an impatient motion. "I don't care what you said. I don't care what's wrong; maybe you're infected with leprosy — are you?"

"No."

"Because Freddy is a little simple? Insanity in the family?"

"No." She turned and walked quickly away. I ran after her.

"Betty — when can I see you again?"

"I don't know."

"Tomorrow night."

"No."

"Yes."

"I can't get out without my father knowing."

"Suppose he does know; what's the odds?"

She said hurriedly, "Very well, tomorrow night — but only for a very short time."

"Where?"

She pointed to one corner of the beach. "There. At nine o'clock. Goodbye."

"Goodbye."

I watched her walk around the road, a tragic figure with dark gold head hanging miserably. Then I turned and looked down at Positano. I had no stomach for anyone, especially Kex. Not to mention this uneasiness, which had reached rather formidable proportions. But I could not stay up here on the road all night. Swallowing the lump in my throat, I set out down the hill.

CHAPTER XIV

I WANDERED DOWN TOWARD the beach, feeling nervous and watchful, like a child playing hide and seek. Signora Umberto peered like a vindictive terrier from her shop, wishing me evil. Where the road turned up the hill by the post office a group of young laborers looked at me sidewise and spat in the dust; and when I had passed I heard gruff mutters. Presumably *l'affaire Chi-Chi* had gone the rounds, and I could expect unfriendliness during the rest of my stay in Positano. Well, with luck I'd get through without a cut throat. I passed one of the local carabinieri, pompous as a turkey-cock in his uniform. Even he gave me a surly glance, as if to say, "No formal charge, my lad, but for a ten lire note I'd clap you in jail anyway."

I went slowly down the side-alley, feeling wan and harried. Ahead of me I saw Hortense step out of her shop, lock the door. An elderly couple, the man in a gray sharkskin suit, high knob-toed shoes, the woman thin as a weasel in a Queen of England hat, stopped her to ask directions. As she paused, swaying to answer, she caught sight of me. I saw her frown, her eyes shining like the eyes of a nervous horse.

She gave the tourist couple an answer; they thanked her with solemn courtesy, and stumped slowly along the lane. Hortense, moving half-away from me, looked coquettishly over her shoulder. "Hello, Mr. Musgrave."

"Hello."

She fell into step beside me. "You're sunburned; you've been out in the sun."

"All day. I climbed up the mountain."

"It's beautiful up there." She stopped by a side-lane. "This is where I live."

"Oh?"

"Yes." She smiled shyly. Or coyly. "Will you have a cup of tea with me? Or a drink?"

I rubbed my chin, my mind a blank, not knowing whether to say yes or no, but under a strong suspicion that whatever I did it would be a mistake.

She stood waiting, calm, attentive, like a saleswoman with an indecisive customer. I scrutinized her from the corner of my eye — lithe as a mink, unmistakably expectant. If I came in to drink, I would wind up on the couch. Here, in Argus-eyed Positano, and ten minutes after saying goodbye to Betty, was not the occasion.

She watched me come to a decision without emotion. "No," I said, "not now, thanks."

She nodded, and her earrings jingled. "I'll see you tonight in any event. You're coming to Buster's party, I imagine?"

"I hadn't heard of it."

She smiled cryptically. "You're practically the guest of honor. Buster says it's a meeting of the Dirty Shirt Club."

"Oh." I felt as if I didn't especially want to be bothered. "Well, maybe I'll see you there."

"Goodbye."

I came out on the esplanade. Positano seemed suspended in a curious trance, an ebb. The sun was low over the hill, shining with the melancholy pale-gold of late afternoon. The sea was generating a small cold breeze that robbed the wan sunlight of what little warmth it possessed.

I went on into the Vistamare. The Marquis and a strange red-haired woman were eating lobster with a bottle of champagne at their elbow. At another table sat Munton and Oleg Vroznek, Munton with a formidable loose-leaf notebook and a briefcase open on the floor beside his chair; Oleg with a book of impressive thickness.

I paused, not particularly anxious to join them, but unwilling to concede that I had no right to do so.

Oleg turned his head, nodded carefully; I went forward as if I were walking into a cold shower, pulled back a chair. Munton glared at me in pain and outrage, head thrown back, nostrils flared like an angry bull. Muttering through his mustache, he stuffed the notebook into his briefcase, bounced to his feet, bowed stiffly, stamped out into the pale afternoon.

Oleg watched him go, faintly smiling. "Munton has conceived a prejudice against you."

"If that's a prejudice, I'd hate to have him really dislike me."

Oleg pursed up his mouth. "He refers to you as a 'damnable meddler'. He mentions horsewhips, and 'drumming out of town'."

"Very British of him."

"I think it is a mistake to think of the British as an unemotional people. Indeed I know of no other race so completely driven by emotion and sentiment. Munton, for instance, is quite beside himself with passion."

"He must have a lot on his conscience."

"Ah." Oleg massaged his long pale chin dreamily. "Why do you say that?"

"Consider the circumstances. I seem to be cast in the role of avenging angel around here. If Munton were clean and innocent he would treat me with more consideration."

Oleg said with a wan, faintly mocking smile, "I'm afraid that I have not completely grasped the sequence of events during the last few days. But offhand I would say that you accept a responsibility I myself would greatly fear." And he sipped his wine, not at all displeased with himself.

I watched him sardonically. "You've got over your own scare, I see."

"Scare? Ha, so, hm, well — I would hardly profess to —" his voice drifted away, he turned a page in his book, looked fixedly at a footnote.

Arturo came to the table; I ordered a bottle of beer. "Perhaps I'm wrong," I said, "but when you opened your letter yesterday you seemed — well, certainly startled."

"Perhaps so," droned Oleg. "Perhaps so."

"I need hardly say that the letter is one of Kex's jokes."

"Yes," said Oleg. "I knew that three minutes after I opened the letter."

"You used your head better than anyone else around here."

Oleg smiled with obvious pleasure. "Perhaps because I have no real guilt, nothing internal to bring disorder to my mind. My fears are objective, I can consider them rationally and therefore, when I find you described as an *agent provocateur*, a Cominform bully-boy sent here to assassinate me, I presently detect the ridiculousness of the situation. I deduced Kex's touch almost immediately."

"Kex was amateurish in your case. He didn't jab you where you'd jump."

"He has not been so in the past," said Oleg carefully, his eyes becoming opaque.

"However he succeeded brilliantly with the Ryens."

"Yes, quite."

There was a short silence. Arturo brought my beer, poured it with true Italian verve from a height of eighteen inches. I watched him with disapproval.

Oleg said suddenly, "A tragic circumstance. Tragic for you —" pointedly "— in a large sense."

"I don't see that I had anything to do with it."

"Well, well," Oleg moved his book, leaned forward. "This is interesting. I wonder how you derive this conviction."

I tried to convey the train of thought which had led me to the conclusion. Oleg listened with flattering concentration, as if he were really interested — which, in fact, he was.

"Then," he said, "you reflect the entire burden of responsibility upon Kex."

"I'd express it a little less bluntly, perhaps, but that's what I mean."

Oleg put the tips of his fingers together, looking the caricature of a schoolmaster. "It makes a fascinating problem. You find yourself to be an instrument of mischief; you profit from the same mischief, but — perhaps rightly — you feel that by attempting to counteract this mischief, you swing yourself away from moral responsibility."

"That's a rather unsympathetic way of putting it — but in the main it follows my line of reasoning."

"In many ways," remarked Oleg, "the pattern of logic is that followed by sensitive high-ranking Nazis during the last war. Their preferential status grounded upon and stemmed from a vileness paralleled in modern times only by the Communist regimes. Certain of these men justified their positions by claiming that they had tempered some of the more flagrant brutalities." And Oleg sipped his wine with an air of placid triumph.

I did not consider the remark tactful. I said coldly, "Your analogy is as full of holes as a Swiss cheese."

"Oh indeed," Oleg hastened to say. "It was not meant to be the mirror image of our present case, but only to shed a measure of illumination —"

"In the first place I'm not a Nazi."

"Of course not; I hardly suggest —"

"In the second place, these Nazis had a choice: acquiescence, deploring, hoping for the best, all negative attitudes — or positive rebellion. I have been positively trying to counter Kex's mischief. I have no positive alternative unless I kill Kex."

"Ah?" asked Oleg solemnly. "You seriously consider this step?"

"No," I said. "I'm not that much of a public benefactor. I'm merely pointing out that I don't need to feel ashamed of myself merely because I'm bleeding Kex of his money."

Oleg drummed his long pale fingers on the table. "Perhaps you have a point." Oleg focused his eyes dreamily on the ceiling. "Let us, as an exercise in moral judgments, consider the following hypothesis: suppose Kex had informed you in Rome exactly what duties would be required of you. Would you have come to Positano under those conditions? In other words, knowing what you know now, would you do the same thing over again?"

I opened my mouth to say, "Yes, certainly," then paused to wonder if this would, after all, be an honest answer. I finally said, "Well — if you insisted on an answer, I think, to be consistent, I'd have to answer 'yes'. Since we're talking hypothetical cases, I might hypothecate Kex hiring some ruffian who would actively enjoy scaring the liver out of people."

"And who," said Oleg gently, "might well find himself in the same kind of trouble Kex is in."

"Is Kex in trouble?"

"I believe that Kex has seriously miscalculated. His previous pranks have never had such serious effects, or aroused such wide alarm. True, he means no great harm, he is not innately vicious; still he must bear the consequences of his acts."

"Legal consequences?"

"Legal, if there are any, which I rather doubt. Certainly he will face a measure of social disapproval here at Positano."

"That won't worry Kex. He'll move to Majorca or Lipari or Taormina or Barcelona if he gets frozen out here."

Oleg nodded judiciously. "Our contemporary way of life makes it easy for what an anthropologist might call the 'breaker of a taboo' to evade the social pressure that formerly acted to keep life flowing in a well-charted course...Well, well, if nothing else, Kex's actions give us material for endless discussion. I suppose that at Blaine's party this evening we'll hear little else. You're coming, of course?"

"I haven't been invited yet."

Oleg made a gesture. "It means nothing; Blaine expects anyone and everyone, so long as he brings a bottle or two. Today it is the Dirty Shirt Club — so Blaine calls it."

"Is Kex coming?"

"I'm not sure. I hardly know. But let us turn to happier subjects. I understand you paint?"

"Not seriously. I play at it."

"Then painting can't be your major interest in life."

"No. I merely tried to develop a technique so I could use a sketch-pad instead of camera."

"Ha." Oleg digested the idea a moment, then came up with the careful comment which I knew was inevitable. "Don't you feel that this is — well, let us say a careless, a superficial, a disrespectful attitude to take toward one of the great arts?"

"Two or three hundred years ago I might have agreed with you."

Oleg deployed himself for argument; his eyes glistened, he licked his lips. "If I understand you correctly, you appear to believe that there is no place in the world today for modern painting."

"You haven't understood me correctly. I just don't think that painting is the career a talented and intelligent young man should pursue."

"Ha! On financial grounds?"

"No. Spiritual — if you don't mind the word. Painting today is all derivative, to use a five-dollar word. There's no life to it. It's not growing; it's saying nothing significant. It's become a minor art."

Oleg shook his head sadly. "My friend, we can hardly shrug off a tradition of almost a thousand years as a minor art."

"It was good while it lasted — but we stopped building pyramids a long time ago, and that was quite a big thing while it lasted too. And look at all the marble statues in Rome and Florence: thugs beating each other with clubs, ninety percent of them. Perhaps that was meaningful one time, but now what does it mean? Nothing."

Oleg asked sarcastically, "And what do you propose as the new fine art? Singing commercials? Comic books?"

"I don't know. It's probably something similar, something that we live with, that's growing and developing under our noses. Cinema, animated cartoons, perhaps. I know it's not going on in Italy and probably not in Europe. In the States we're too close to the forest to see the trees. Five hundred years from now the art critics may look back and single out men we've never heard of, who are doing things we'd consider trivial, unnecessary, like designing manhole covers or playing the ocarina, or writing copy for fashion ads, or thinking up names for new brands of lipstick. And one thing I'd bet my next year's salary on — that the so-called *avant-garde* turns out, in retrospect, to be fairly rear-guard material."

"I should imagine," said Oleg heavily, "that a great deal depends on the way the world takes. For instance, if the Russians succeed in their mission, our entire western culture becomes of no more than didactic interest. If the United States completes its spiritual invasion of Europe —"

"You mean, if Europe continues to suck spiritual strength from the States."

"— then our heritage likewise becomes a golden memory."

And so we argued, and time went past. We ate dinner, and drank wine. About eight o'clock Munton stalked into the room, shot me a red-eyed look, seated himself at the bar, and consumed a gin and tonic.

Ten minutes later Blaine looked in. "Come on over," he said. "I've got the place cleaned, and my maid has put flowers in the vase and my bed's made, and I'm getting restless. Let's get the party going."

Apparently I was included in the invitation; Blaine seemed to take it for granted. I said, "Wait till I pick up a bottle, and I'll be with you."

"First annual meeting of the Dirty Shirt Club," sang out Blaine. "Now convening; bring your shivs and bottles of acid; it's gonna wind-up a free-for-all or my name ain't Buster Barbecue Blaine."

CHAPTER XV

MUNTON, SULKING AT THE BAR, wouldn't come with us. "Can't see my way clear," he muttered, glaring at me out of the corner of his eye.

"Hell," said Blaine, "don't blame young Musgrave. He's as much an injured party as any of us."

"Pull a stunt like that in England," growled Munton, obviously not heeding Blaine in the slightest, "man wouldn't be allowed in the streets."

"Well, come or not, as you like," said Blaine. "It's a meeting of the most exclusive club in Positano — the Dirty Shirt Club."

"Don't believe I quite getcha."

Oleg put in gently, "All of us share essentially the same predicament."

Munton blinked. "Then why don't we band together and put this damned outsider in his place?" And he jerked his thumb at me. "I know what kind of chap he is; I've got secret information; damned paid snoop, worst kind of rotter."

If it hadn't been comic I would have become peeved. Blaine pulled a droll face at me, even Oleg smiled faintly. "It's not Musgrave," said Blaine, "it's Kex."

"Who? Him? Nonsense. I know Kex."

It was clear that Munton's bitterness had made him more obtuse than usual. He was under compulsion to hit out at something; I was the most obvious target.

"Well," said Blaine, "Kex got hold of whatever it is you're afraid of coming out —" he paused. "Oh hell. Come to the party."

"Will this man be there?"

"Yes. So will Kex, I hope."

Oleg looked at Blaine in mild surprise. "Is Kex really coming?"

Blaine said, "What would a meeting of the Dirty Shirt Club be like without its founder?"

"I would hardly think that he'd be likely to come."

"Kex seemed to enjoy the idea."

"Sometimes," said Oleg, "I think that Kex must be victim to manic delusions — utterly solipsistic."

"Come, come," Munton snapped. "Talk English; can't go this psychology jargon."

"I'll translate for you, if you like," I said. "He means that Kex must be crazy to think he can get away with a stunt like this. He thinks it's because Kex is so completely immersed in his own thoughts he can't imagine anyone or anything running seriously counter to his wishes."

"Save it," said Blaine. "This is part of the minutes of the club meeting." He looked at Munton. "Are you coming or not?"

"It's just possible I might look in for a bit."

"Bring a bottle," said Blaine laconically.

We left the Vistamare, Blaine first, then Oleg, then myself, and climbed the lane to his flat. The kitchen smelled of soap and bleach, a bare bulb shone on gray plaster walls. Blaine led the way into his bed-sitting room where the light also burnt. Curled up in Blaine's bed was a thin tousle-haired woman in a blue sweatshirt, a gray skirt: Alma. She lifted her head, spoke in a blurred voice, "Whussa trouble?"

"Alma," said Blaine, "you've been at the brandy."

"So what? Sposen I have?" Her eyes flicked past to Oleg and me. She asked in a plaintive voice, "Couldn't you find anyone better than Professor Pussyfoot and young Claptrap?"

I was evidently young Claptrap. Professor Pussyfoot looked inexpressibly pained.

Blaine grinned, reached down, gave her a spank where the skirt stretched tight across her rump. "They're full-fledged members of the club; get up now and act a lady. Serve us a drink."

"I'll do nothing of the sort." She put her head back down on her arms, pretended to sleep.

"Don't mind her," said Blaine. "She's drunk as usual. God knows how she got in here; I had the door locked."

"There's a bad smell up in my flat," whined Alma, like a spoiled child.

"I couldn't stand it. It's no better down here — worse now that you've brought in your smelly friends."

Blaine laughed with indulgent good humor. "You're not so much drunk as you are mean. Why don't you save it?"

"Why save it? I've got lots more."

Blaine said to Oleg and myself, who were standing uncomfortably just inside the door, "Don't pay any attention to her. She's a little drunk and a little crazy, and the rest exhibitionist."

"Pooh!" And Alma laughed, a silly high-pitched fluting.

"Here," said Blaine, pouring three inches of brandy into a glass. "Have a drink."

She looked at it suspiciously. "What is it?"

"Brandy. What do you think it is?"

"I'll tell you what it looks like." She told us. "I wouldn't put it past you either, Buster... Big-hearted Buster — used to tend bar in San Francisco till they ran him out for cutting the booze with wee-wee." Again she yelped in laughter.

Blaine's long face twitched and twisted. "In a kind of bitchy mood tonight, ain't you?"

"Me? Never!" She raised up on an elbow, sipped the brandy, wrinkled her nose. "First, last, always a lady."

I heard the outside door open. "Hoo-hoo," came a voice.

Blaine winked at me. "Now Alma will behave; it's Countess Margaret d'Egliari."

"Countess, my left nose," muttered Alma. She took a sullen gulp of the brandy.

Countess Margaret appeared in the door, two flaring spots of rouge on her doughy cheeks. "I thought you were coming to pick me up, Buster," she said plaintively. "You told me that —" She took in Alma on the couch. "Oh." She took note of me. "Oh?" And insulted Oleg with a glance.

Blaine said smoothly, "As you see, my dear Countess, I was busy; I couldn't make it. Take a seat — have a drink."

She settled herself in a chair beside the bed, raised her eyebrows at Alma's feet. "My dear, did you know you've got a hole in your sole?"

"Oh, these old things." She kicked them off. "Usually I take my shoes off in strange beds."

"The lady-like thing to do," agreed Blaine. He brought glasses from a cupboard, set them on the table. "Help yourself. I'm damned if I'm gonna run around all night pouring liquor."

Oleg and I each made ourselves a highball, retreated to the corner opposite Countess Margaret. I said in an undertone, "I don't quite know how to handle these Positano females. They're a breed in themselves."

"Ignore them," said Oleg. "They're really sick mentally."

Countess Margaret said in a practical voice, "Just what's the idea of this party, Buster?"

"It's a meeting of the Dirty Shirt Club."

"Speak for yourself, Buster. I wash once in a while myself."

"You're a member, whether you wash or not."

"I don't want to be a member. Call me a snob if you like, but I prefer to pick my own friends."

"You're drunk," called Alma. No one paid attention.

Blaine took his drink, seated himself on the bed with his back to Alma. "You're in, Countess, automatically. It's honorary — no dues, no nothing."

"I don't want to be in." She shot a venomous glance in my direction. "In fact I'm leaving here in about ten minutes. It's a bore, deadly dull. One thing I can't forgive, that's dullness."

Alma kicked Blaine on his rump. He paid no attention. "Countess, may I ask a personal question?"

"Since when you been so considerate, asking my permission?"

"I want to ask you, did you get a letter in a blue envelope, warning you that Chuck over here is hot on your trail?"

Orange-pink blood rose into Countess Margaret's cheeks. She lit a cigarette with shaking fingers. "No, of course not. I don't need a letter." She darted me another malevolent look. "Suppose I did get a letter — which I didn't — what of it?"

"That makes you a member of the Dirty Shirt Club."

"Is that right."

Alma, wanting some attention, gave Blaine another kick, which he ignored with tremendous dignity. "I'll say one word," said Blaine, "which should explain everything: Kex."

Countess Margaret puffed her cigarette, pursed flabby lips, tried to blow a smoke ring.

"Hell," said Blaine. "Why do I keep going over this old song and dance. There's Hortense still to come and Leibnitz and Munton."

"And that's the membership in this Dirty Underwear Club of yours?"

"Well, no. There's quite a few more but they won't be here. Piombino — he's left town. Something tells me we won't be seeing him again. There's the Dannister family."

"I like Freddy Dannister!" called Alma.

"There's Pamela and Hester Ryen," continued Blaine. "They should be here."

"Maybe they are here," Oleg said suddenly, in a clear baritone.

Countess Margaret shuddered. "Don't start talking spooks; I'm superstitious."

"Last but not least," said Blaine, "there's the founder and preceptor of our order: Kex."

"I want Freddy Dannister!" cried Alma, kicking Blaine.

"You'll get a right cross to the kisser if you don't keep your feet off my ass," Blaine advised her.

"Give her another brandy," sniffed Countess Margaret.

Alma raised up on her elbow, her sharp python face congested with drunken anger. A knock sounded on the outer door. A sharp staccato *rat-tat-tat.*

Blaine rose to his feet, stalked with long strides through his kitchen. He opened the door. "Come in, come in."

First Leibnitz, the sharp red-haired painter, then Munton entered the room. Blaine swung chairs out from the table; with a side glance toward me, Munton sat down. Leibnitz walked over to the bed, looked searchingly down at Alma, who smiled cozily up at him. Then he returned to his chair, smartly seated himself. Blaine said, "Help yourselves to the booze. You bring a bottle?" He craned his long neck, peered at the table. "No," he sighed, "I see you didn't. Well, there's enough liquor to grease the wheels." He looked from face to face. "We're just about all assembled, I should say."

"What's the enormous mystery?" demanded Leibnitz. He had a sharp ringing voice, voicing his words with an accent I won't try to reproduce.

"No mystery," said Countess Margaret, dropping her cigarette butt to the floor with a regal gesture. "This is Buster's new social organization, nice balanced group, everybody nuts about everybody else."

"My God, woman," said Blaine, exasperated at last, "give me a chance. Do you think I'd invite you anywhere but a dog-fight if I didn't have a good reason?"

"Well, for Heaven's sake, get on with it. I still want to wash my hair tonight."

Blaine sighed. "I can see this idea isn't going to work out."

"What was the idea?" asked Leibnitz.

"This is supposed to be —" The outer door opened, Hortense slipped quietly into the kitchen, crossed in three lithe steps, for an instant stood in the archway, radiating life and passion, and every man moved in his seat. "Good evening, everybody." She slipped around the table, took a seat on the bed leaning against the wall. Alma groaned, kicked both legs into the air, subsided. Countess Margaret hulked into the wicker armchair, a pasty mass with a sour mouth.

"Well, we're all here now," said Blaine jovially. With Hortense a new atmosphere had come into the room; the party was taking on strength. "Have a drink, kid; take off your hat and pants."

Hortense demurely accepted a drink. "Is this everybody who's got the letters?"

"Not all. The Dannisters, Piombino aren't here. The Ryens are dead."

"Bad show that," muttered Munton. "Wonder what the real story there is."

Blaine looked at him, his eyebrows twisted into odd quizzical shapes. "So far as I see it, they got one of Kex's letters, and it scared them so bad they decided it was better to go fast."

The room was silent five seconds. Hortense shook her head; Munton gazed at his glass of brandy with an air of bemusement, not sure what kind of expression was suitable. Leibnitz said in his sharp voice, "How do you know Kex sent the letters?"

Everyone spoke at once. "Who else but Kex?" This was Blaine.

"Serious charge, serious charge indeed." — Munton. Alma vented a sepulchral groan. "There's no possible doubt; he's what might be called a public enemy," said Oleg. "Poor old Kex," sighed Countess Margaret.

"Where's Freddy Dannister?" called Alma. Hortense turned her head, looked speculatively along Alma's curled up body.

Blaine rose to his feet, poured himself a brandy. His face was becoming pink. Nothing was going the way he had conceived. Perhaps he had pictured a group of serious citizens, each alert and dynamic, guided by his easy but acute chairmanship, arriving by rational progress to a logical conclusion. Poor Buster Barbecue Blaine; his plans were coming open at the elbows. Munton was fatuous and obstinate, Alma drunk, Oleg pedantic, Countess Margaret sulky and inattentive, Leibnitz waspish and repressed, I was watching Hortense, Hortense was musing on something far away. Even the ghosts of Pamela and Hester could not intervene to coagulate the meeting.

But brandy began to slide down throats; concentrations of alcohol in blood began to rise toward the 0.5% line. Blaine sat down, Alma kicked him several times. Hortense and I exchanged languorous looks, Munton chuffed and puffed, Leibnitz pounded the table, his eyes glittering, his red hair tufted at all angles.

Blaine presently recollected his plans. Once more he rose to his feet. "Ladies and gentlemen, we are gathered here tonight to discuss one of the biggest stinkers the world has ever seen —"

Oleg waved a hand. "I think we ought to know just what's in our own minds. After all, it's really not that Kex is an evil man; he's merely thoughtless and egotistical and bored —"

"My God," I cried, "what do you mean he's not evil? What else do you mean by evil? Of course, he's evil! He's the very definition of evil!"

"Well, well," said Oleg, "that statement needs some consideration."

"He's depraved. He's hounded two women to death; he makes eight or ten others miserable. He's homosexual. He's corrupted God knows how many men and women, and to what purpose? To amuse himself. To dispel his boredom. What is that if it isn't evil?"

"Well, perhaps 'evil' isn't the most useful word —" began Oleg.

"Is homosexuality evil?" Hortense put in mildly.

"Of course it's evil," snapped Countess Margaret. "I've never yet seen a fruit that was worth spitting on."

Hortense shrugged. "I don't see what difference it makes."

"It's just plain nasty."

"I agree," said Munton. "Bounders for the most part, West End's full of 'em. Damned continental notion."

"I agree also," said Oleg, "but for different reasons. Homosexuality is the denial of the future; homosexuality is suicide, negativity, futility."

"But isn't the world a futile place to begin with?" Hortense asked.

"That leads us into the doctrines and anti-doctrines of existentialists."

"Poof." Leibnitz waved a hand. "I know Sartre well. Does he practice the creed? Hardly. Let me tell you an anecdote —"

Blaine pounded the table. "What in God's name are we talking about! Who gives a big rat's ass whether Kex is fruit or whether Sartre exists? I agree with Chuck. Kex is evil. Let's start from there."

A new voice said suavely, "Excellent. An admirable jumping-off place. Let's start from there." Kex came a step into the room. "I'd like to help develop the idea. It's one on which I frequently speculate myself. I'll take either affirmative or negative, as the trend of argument requires."

CHAPTER XVI

KEX WAS WEARING the nattiest of outfits, gray flannel slacks, a navy-blue jacket with brass buttons, a white scarf, a white yachting-cap. His face was pink, pomaded and powdered, his mustache was well-tended, precise, sporty; his eyes were clear, inquiring, candid as a kitten's.

He looked around the room, nodded politely here and there. "Hortense…Good evening, Oleg…Chuck…Countess."

"Find a seat, Kex," said Blaine. "Pour yourself a drink."

Kex went to the table, lifted one or two bottles, peered at the labels, pulled a cork, sniffed, picked up a glass, scrutinized the interior sharply, poured himself a modest half-inch.

The entire room watched in silence.

Kex went to a chair by the window, hitched up his trousers, sat down, crossed his legs comfortably. "Weather's changing. Spot of rain before morning unless I'm much mistaken."

The room was still silent. Then Alma began to giggle. Kex inspected her with mild inquiry. Blaine cleared his throat, started to speak, then stopped. I thought, whatever Kex has on Blaine, it's pretty good, and Blaine doesn't want to run too many risks.

Oleg, looking from Blaine to Kex, leaned back in his chair, patted the top of his head with his long white fingers. "There is no need to dissemble, to hide our faces from one another. As I see it we in this room are some of the victims to one of your —" he looked at Kex "— particularly vicious jokes. If joke is the correct word."

"Sadistic experiments," I volunteered, and Kex flashed me a moist reproachful look.

Leibnitz rose to his feet, reached in his pocket, waved a blue envelope at Kex. "Yes or no," he shouted. "Did you write this letter? Yes or no?"

"Gentlemen, gentlemen," said Kex, looking pained. "What is this, an inquisition?"

"Yes, by God!" trumpeted Munton, looking more like a rhinoceros than I would have thought it possible for a man to look. "There's been some ugly rumors circulating; I want to pin down their source. I won't stand for these monkey-tricks!"

"Ugly rumors?" asked Kex, raising his fine white eyebrows. "My word! To what effect?"

Munton opened his mouth, closed it, blinked his rhinoceros eyes angrily. "No matter what these rumors might be —"

"Could they be the truth?"

"Pah!" Munton's throat was corded.

I said, "Watch your blood-pressure, man. There's no use you popping off too."

"By all means," said Kex. "Whatever the issue, there's no cause for acrimony."

"That's debatable," said Oleg.

"It's not debatable at all," cried Leibnitz. "It's —"

"Kex is a son of a bitch," said Alma sleepily. "Why don't we let it go at that."

"For one thing," said Oleg, "two innocent women have died."

"And I've been threatened and had my face slapped," I said.

Kex smiled. "You're not doing so badly."

"If I stopped six inches of knife, you'd say, 'poor Chuck — he gambled and he lost'."

"From my viewpoint you've taken excellent care to see that nothing of the sort occurs."

"That's what I told you I was going to do. I'd be a damned fool to do otherwise."

"You may consider your employment by me at an end, as of this minute."

"Ho," cried Blaine, "then you admit that you masterminded this whole affair?"

"Have you ever had any doubts?"

Blaine shook his head in rueful admiration. "For sheer cat-pot meanness you take the cake."

Oleg asked, "How do you reconcile your conscience to the death of those two poor women?"

Kex stared around the group, pained and indignant, then breaking into a laugh of bitter amusement. "I'm honestly so dumbfounded, so astonished, that I can't find words."

" 'Dumbfounded'? 'Astonished'?" Oleg leaned forward. "Those are hardly the —"

"I sit here, I look out over this room full of mealy-mouthed hypocrites — I can hardly find words to express my disgust and contempt." He looked around the room, now frankly at bay. To his back was the balcony, then counter-clockwise, on his right was first Oleg and myself, Munton and Leibnitz at the table, Countess Margaret in the far corner, on the bed Blaine, and directly to his left Hortense, with Alma curled in foetal position behind them. Every eye was fixed on him, every mind tumescent and swollen.

Kex relaxed, lit a cigarette, surveyed the group with quizzical equanimity.

Blaine shook his head. "You'll have us apologizing to you next."

Oleg said, "You honestly find your conduct defensible?"

Kex waved his hand breezily. " 'Defensible' is too strong a word."

"Would you set the same forces in motion if you knew what their consequences might be?"

Kex shrugged. "Why all this ridiculous moralizing? No one knows what the consequences of any of their actions are. Blaine here writes murder stories. How many people does he influence to commit successful murders? Hortense goes to bed with young Freddy Dannister and gets him pregnant —"

"I want Freddy," called Alma in a muffled voice.

"What I'm trying to say is that if we tried to explore every conceivable avenue of the future we'd go crazy."

"There's a difference between acts of omission and those of commission. I would say that you deliberately hoped for violence, distress, anxiety."

"Merely because I found this pot of filth here and gave it a stir? Nonsense!"

"You went to a great deal of trouble," observed Munton, with rare restraint. "How did you find out that — well, what were your sources of information?"

"I hired detectives. Two months ago. Originally I planned a party — a very novel party, one that the most jaded of cosmopolites would remember a long time. My original intent was to invite all the participants to the game, and each would pick a dossier out of a hat. Each in turn would read it aloud — the names and places would be concealed — and then the party at large would try to guess to whom the dossier referred."

"Cute," said Blaine. "Very cute."

"Yes, isn't it?" sniffed Countess Margaret. "Cute as a scorpion."

Kex acknowledged the compliment with an airy smile. "I think it would have made quite a splash."

"You would have made quite a splash too," muttered Countess Margaret. "When we tossed you in the sea."

Kex ignored her. "I changed my original concept when I ran into Chuck, who closely resembles one of the principals in the case. I acted on impulse and now I'm rather sorry I didn't stick to my first plan; I'm afraid that Chuck hasn't cooperated the way I expected him to, and the game has lost something of its punch."

"What I can't understand," remarked Blaine conversationally, "is why you picked on us, and not a dozen others around here? I mean, we're the average denizens of the place — not even the crazy ones. Take Marsden the Buddhist, for instance, or Baron von Asparagus or whatever his name is, or Boulville or Paul Prie. Why pick on us? I mean it makes a peculiar assortment — the Ryens, the Dannisters, me, Countess M, Alma, Hortense, Munton, Leibnitz, Oleg."

"Ha, ha," laughed Kex waggishly. "I didn't choose the assortment, the assortment chose itself. My detectives got a quick line on the entire foreign colony. Some were easy to trace back, others not. Some had particularly colorless backgrounds. Paul Prie, for instance. Beyond the fact that he spent three years in a lunatic asylum, there was no *point d'appui*."

I said sarcastically, "You could always have represented me as one of the orderlies come down to yank him back to the asylum."

"Yes," said Kex coolly, "perhaps I might. But events worked themselves out in the fashion we know of."

"But why," asked Blaine, "*why* did you pull a stunt like this?"

"Yes, why?" echoed Oleg.

"Why?" Kex's lips twitched in irritation. "Why does a man do anything? Why does he go to the theater, read a book; why does he live at Positano instead of Bermuda? No reason at all, which is every reason in the world."

"Damned perversity," muttered Munton.

Blaine said seriously, "Doesn't your conscience give you any pangs whatever? After all two innocent women are dead —"

"*Innocent!*" barked Kex. "Innocent like all the rest of you papmouthed sanctimonious fakers! Why did they kill themselves if they were innocent?"

"I'm sure it couldn't have been anything very wrong," said Countess Margaret hopefully.

Kex laughed. "Nothing very wrong. They just got rid of a couple of brats Hester spawned after a night on the tiles. Set fire to the crib, blamed it on the gas heater. Verdict — not proved. What do you think of that?" He sipped his drink. "What do you think of that, Munton? Eh, Blaine? And you, Leibnitz?"

"Well," said Blaine lamely, "it surprises me. They hardly seemed the type."

"None of us look the type, do we?"

"Well, now, the human face is a funny thing —"

Kex laughed. "It is indeed. It's a constant wonder to me. I sit here, I look around at your faces, knowing what I know about you —"

Alma laughed shrilly, kicked out with both feet. Blaine gave her an injured look. "Priceless, priceless, priceless," yelled Alma. "Wonderful, wonderful, wonderful! Go on spill it — get it off your guts — you're dying to!"

Kex pursed his pink mouth. "There's really not much to spill. Just an ordinary spectrum — nothing much more depraved than Munton's punishing native chicken-thieves, when he was district commissioner in Nigeria, by flogging them with his own hand and his special whip. Munton took pride and pleasure in his skill; and his zeal upholding the statutes, on at least three occasions, resulted in the deaths of wrongdoers. They talk of him yet in Kapami."

Munton was sitting like a stump, gray and mottled. His fingers clung to his glass, he stared at Kex and his mouth moved, but no words came.

No one else moved; no one spoke. Everyone sat tense, horrified and fascinated, afraid and yet eager. The room was warm and yet gave an impression of icy cold, and there was a sense of evil afoot. I thought, Kex is the devil, Kex is Satan in a trim white mustache and a yachting costume; the devil is conferring with his acolytes.

"Shall I go on?" asked Kex. No one spoke. Munton gasped thickly, "It's a lie," but no one heard him. "A peccadillo here, a misstep there. Hortense, for instance — I've bought a marvelous sixteen millimeter reel in which Hortense acts one of the leading parts. She looks about seventeen or eighteen. I couldn't show it here, mixed company, you know, but it was filmed in Germany, and it displays the peculiar German thoroughness in everything they touch, even depravity. Hortense, I salute your virtuosity; I never appreciated exactly how far your talents extended."

"Swine," said Hortense in a low voice.

"Ha, ha," laughed Kex, "and Blaine — look at Buster Blaine. In Los Angeles they call him the Marrying Bartender, the Ding Dong Daddy of the Dandy Bar. Eighteen wives has Blaine, think of it, eighteen Mrs. Buster Barbecue Blaines, all yearning to find their evasive husband. All at once, mind you. I think this is an American record. Buster just couldn't seem to resist the call; he loved the scent of orange blossoms."

Blaine was red as raw meat.

"Only a peccadillo, you say, you're disappointed. No murders, no killing. But I didn't plan a Grand Guignol. This is just our little game. Who's next? Leibnitz? There's not very much we can say about Leibnitz, because Leibnitz is a demonstrable patriot. His devotion to Germany took him to selfless heights of service. Leibnitz is a Jew, who during the late unpleasantness, assisted the German government in uncovering underground escape routes; I understand he worked closely with the Gestapo, and for that reason is reluctant to return to Germany, nor does he wish to visit Israel, where the remnants of his race have found a home."

Silence.

"Oleg hates Communists. Perhaps because every year, while Oleg studied the classics and pondered the meaning of right and wrong in his ancestral castle in Poland, perhaps ten, perhaps twenty, perhaps fifty of his serfs died of hunger, exposure, disease. Oleg was not a first-class landlord. His castle is a government rest-home now, and the two hundred thousand-acre Vroznek estate is a collective farm. But the peasants still spit when they hear the name Oleg Vroznek."

"Nonsense," said Oleg excitedly. "You talk tommyrot. I did as well for the peasants as I had time for. This is Communist propaganda; they hate me because I was one of the old land-owners."

Kex shrugged. "Possibly. The information was gathered among the Polish colony in London, however. But no matter — where do we go from here? Alma? Countess Margaret? No need to particularize."

"Don't you dare!" shrieked Countess Margaret.

"Why not?" asked Kex smoothly. "Are you ashamed of your career as a prostitute? You earned your passage from Winfield, Kansas, to Italy, where you met and captivated Count Alessandro d'Egliari… And you, Chuck — I've had some late advices."

Now I knew how the others had felt; my heart seemed to pause inside a cold cage, my throat was dry. And Kex, hateful, vile creature peered at me with a smiling complacency that I would have cut loose from his face with a knife.

"Chuck's errors, like Leibnitz's, were due to misdirected zeal. A few years ago Chuck was a cadet at West Point Military Academy, and quite a skillful football player. Unfortunately, he found that football interfered with his studies, or perhaps it was the other way around; in any event there did not seem to be time for both. Chuck decided — rightly or wrongly, who is to judge? — that while he could always repair the deficiencies in his learning, if he missed football practice he might lose his place on the team, and so he passed his examinations the easy way. He was unlucky enough to be detected and expelled. Nothing serious, a minor delinquency. What's a bit of dishonor, or sadism, or infanticide, or bigamy, or whoring? Let him who is without sin cast the first stone."

Kex looked around the room, solemnly complacent. "Each of us uses at least three levels of thought — first his overt self, more or less socially correct; second, his secret mind, where he judges, hates and condemns his fellows, while he assures himself that his own delinquencies are minor affairs, to be sympathetically glossed over. The third level is his subconscious, where he knows that this is balderdash, and that he really indeed is as wicked as he fears he is."

Blaine took a heroic gulp from his glass. "That makes twenty-seven of us."

Silence. Someone moved, someone else scraped his feet. No one knew where to look, fearful of meeting someone else's eyes. If Kex had wanted to strip us all naked, to show us all to each other and ourselves, he had succeeded. Piombino, I thought, had got off easy. The Ryens had killed themselves. The Dannisters — what of the Dannisters? Kex had not mentioned the Dannisters or James Hilfstone. Was he saving that for the last? I desperately wanted to know... But now Kex rose to his feet. "I think I'll say good evening, Buster. This has been a wonderful party and I've had a marvelous time. I've got a few things to attend to or I'd stay longer."

He rounded the table. Blaine rose, took a few uncertain steps after him. "Don't bother," Kex begged him with effusive affability, "I can find my way out."

He left the room. We heard the door open, close. Kex was gone. Everyone in the room took a deep breath.

CHAPTER XVII

THERE WAS GENERAL CLEARING of throats, indecisive mutterings, a considering of empty glasses. Blaine carried the bottle around, a subdued droop to his shoulders.

Alma gingerly swung her legs over the edge of the bed, sat up, smoothed her snarled black hair. Munton glared fiercely toward the door. Hortense lit a cigarette, puffed smoke thoughtfully at her knees. Blaine set the empty bottle on the table with a thump, bravely lifted his glass, "Here's to crime."

There was silence, while the Dirty Shirt Club took stock of itself.

Oleg cleared his throat. "An interesting evening — interesting to observe oneself from so strange a vantage point."

"Interesting, be damned," muttered Munton, evading eyes. "A pack of lies, at least what he told about me. Gave quite the wrong impression, a complete distortion. A man in nigger country's got to enforce discipline; otherwise he's had it. Did what was necessary, no more."

There was a sudden babble, like half a dozen stations on a radio.

"Slanderous blackguard," gritted Leibnitz. "I can go to live in Germany any time I wish; what stupid nonsense he talks about me and the Gestapo! Never —"

"Not that I'm any tin-pot angel," Countess Margaret told the room, "not that I care what anyone thinks, but whoever lies like that about me, he's in for trouble. I don't care who knows it; after all there's a limit."

"Drunken skunk," called Alma. "Damned drunken old he-whore. Where's he get that stuff?" She peered blearily from face to face. "Buster," she yelped, "that man again!" — meaning me.

"People don't realize the strain on a football player," I told Oleg and Blaine. "Not so much a matter of cheating; hell, seven-eighths the squad was doing the same, only worse; I was unlucky enough to get caught."

At the same time Blaine was explaining, "What's a little marriage ceremony between friends? I was doing 'em a favor; lots of guys would have laid 'em without benefit of clergy. I left 'em with their egos in one piece."

Oleg nodded at judicious intervals. "Certainly a marvelous performance — tinged with exaggeration in my own case, certainly. Conditions were never like that on our holdings. We ran a model estate. Indeed, we kept hundreds of people alive who might well have starved. The Communists, they have distorted, turned our old people against us."

Hortense smiled her faint secret smile, tilted her glass, drank slowly. I was talking again, everyone was talking: explanations, refutals, vindications, arguments to which no one listened. I wondered if everyone felt as heated and embarrassed as myself; I wanted to stop talking but the words kept pulling out of my mouth as if they were tied to a long string.

Talk and more talk, till the room vibrated. The brandy went low in the bottles and Munton went to the Vistamare, expansively returning with three new bottles. "I'd like to have Kex for three months in Nigeria, make him toe the line! By George, he'd be a different man for a stripe or two; a better man!"

"He'd be a better man if he were dead," said Countess Margaret. She had slumped into her chair, her knees spread apart, a white toad in a blonde wig.

"That's a damn good idea," said Blaine huskily.

"Man misusing his life like that doesn't deserve to live," Munton told us.

"If I had a gun I would pull the trigger," cried Leibnitz, his eyes flaring, "personally, with these two hands." He held up dramatically contracted hands.

"There does come a time," said Oleg, "when the ordinary processes of justice seem inadequate."

"If I was a man," said Countess Margaret, "I'd do something about him."

Blaine said scornfully, "You don't have to be a man; you can do the business just like anyone else."

Alma yelped, "Let's kill the son of a bitch!"

There was a sudden cautious silence, then Blaine said, "There's no doubt the son of a bitch needs killing. He's misery to enough people. As good as murdered the two Ryen girls with his own hand."

"Damn shame," rumbled Munton. "I'd know what to do if I had him out on a hunting trip."

"All you need is an accident," said Blaine. "Just one simple little accident."

Oleg's mouth twitched uneasily. "Naturally we don't seriously intend —" he paused, thoughtfully sipped at his drink. "And on the other hand —"

"I say, kill the son of a bitch," declared Blaine.

"I say so too," cried Leibnitz. "A blot on the earth, a public service to take him off."

Munton winked slyly. "Case like this, it's always wise to have an alibi, eh? Well, here's eight reputable citizens, ready to swear that, ahem, whoever does the business was drinking wine, everybody, all together. Chap naturally can't allow himself to be seen, of course, has to use rudimentary caution; can't have any misunderstandings."

Blaine rose to his feet, looked around the circle of faces. "It seems to me that we're all talking the same language. I don't hear anybody pleading for Kex."

Silence.

"Anybody got any objections to speeding Kex on to his reward?"

Silence, with everyone looking belligerent and dedicated.

"I think that Kex has given us all the dirt a civilized man ought to take; I think we ought to do something about it."

"In union there is strength," said Oleg.

Hortense smiled her faint smile. I thought of Kex's sixteen millimeter films. At seventeen Hortense must have been an eyeful. Hortense noticed me watching her, and knew what I was thinking.

The brandy flowed; faces became mobile, earnest, detached from the body below. Personalities blew up like balloons, larger than life. The light was high and yellow, like a Van Gogh sunflower. The room became larger, people sat closer together.

There was talk of ways and means. Alma's idea was impractical:

"Kick him on his fat rump until his brains spill out." Leibnitz spoke of a gun, but Blaine shook his head. "It's got to look like an accident. Why all these stairs around here if we're going to waste them?"

Said Oleg wisely, "The simplest way is the best."

"First," said Blaine, "we've got to decide who's going to pull the stunt. That'll make a difference."

"Right," cried Munton, "first things first." He glanced around inquiringly. "Well, who's for it?"

Everyone was drinking brandy and water; everyone appeared to be deep in thought.

"Ha, ha!" cried Hortense, her first words for twenty minutes. "Who will bell the cat?"

There was silence, disturbed only by Alma's hiccups.

"Well," asked Blaine, "any ideas?"

Munton coughed, shook his finger, drank some brandy, as if to relieve the cough.

"It's about as I thought," said Blaine sadly. "Not one of us has the guts. If we had, we wouldn't be here." He slumped into his chair.

Alma made an irrational sound, half-gurgle, half-laugh. "Let's go out and run a foot-race. Let's have a foot-race."

"No," said Blaine, "but here's what we can do. Everybody up to the table; we'll deal out the cards."

"What are the conditions?" asked Oleg warily.

"Ace of spades does the business."

"When?"

"That's what we'll figure out. Whenever the time is ripe. Anybody got any objections?"

Hortense, weaving only slightly, slid from her seat on the bench, brought a chair to the table; Countess Margaret, glowering at her and resolved that Hortense should take no glory to herself, was quick to join her. "Come on, come on," she growled to Oleg and myself, who were both hanging back; "let's get on with it."

"Somebody's got to kill the son of a bitch," said Blaine, "and we're all in it together."

By no conscious will of my own, I found myself sitting at the table, Oleg on my left, Munton on my right. Blaine produced cards, which each of us in turn solemnly shuffled. It made a fine picture, the eight of us crowded around the table, brandy bottles in the center, naked bulb glaring down, making faces look long and haggard.

Blaine said, "Each of us takes a card off the top. High card, ace high, gets the first card in the main deal, and clockwise afterwards. O.K."

Alma reached, took a card: six of clubs. The rest of us followed; Munton was high with the queen of hearts. "Well, that's just preliminary," said Blaine. So Munton was first, with me second, then Oleg, Hortense, Blaine, Alma, Countess Margaret and last Leibnitz.

We all shuffled again, the cards were placed in the center of the table.

"Go ahead, draw," said Blaine. Munton licked his lips, took a card. Three of spades.

I drew…Ten of hearts. Oleg put his hand cautiously forth as if he were reaching for a dozing snake. He raised a corner, peered underneath. King of diamonds. Hortense nonchalantly flipped over her card. Deuce of diamonds.

Blaine got the five of clubs; Alma, fumbling, came up with the queen of clubs; Countess Margaret drew the jack of spades, and Leibnitz the four of clubs.

It was now Munton's turn again. Cautiously he drew, peered under the corner, turned it over with a triumphant grin. Ace of clubs. "There's one of 'em gone."

My draw. The deck looked sinister and big, like a close-up in a crime movie. I reached out, took hold of a card — it seemed terribly important — flipped it over. Six of spades. I sighed and watched Oleg sneak a look at his card. Five of hearts. Hortense twitched over hers calmly. Eight of diamonds. Blaine carefully drew the king of spades, Alma the seven of diamonds, Countess Margaret the three of hearts, Leibnitz the eight of clubs, and it was back to Munton again.

Grinning, showing yellow teeth he drew the ace of hearts. "There's another of 'em."

I felt very sober and very light-headed together and at the same time. The deck waited for me. I drew. Queen of spades.

"After all," said Blaine, "it's a privilege, not a sacrifice."

Oleg drew the four of diamonds and looked at it in a subdued manner. Hortense flipped over the jack of diamonds.

"It's a privilege," said Blaine hollowly. He turned over the nine of hearts. "Where's the ace?"

"Here," said Alma. But she had the ten of clubs.

"Here," said Countess Margaret. She had the six of hearts.

"One of these times," said Blaine, "you're going to yell 'here' and be right."

Leibnitz said, "I won't say anything." He drew the seven of spades.

Munton went after his card with a jerk, lifted it, stared at it. "I seem to be getting all of 'em." It was the ace of diamonds.

Now it was getting grim. I got the deuce of spades. Oleg got the three of clubs. Hortense got the jack of clubs.

Blaine said, "Come on you," and turned up the eight of spades. "Come on you," said Alma and got the six of clubs. Countess Margaret got the nine of diamonds, Leibnitz the five of spades, and it was back to Munton.

He laid his hand on the deck. "I've got 'em all so far, here's the ace of spades." He looked from face to face. "The ace of spades." He turned it over. The nine of spades. I drew — I looked. The ace of spades. Big and black as a coal-scuttle.

The Ace of Spades.

So I was chosen to kill Kex. I studied the card. The Ace of Spades beyond argument. I heard everyone relaxing, laughing, and drinking their brandy.

"Well, that's taken care of," said Blaine cheerfully. "Now as to ways and means."

"It's got to be an accident," said Munton, once more regimental. "Can't do things any old way, learned a trick or two myself in Nigeria. The niggers teach you a thing or two along these lines."

Oleg said judicially, "It's primarily a question of opportunity, and perhaps we'd better adjourn until —"

Leibnitz pounded the table. "No, no, no. I say, make the opportunity, rid the earth of this stench!"

There was general agreement, now that a mouse had been elected to bell the cat. At the moment I was drunk enough to be worried.

Blaine said importantly, "That's all well and good, but you can't go up to a man on the Vistamare terrace and 'accident' him; there's got to be a time and a place. And don't forget we're all in this together; if there's a slip-up it's not just Chuck's ass, it's all of us. We've got to work together."

Munton huffed and blew out his cheeks. "Shouldn't work quite that way; no use involving the whole group."

"Well, we've got to work up an alibi."

"Humph, yes, I suppose that's true."

Blaine said in a thick voice, "Well, let's drink up. Here's to crime."

"Here's to crime," said Oleg with drunken abandon.

Alma had passed out; Hortense's eyes were glazed; Countess Margaret was more puffed and moist than ever.

"Here's to Kex's funeral!" cried Leibnitz with spirit. "Here's to crime!"

Chapter XVIII

EVENTS BEGAN TO GO VAGUE. There was a swimming in my eyes, a sour exhalation in my throat, a drumming in my ears like surf — and which, in fact, *was* the surf, about a hundred yards south. There was boisterous talk, some breaking glass. Oleg sang a whimsical song in Polish in response to a challenge from Countess Margaret, which he refused to translate. Blaine became annoyed when Alma refused to come alive. Munton, with heavy gallantry, at last lifted her to her feet, and in spite of her querulous complaining, took her out the door and in the direction of the Luxa Hotel.

Oleg and I argued about the future of civilization, to be interrupted by Leibnitz and Countess Margaret shouting obscenities at each other. Blaine looked up from the bed where he was toying with Hortense and ordered everyone out.

Oleg and I wandered drunkenly down along the beach and finally with dawn breaking open the east stumbled up the Vistamare stairs and into bed.

When I awoke it was Monday morning. I had a horrible taste in my mouth but otherwise no hangover. I lay torpid five or ten minutes, and recollections of the night began to seep out of my subconscious bank to surface, and I was not sure whether I should feel amusement or embarrassment... But there were other matters more urgent than last night's drunk; when I thought of them I jumped to my feet, and scrambled into my clothes.

It was unexpectedly early, ten o'clock. I ran downstairs, and without waiting for breakfast I ran up the hill, and to Kex's flat. The big Chrysler waited in front — my Chrysler. I slotted the rotor back into the distributor — my rotor, my distributor — jumped into the front seat, started the engine, and drove off downhill, past the post office, up the hill toward Sorrento.

Positano lay behind; ahead was the stone wall and the wrought-iron gate with the lantern and the plaque 'Villa Serenia'.

I slowed as I passed, looked through the gate. A flicker of motion, a flash of white? I jammed on the brakes; the Chrysler came to an elastic halt. I backed up, and met Betty opening the gate. She was in her white blouse and blue jeans, with an old rose sweater slung over her arm. She looked first at me, then the car with sardonic eyebrows.

"Good morning," I said politely.

"Good morning." The temperature was low.

"Where are you going?"

"Up over the mountain."

"Like to come for a ride?"

"No, thank you."

"You're very formal today."

"Am I?"

"Very much so."

She looked away, up the hill.

"Are you annoyed at me again?"

"No, why should I be?"

"No reason at all — so get in, and come along."

"Where are you going?"

"Naples."

"I can't go." She looked over her shoulder through the gate. "I shouldn't be talking to you."

"I can't be that bad."

She made no reply. After a moment she looked speculatively through the gate, then walked around the car; I opened the door, she jumped in. "I'll ride with you a little way."

We started out, the car gliding over the road smooth as a big green canoe.

She sat rigidly on the edge of the seat, knees tight together. "I've never ridden in a car like this before," she said. "It's an American car, isn't it?"

"Yes."

"It's Kex's — isn't it?" She looked at me, slyly challenging.

"No. It's mine." I explained.

She digested the information in silence. "Why are you going into Naples?"

"I want to cash Kex's checks before he gets the idea of stopping them. I'm not working for him anymore. He fired me last night."

"Oh."

There was no response to be made. I drove on. "I'd better get out here," said Betty suddenly.

I slowed the car, looked at her. "Oh, come on into Naples. It's a beautiful day."

For an answer she gave me a faintly scornful look.

"O.K.?" I asked.

"No, of course not. I'm not dressed for Naples in the first place."

"I'll buy you new clothes, from the skin out."

"Now you're being silly." But she was not displeased.

"Try me and see."

There was a pause.

"I shouldn't, really," she said thoughtfully.

I took this for assent. "Do you have to be back at any particular time?"

"No. No one notices whether I'm in or out."

"Don't you get on well with your parents?"

"We tolerate each other. They — have their problems — I have mine." This was quietly said. She sat back into the seat, relaxed a trifle. After a moment she switched on the radio, turned from station to station, but finding nothing but static, turned it off.

I studied her profile covertly. She looked almost happy. I said on wild impulse. "Let's not stop at Naples, let's keep on going. To Paris. And then home — to the States."

She looked at me startled, opened her mouth to speak, closed it again. Finally she said dryly, "What makes you think I — like you?"

"The only way to find out is to ask."

Leaning her head back on the leather cushion she watched the limestone crags go by. Then after a moment she said softly, "Well, I don't." And a moment later, "I wouldn't get very far without my passport."

"Oh, that could be arranged somehow."

"I almost wish I could... I want to leave Positano — more than anything else in the world."

"Then — we'll leave. We have this car, we have eighty-five hundred dollars besides my bank account."

"It's — it's impossible."

"Why?"

"I can't leave my family."

"Like I told you before, thousands of girls do it every year."

"Not families like mine."

"I wish I understood what you were talking about."

"If you did, you might not be so anxious to seduce me."

" 'Seduce'? Hell, I want to marry you."

She laughed. "You'd be even less anxious. I'm never going to be married."

"You talk like a girl who's afraid."

"I am."

"Afraid of what? As your fiancé I have a right to know."

"You're not my fiancé."

"But you are afraid?"

"I suppose so."

"Of whom? Your father?"

She hesitated an instant. "No."

"Your mother? Freddy?"

"No."

"Who then?"

"No one in particular. Just — of circumstances. Of the way my life is going. Something terrible is going to happen." She paused, then said, "Hilfstone is in Positano. He's staying at our house."

"What's he want?"

"I don't know for sure. I heard him say something about Kex."

"It may interest you to know that I'm supposed to kill Kex."

She looked at me in surprise.

"I was appointed last night, by the Dirty Shirt Club; you should have been there." I told her about the party.

"And are you going to kill Kex?"

I laughed shortly. "Of course not. No question but what he deserves it — but damned if I'm going to do it. Last night we were all drunk. It seemed real then; it's daytime now, and I'm not drunk. If Buster Blaine wants to part Kex's hair with an axe and make it look like an accident, he's welcome to. But not me."

"I'd kill him if I had the chance," said Betty, looking straight ahead.

"Life's too short. The sooner I get you away from Positano the better."

She made no response. And the big green convertible flew over the hills, and the peasants looking up from their artichoke patches knew us for millionaires. We crossed the ridge, coasted down toward Sorrento. The road to Naples lay to the right, up around more hills, with the Bay of Naples below, Capri in the distance, and Naples, miraculously cleansed by distance, sprinkled around the far shore.

The road was narrow, congested with donkey-carts, buses and motor scooters — it was quarter to twelve before we reached Naples. I broke speed laws getting to the American Express, on which Kex's check was drawn, and which by the greatest good fortune carried my own trifling account, and ran in almost as the doors were being closed for the daily two hour siesta.

I banked Kex's checks, Piombino's cash, and came out a man much more secure in my wealth. Betty once again deprecated her clothes when I wanted to take her to one of the big hotels along the seafront.

I said, "What's the difference? We're just two more mad Americans, and as long as we have money, we can't do any wrong."

So we had a long lunch, with *Cannelloni alla Genovese* and lobster and pheasant and avocados air-freighted from Mexico, with three bottles of champagne, and the waiters were sure that we were particularly mad Americans. We flirted across the table and held hands and the world was a wonderful place.

After lunch we argued whether or not I should buy her an afternoon frock, because we had decided that it would be a poor business to return to Positano so soon. We came to a compromise on the frock; she would borrow the money from me until we arrived home, so we went to an expensive-looking store on the Via Roma and came out with Betty in black and white, looking amazingly happy, astonishingly pretty. When she jumped into the car, I kissed her, and after an instant's hesitation, she went warm and melting. I said, "Betty, you'll marry me, won't you?"

"No, Chuck."

"I love you."

She was crying. Passersby were staring into the car. I drove out Via Roma to the waterfront, where it was sunny and isolated. She was sitting close up against me. "Chuck, I want to marry you — I want to go away — but I can't, so please don't ask. If you must know..." she hesitated.

"Well?"

"There's insanity in the family."

"But you're not insane."

She said with a wry sidelong smile, "You've seen Freddy."

I could hardly insist that Freddy had all his marbles at hand. I conceded that perhaps he was a little easy-going.

"Easy-going! He's just the reverse; he has tantrums like a baby!"

"A little simple, then. But," I added stubbornly, "there's nothing wrong with you."

"You can't be sure."

"I'm not sure that I'm completely right myself."

She studied me with her peculiar dispassionate speculation. "I think you're very sane, very practical."

"I'm not so sure. What's sanity to begin with? A state of mind relative to other states of mind."

She smiled wistfully. "But you don't know what goes on in my mind. I have thoughts I could never tell anybody. And sometimes when I'm half-awake I see, well, visions I suppose you'd call them. Like a color cinema, as if I'd been smoking opium."

"What for instance?"

"Oh —" she hesitated. "One time it was as if I were underwater, among blossoming seaweeds, purple, pink, green, and they grew and expanded and changed, like a kaleidoscope."

"I'd like to see something like that myself."

"Another time was inside an enormous hollow pearl or a moonstone, and it turned itself inside out — it sounds impossible — but I saw it, all of it, and I was on the outside, and the pearl had become a soap bubble. And I've seen things like demons, and fairies — as plain as I see you! Sane people don't see things like that!"

"Sure they do! Why not? You've just got a strong visual imagination."

"I wish I could think so."

"I think so, and anyway you're what I want."

"You say that now, Chuck, but later you might think otherwise."

"But —"

She put her hand over my mouth. "No, Chuck, it's a nice thought, but I won't marry you."

"Yes, you will too."

"No, Chuck."

"Yes."

"No."

"Yes."

She laughed, and in a sad voice said, "We could keep this up all afternoon."

"Until you say yes."

"I can't. I won't."

"You can. Do you love me?"

"I — I think so...Yes."

"Then that's all there is to it."

She said nothing. I kissed her again.

Two women pushing baby-carriages stopped to stare, eyes coming out like the eyes of a lobster. I gave them a dirty look, put the car into gear, drove on around the waterfront, and into the Via Partenope, where we parked and walked down to the Cafe Bersaglieri and sat in the afternoon sun, with tall glasses of wine and soda. They cast a rich red shadow, and bubbles rising up in the glass produced hurrying little motes along the tablecloth.

I asked suddenly, "Who is James Hilfstone?"

There was the usual hesitation, the inner weighing; then, meeting my eyes, she said, "He's my mother's half-brother...But please, let's not talk about him. This is wonderful here, so peaceful."

So we sat holding hands through one of those halcyon instants that hang lifelong in the memory, when air and light and shape and color take on sudden marvelous richness, when even the motes fleeing east through the two ruby puddles on the tablecloth came alive with symbolic meaning. A precious fragile shell of the moment, with time and beauty and the universe trembling just out of grasp.

Then clouds covered the sun and a cold wind arose. We left the cafe and crossed the street to the Hotel Montfalcone. A *thé dansant* was in progress; we drank two Martinis apiece and danced and held hands and looked into each other's eyes. The afternoon went like a boat sailing into a moving wall of mist, with the widening wake left behind for our contemplation, should we care to look. Preoccupied with the sweet present, we hardly felt the motion, and presently it was dinnertime.

We had chateaubriand garnished with truffles, a salad and more champagne, and when I looked at my watch it was after ten. I asked, "What will your father do if you're not home?"

"He won't know; he goes into his study and never comes out until morning."

"What about your mother?"

"She doesn't care what happens to me."

"You don't have much of a home life."

"I've always liked being by myself. They know I'm not — wild."

"But you are, in a way."

"This is the first time."

We had a room on the top floor with the dying moon peering through the window and the lights of Naples strewn around the shore.

At midnight Betty whispered through the dark, "If my father knew, he'd kill me." And a moment later she said hesitantly, "You're — *sure* there won't be any children?"

"No. There won't be any children." The moon dwindled behind a wrack of dreaming clouds, and presently sank. We lay close together, face to face.

I said, "Tomorrow we'll get your passport and then we'll leave Positano and never go back."

"I wish I could, Chuck."

"If you want to, that's all there is to it."

"I can't."

"But you can."

"No. You — don't know me, you don't know anything about me."

"Then let's have it; get it off your chest!"

She took my hand, held it to the smooth skin of her hip. I felt a scar. She opened her mouth to speak, but no words came. Her face began to wrench and twist.

I said, in something like alarm, "Don't talk if you don't want to, Betty."

She let out her breath in a gasp. "I want to — but I can't. When I try to talk, something reaches out and takes hold of my brain."

I tried to soothe her. "It's not important anyway; nothing behind us is important, just what's ahead."

"I know," she said in a low voice. "It's what's ahead I'm afraid of. There's something awful coming toward us, that we can't get out of the way of, like a train…"

"You're having nightmares."

"No, no, no, I feel it, Chuck!"

I could say nothing, my heart was too full.

At three or four, sometime in the early morning, we left the hotel, climbed into the car, and started back south. The roads were empty, the Chrysler boomed effortlessly over the narrow roads, the headlights shining for single instants on the dismal little houses, the blank windows, behind which men and women and children lay rapt in sleep, as far out of touch with our lives as if we were spirits.

We met the dawn at Sorrento and drove along the coast road into the brightening east. I let Betty off in front of her gate as the first tip of the sun sparkled over the gray water.

"Are you sure you're all right?" I whispered, and my voice sounded loud in the cool stillness.

"Yes."

"When will I see you?"

"I'm not sure. I'll let you know."

I watched her through the gate and down the hill. How quiet it was this morning! I coasted on around the road, rolled to a stop near the post office, parked, went on foot down to the Vistamare. I got to bed about quarter to six and slept till one-thirty in the afternoon.

I arose in a rather unsteady frame of mind, full of trouble, uncertainty, foreboding. I showered, shaved and went down to pick up a cup of coffee.

There was an air of excitement in the dining room. The waiters were leaning over the back table, where the customary local group played cards. Chi-Chi gave me a slant-wise look, which I ignored.

At a table near the door Munton sat, pretending not to see me. From sheer perversity I dropped into the chair beside him.

He cocked his head to the side, lifted his lip, raised his eyebrows, like a dog preparing to snap. I said carelessly, "What's new this morning?"

"What's new, eh? That's a good one." He laughed hollowly. I looked at him in surprise. His purple-gray lips were wet, his hands shook nervously. "I'll give you credit, you American blokes, you work fast."

"Hey? What are you talking about?"

"Don't know what insanity got me within hearing distance of your crazy idea. But don't forget, I fought it all the way. I won't be involved —" he banged his fist on the table, "— in any manner, shape or form." He rose to his feet, jerked his head, strode from the room.

I watched the stocky figure vanish down the steps in complete puzzlement. I looked up to find Arturo with my coffee. "What's all the excitement, Arturo?"

"Ah, signor, the tragic affair." He gave me a sly unctuous look.

"What tragic affair? I've just got up."

"Our good friend Kex —" Arturo poured the coffee. "He is dead. Killed!"

I stared up at him. "But how?"

Arturo smiled, a meaningful intimate smile. He said formally, "Signor Musgrave of course would not know; he has just arisen."

"Of course I wouldn't know!"

"It was a rock, signor — a great stone rock, dropped on the head of Kex." He bowed with exquisite finesse, turned on his heel, departed.

CHAPTER XIX

I SIPPED MY COFFEE. I looked at my hand; it was shaking. Kex was dead. I understood why Munton had fought shy of me. He thought that I had taken my commission for the Dirty Shirt Club seriously; he thought I rushed out to wreak a bloody revenge. I managed a wry smile. It could be no mystery who had killed Kex. Here in Positano everybody knew everything. I'd find out later in the day; at the moment it made not too much difference. I had other things on my mind. How could Kex's death affect me personally? I had banked the checks before he died; my title to the car could hardly be challenged...There was Betty. Kex's death would scarcely lessen her dread of Hilfstone.

Thinking of Betty I felt an overpowering urge to see her, so strong I nearly rose from my seat and ran out the door. No question, I had it bad.

But back to Kex. Blaine, I thought would know the details. I finished my coffee in a gulp, climbed the hill to his flat, knocked on the door.

A moment later I heard a cautious voice, "Who's that?"

"Chuck."

The door opened two inches; Blaine, wearing a shabby brown bathrobe, looked forth like a fox reconnoitering from its den.

"Hello," said Blaine in a colorless voice. "What'll you have?"

"I'd like to talk a little bit."

Blaine clearly shared all of Munton's convictions. I was guilty — the man who killed Kex.

Blaine looked up and down the lane, his long clown's face set in glum folds. "I wonder if it's a wise move right now. Might not be a good idea to be seen together."

"I'll take the chance."

Blaine saw my face. "Well, don't get huffy. I was just trying to —" I pushed past his long bony form. He made an indecisive movement to stop me, peered once more up and down the alley, shut the door.

"That damn Molino in the fish shop, he's got an eye like a knife," said Blaine querulously, "watches every move I make."

I went to the window, stepped out on the balcony. There was a gray overcast, clouds curled low over the mountains. A drop of rain hit my cheek; the beach was gray and empty, the surf groaned mournfully. Behind me, Blaine stood making anxious gestures. "Come back in, for Christ sakes! The whole town will see you!"

I returned inside. "Why shouldn't they? Aren't we in this thing together?"

"Hell," said Blaine nervously, "I didn't know you were, well, going to act so sudden. And why do it with half the town looking on?"

"Oho!" This was something new. I thought it over. "There were witnesses?"

Blaine said limply, "It's all over town…"

"Somebody saw me kill Kex?"

Blaine nodded. "A young Italian couple — I don't know their names. They turned you in."

I considered carefully. "Me, Chuck Musgrave?"

"Just like that."

"Well, well." In a way I was relieved; I knew who had killed Kex. There was only one man it could be. He was staying at the Villa Sirenia.

Blaine was eyeing me anxiously, wondering how best to get rid of me.

I said maliciously, "I'm going to say I was in here with you all evening."

Blaine's face became agonized. "God damn it, Chuck, don't drag me into this mess!"

"I thought we were going to stick together."

"Hell, man, that was party-time; you can't expect a man to talk sense on a snootful." He eyed me warily. "I didn't know you were quite so ready."

I sat down, lit a cigarette. Blaine wandered along the periphery of the room, a long brown weevil with tremulous antenna.

I grinned sourly. "Lucky we're all in this together; that's the value of organization. One for all, all for one."

Blaine draped himself into a chair, elbows and knees at random angles. "Hell, Chuck," he cried, "I can't afford to be mixed up in a thing like this. This isn't a joke. This is — this is murder!"

"That's what it figured to be. We called it 'execution', of course. So now — hang one of us, hang us all."

"Gad!" he gasped, "you're a cold-blooded devil!"

There was a scratching at the outside door. Blaine leapt grotesquely to his feet, ran into the kitchen. He opened the door a crack. "Hello?"

A female voice muttered something indistinguishable.

"No, no," said Blaine. "Not now."

In response the door gave a sudden lurch; Blaine clapped his hand to his nose, staggered back. Alma stood in the doorway, her hair was combed neatly in an unflattering style. She seemed to be quite sober and stood rigidly, eyes fixed on me. She swayed back, accused Blaine with a fierce look, turned slowly, left my line of vision.

Blaine shut the door, came back with his face screwed up into a frantic mask. The fun, such as it was, was over; besides my own curiosity was getting out of hand. "Well, Buster, just to put your mind at rest, I didn't do it."

Blaine halted in his tracks; his face changed comically, his big maw of a mouth gaped open. "What's that you say?"

"I didn't kill Kex; I haven't been within miles of him."

"But, Christ! Chuck! They saw you!"

"They saw someone who looks like me."

"Mumph." Blaine cocked his head critically. "That's hard to take."

"Kex gave you the whole story the other night."

"You mean the guy you're supposed to look like?"

I nodded. "His name is Hilfstone. James Powan Hilfstone."

"How do you know he's around?"

"I know."

Blaine considered several seconds. "Well," he said dubiously, "it makes a nice angle."

"But you don't buy it?"

He made a helpless gesture. "Don't get me wrong, Chuck — I'm *for* you! But at the session the other night —"

I said in a weary voice, "Do you think I'd be sucker enough to stick my neck that far out? Give me credit for a few brains."

Blaine thought it over. I could read his mind: if I were telling the truth, there would be no criminal conspiracy. "Eyewitnesses don't always see things right," he mused, "it might be most anybody."

"Maybe you got him yourself," I suggested.

Blaine jerked in his seat. "Not me, no sir! I'm a peaceable man."

"It was your idea."

"Forget that fool talk — you'll get us all in hot water. If you say it's Hilfstone, it's Hilfstone."

"I'm saying it wasn't me. The rest is deduction. Incidentally, what time did it happen?"

"Late last night, I suppose."

"That lets me out definitely," I said. "I was in Naples; I can prove it." I thought again. Maybe I couldn't prove it. I heard Betty's husky whisper, "If my father knew he'd kill me."

Blaine looked a little more cheerful. "You can prove it, you say?"

"Well — if I had to. I didn't get home till this morning."

Blaine massaged the lean flanks of his face, pursing out his lips. "If they can't find Hilfstone — then what?"

"They'll throw out the dragnet. Are you in the clear?"

He looked injured. "Why should anyone think I did it?"

"Why not? You had lots of cause to hate him."

"So does Oleg. So do lots of people."

"Everybody on the Dirty Shirt List. If that deal comes out —"

"What do you mean 'if'?" asked Blaine gloomily.

"— everybody on the list will be under suspicion."

Blaine pulled uneasily at his chin. "You don't know these Italian police. They don't go in for much Sherlock Holmes stuff. All they give a damn for is striding around in their uniforms. They'll grab the first son of a bitch that looks likely and let it go at that. One crime, one prisoner. Whether he's guilty or not is secondary." He stalked to his cupboard. "Have a drink?"

"No, thanks."

I got to my feet, but before I could leave, the outer door swung open, and Alma slipped in. Blaine stood in the arch, looking at her. "Now what?"

"Is he still here?"

"What if he is?"

"He'd better clear out. Margaret's gone up to the carabinieri and had an emotional orgy. She spilled the beans about your little party, and they're taking a dim view."

"Oh God, oh God," prayed Blaine, "if I don't go on the wagon after this my name ain't Buster Blaine!"

He tottered into the room, sat on his bed. Alma in the doorway, examining me without emotion.

Blaine groaned, "What the devil got into her? What —"

"She thinks she'll duck free while the ducking's good."

"How in God's name did you hear all this?"

"Margaret told me. I've just been up to her room."

"So help me," said Blaine, "if I ever buy that babe another drink or so much as pinch her bottom…"

Alma looked at me with slowly dawning interest, and what might be called contemptuous respect. "You seem to be taking this thing pretty coolly."

"Mainly because I had nothing to do with it."

"Really." Alma shrugged. "That makes a good story."

I laughed grimly. "The innocence, the naïveté of you people astonishes me. We draw cards to see who kills Kex. Not one of us intends to follow it up; but when Kex is killed then you jump to the conclusion that I who drew the ace performed the act."

"You were seen," she said coldly.

"Hell," I said, "it stands to reason that I'd be *least* likely to kill him after that party."

Blaine said to Alma, "He was in Naples all last night. He says he can prove it."

"Oh yeah? Ha ha!"

There was a sharp rap on the door. Blaine licked his lips. "My God, I think I'll rent me another room; this place is like a longshoremen's hiring hall."

He swung open the door; behind him I saw the flash of brass buttons. Blaine's manner changed. "Hello."

There was staccato talk in Italian.

"No savvy," said Blaine. "No comprendez."

The man in uniform repeated himself, in louder higher voice. It was not a friendly statement. Blaine's shoulders drooped.

"Me Americano," he said. "I don't know what you're talking about."

There was disgusted murmur, and then silence. Blaine said nervously over his shoulder, "I guess they took all that talk seriously…They're coming back with Vittorio; he speaks English." He turned back to the open door, "Hi, Vittorio, what's the trouble?"

Vittorio evidently addressed himself to the carabinieri, and after eliciting a reply, turned back to Blaine. "It'sa very bad, Mr. Blaine. They say the guy that kill Kex is here. They want him to come out."

Blaine said in a frenzy of anxiety, "No, no, Vittorio — you tell him he's all wrong. Tell him he doesn't want to pay any attention to that Countess Margaret, she's hysterical — crazy."

Vittorio explained to the carabinieri. I rose to my feet, went to stand in the doorway. The carabinieri listened with glowering faces, as if crime of any sort were an offense against their personal prestige and dignity.

Vittorio's mobile face contracted, expanded, sucked in and out with the earnestness of his speech. The carabiniere replied in a sharp volley, waving his hand arrogantly, pointing over Blaine's shoulder at me. Across the street the fish peddler came to stand in his doorway; two fat women and a dozen ragged urchins gaped from the street.

Vittorio said, "They say they come to arrest a man call Musgruff."

"But why?" cried Blaine. "They can't arrest him merely on some weird story of Countess Margaret's."

There was further argument and counter-argument. Vittorio turned back to Blaine. "They say they don't care for this Countess Margaret; she makes no difference. They were coming for this Musgruff even before Countess Margaret. They say Musgruff kill Kex."

I came forward. "You tell them they're crazy; I had nothing to do with it."

"They say they got people who saw you. Two people, last night, they see you drop a rock on Kex!"

Blaine's confidence in me wavered. He glanced fearfully over his shoulder. "Tell 'em, Chuck! Tell 'em who really did it!"

"I didn't do it — that's all I know for sure!"

"But they *saw* you," said Vittorio, now spokesman for the carabinieri who nodded angrily. They spoke in sharp voices.

Blaine said desperately, "Tell 'em, Chuck — you were in Naples. Tell 'em!"

I didn't want to say anything about Naples. They looked at me expectantly. I kept silent. Their voices rose again.

Vittorio said, "They want you to come; they're gonna put you in jail. They think you killed Kex." He looked at Blaine, laughed in nervous glee. "Lots of excitement, huh? Like tourist season already. Every year it gets worse."

Chapter XX

Protesting, angry, apprehensive, I went with them, through the smelly narrow ways, past the staring shopkeepers, the laborers with loads on their backs, the awed children, up to the carabinieri headquarters, up the road from the post office. They marched me up the steps with an unpleasant air of rectitude as much as to say, "One more evildoer tripped up and ready for his just deserts." We entered a bare dirty room smelling of tobacco and carbolic acid. A pair of rough benches faced each other; there was a bulletin board covered with appeals and advertisements, with a bellicose photograph of Mussolini pinned neatly in the lower left-hand corner.

I was taken through a door into a second room, with a high arched ceiling and marble floor. Behind a desk sat a handsome young man in immaculate uniform, sitting with an air of studied insolence. His forehead was high, his hair cut back from the temple in a line like that of an old-time Japanese warrior. His eyes were hooded like a falcon's, his mouth was languid under a spruce mustache, he looked sardonic, egotistical, unsympathetic.

The carabinieri took my arm with unnecessary firmness, led me forward so that I looked like a felon already convicted and stumbling up to the tribunal to hear my just, if severe, sentence.

To my relief the man behind the desk spoke excellent English. He rose to his feet, bowed formally. "I am Assistant Chief Detective-Inspector for the Province of Salerno; you may address me as Lieutenant Piretti."

He sank elegantly back into his seat, pointed to a straight-back chair beside the desk. "Kindly be seated.

"You are here on a most serious charge, Mr. Musgrave. Let me be concise. The body of a distinguished resident was found on Via Bianchini, his head crushed by a large rock. The circumstances indicate murder; witnesses have come forward to identify you as the guilty man, and we have no alternative but to charge you with the crime."

I said as politely and firmly as I was able, "There must be some mistake. I had nothing to do with Kex's death, in any way whatever."

Lieutenant Piretti raised his eyebrows. "You can prove your assertion?"

Lieutenant Piretti, I thought, was determined to make good theater out of the scene. A production rigidly conventionalized, with me the desperate but still dangerously clever criminal to be played like a game fish, inexorably confused and trapped by the easy brilliance of Lieutenant Piretti. He repeated, "You can prove this assertion?"

I glared at him, unable to collect my wits. If I stated my alibi Positano gossip would crucify Betty. Although she seemed to fear gossip less than her father.

I said firmly, "In the United States, we're assumed innocent until proven guilty."

Lieutenant Piretti gave his head a cynical jerk. "No more than a pious hope. I am well acquainted with your methods; I studied criminology at the University of Chicago. I saw your police in operation. But this —" he made an important gesture "— is all academic. In the case of this crime we can prove you guilty; indeed," he nodded a hand at one of the carabinieri, "I intend to do so."

A door opened; a young couple, pale and uncertain, were led into the room. The young man wore a brown suit, the girl wore a neat gray dress and black coat. They were troubled and nervous, but appeared responsible, honest and reasonably intelligent.

Lieutenant Piretti spoke in clipped Italian; they looked at me, walked around me. I stood sweating, with a sinking feeling in the pit of my stomach.

The two spoke together; nodded emphatically. Lieutenant Piretti looked at me with careless triumph. "As you see…"

I snapped, "If you studied at the University of Chicago, you know that an identification outside a line-up doesn't mean much."

"Ah, but this identification was better than that!" Lieutenant Piretti relaxed. "Let me explain. I came here this morning to investigate a strange murder. First I must listen to a mad woman who tells me a sinister tale. It seems a cabal has been formed, and you are appointed the instrument in destroying the man Kex. I ignore her temporarily. Next I am approached by these two people. They are more circumstantial. It seems that, recently engaged, they were last night enjoying a midnight chat, making plans for the future. They sat in the dark overlooking Via Moresco. At one o'clock, they report seeing a man run quietly along the road, looking over the wall from time to time. Here — as no doubt you are aware," and Lieutenant Piretti smiled meaningfully, "the Via Moresco passes parallel directly above Via Bianchini; the two in fact joining a short distance further along. At a spot directly below the two witnesses here — Signor Printicci and Signorina Campaglio — this man selected a rock from a pile of building materials, went stealthily to the wall, waited several seconds, then dropped the rock. Then, turning, he ran back the way he had come. Signor Printicci, recognizing his duty, ran down upon Via Moresco, looked over the wall, down at Via Bianchini, twenty feet below. Here he spied a recumbent body. He immediately notified the police. Significantly, at this time they named you as the assailant, having seen and remarked you a number of times around Positano. Both appear to have excellent eyesight. A streetlight not too far distant provides a sufficiency of illumination. Now," he eyed me with debonair inquiry, "what do you say to that?"

"I say they're mistaken."

"They are quite positive."

"Ask what I was wearing."

"I have done so already. They are not completely certain, but think it was a dark blue suit."

"Ask them again, now."

Lieutenant Piretti shrugged, and spoke to Signor Printicci, who responded hesitantly.

Lieutenant Piretti at last turned to me, his mouth twisted in dissatisfaction. "They say it was a dark suit; of the color they can not be certain. Natural enough, under the streetlight."

"But it was a dark suit?"

"Yes."

I nodded with grim satisfaction. "Well, I don't have a dark suit. Only medium gray flannels — I'm wearing the trousers now — and this sport coat."

Lieutenant Piretti waved a hand languidly. "A detail."

"A detail? It doesn't sound like a detail to me. It means that the man they saw wasn't me!"

"They are certain as to your face, signor, and are content merely to describe an impression of your clothes."

"They're wrong."

"Perhaps you can show that you were somewhere else at the time?"

"Yes, I could. But it involves a lady I don't want to embarrass."

Lieutenant Piretti nodded gravely. He turned to Signor Printicci and his fiancée, spoke in Italian. They bowed and left the room.

"According to Officer San Marco, you explained that you were in Naples at the time of the incident."

Nothing would have infuriated Kex so much as having his murder referred to as an incident. "Yes," I said. "That's what I told him."

"Naples is a large city; however a foreigner is always noticed. If you describe your movements, I will undertake to check them. You may be assured of our discretion."

Lieutenant Piretti's discretion would not be discreet enough. If I told Lieutenant Piretti where and how to check my alibi, no power on earth could prevent the story from percolating down through various levels, through carabinieri and their wives and the storekeepers, to loafers and fishermen and servants, from servants back up to masters.

"Well?" asked Lieutenant Piretti. "I am waiting."

"I don't think I'd better say anything at this time."

Piretti shrugged. "If you are innocent, you are making a mistake. You realize that I have no choice but to detain you?"

"I assume as much."

"Please describe to me your relationship with the deceased."

"He hired me to make some charcoal sketches of Positano." It seemed a long time ago.

"Hm." Lieutenant Piretti raised his eyebrows skeptically. "I understand you were on terms of intimate friendship."

I laughed bitterly. "You got that from my friend Countess Margaret."

Lieutenant Piretti pursed his lips. "Do I understand that you admit to the situation?"

"Of course not. It's not true. Countess Margaret is — well, she's not so much a liar as she is a little crazy. She's got a fixation."

"You say that the deceased hired you to make charcoal sketches. Where was this?"

I described my meeting with Kex, at the Artists and Models Club in Rome. "A rather peculiar aspect to the situation —" I paused, changed the direction of my thoughts.

"What is 'peculiar'?"

"Oh — that Kex was willing to pay so high for what was hardly more than commercial art. The peculiarity however was cleared up after I arrived."

"In what way?"

I explained Kex's idea of a joke; Lieutenant Piretti seemed much amused and rather impressed. "This joke, as you call it, must have cost Kex a great deal of money."

"He could afford it. As soon as I found out what Kex was up to, I hit him up for more money."

"Ah ha!" exclaimed Lieutenant Piretti. "And Kex refused to pay you?"

"On the contrary."

Lieutenant Piretti sank back into his seat, biting his lips in vexation.

"Go on, if you please. Tell me about this Dirty Shirt Club." And he grimaced with fastidious disdain.

I told him; Piretti took a note of names. "And this secret meeting?"

"It wasn't secret and it wasn't a meeting."

"As you wish."

"In fact Kex showed up himself."

"Suppose you give me your version of this affair."

As well as I could remember, I described the party, up to and including the draw of cards.

"So then," said Lieutenant Piretti with exaggerated patience and restraint, a man trying to be reasonable, but meeting irrationality on all sides, "you admit that you accepted this solemn charge to kill Kex?"

"Accept hell! The honor was thrust on me. And also," I said in irritation, "forget this idea about a solemn charge. It was not anything of the sort; it was a drunken party. At the time we were all up in the air, but the next day it was water under the bridge."

"In view of subsequent events," said Lieutenant Piretti ponderously, "I find it hard to accept this interpretation."

"My God man, give me credit for more intelligence."

"Would you have killed him, even if you hadn't drawn the ace?" asked Lieutenant Piretti innocently.

"Come again, Lieutenant. I didn't kill the bloke."

Lieutenant Piretti lit a long yellow cigarette. "One other matter. Shortly after you arrived in Positano, you hung a sign on the door of your residence, stating that you were not 'James Hilfstone'. Who is this man?"

"I don't know."

"This can't be true!" exclaimed Lieutenant Piretti angrily.

"I've never met the man; I've never even seen him."

"Then how did you learn the man's identity?"

"Kex wanted me to use the name while I was at Positano. I refused."

"Surely," Lieutenant Piretti said smoothly, "a man of your inquiring nature would have sought details."

"I asked Kex a few questions, but he never gave me any answers."

"Hmph." Lieutenant Piretti sat staring out the window, a petulant look on his face. "Well, this talk has resolved nothing. You are still the man who has been positively identified as a murderer. Come now," he pleaded, his eyes going soft and feminine, "confess your guilt to me, and we will save very much bother."

"I didn't kill Kex. Why should I confess?"

Lieutenant Piretti struck his fist angrily on the table. "You have been identified!"

"They're wrong. They saw somebody else."

He peered at me suspiciously. "The tone of your voice suggests that you know more about this crime than you are revealing to me."

"It's no surprise to you," I said after a slight pause, "that Kex had many enemies."

"No surprise whatever." He rose to his feet, strode up and down the room. I watched him pace, my brain heavy with a dread. I knew he'd hit on the right track eventually. It would lead through Hilfstone to the Villa Sirenia. And then — I experienced a curious mental image, half-felt, half-seen, an involuntary metaphor. I sensed a tall building — delicate, fragile, airy, spire-shaped, something like a skyscraper, crumbling apart, toppling, sliding toward the ground. It was symbolic of the existence Alfred Dannister had built in Positano; it was toppling, falling, falling, with glorious and tragic certainty.

Lieutenant Piretti came to a halt. "I have no choice but to hold you pending further investigation."

"Am I under arrest?"

Lieutenant Piretti smiled politely, and spoke as one man of the world to another. "You are assisting us by submitting to interrogation. Several points have arisen which require verification, and you have consented to wait while the investigations are pursued. During this time you are our guest and we hope you will be quite comfortable. The case admittedly is one of great complexity and interest; it would be foolhardy to strike for the first bait, which is yourself." He bowed. "And now, if you will be so good as to follow Officer San Marco, he will take you to the chamber which has been prepared —" he grinned with a flash of white teeth "— for your visit."

My cell was clean enough. The walls were white-washed, the concrete floor smelled strongly of disinfectant. The bed of iron pipe was covered with a straw mattress and a rough canvas sheet, quite clean. There was a rough chair, a shelf, a washstand, basin and pitcher. The window gave me a view of the mountainside.

Light left the sky, the cell became dark. I paced the floor after the traditional manner, becoming more and more indignant. The lights went on, a sudden glare that nearly blinded me, the door opened, my dinner was rolled in on a tea wagon: a quite passable meal.

When I had finished, a porter brought in three clean blankets, wordlessly made the bed, rolled out the tea wagon, and ten minutes later the lights went off.

After another half hour of furious pacing I took off my outer clothes, climbed into bed, and gradually relaxed.

Kex. Dead. That last and best of his jokes, with me as the butt. Via Moresco — that would be up the hill from his house; a man walking the upper road from Villa Sirenia to Kex's flat would normally follow first Via Moresco, then double back along Via Bianchini directly below.

One thing still not clear — why had Kex got it from Hilfstone? What in Hilfstone's past had driven him to such swift and decisive action? He had only arrived a day before. I pictured the wrought-iron gate, the graceful loop of wrought iron, the lantern illuminating a bronze plaque: Villa Sirenia. By now the Dannisters would know of Kex's murder. They might even know of Hilfstone's involvement, his guilt. What would Betty think of this? One more weight, one more torment; my heart went out through the darkness and tried to feel for hers. She must be weltering in dread at the moment; she would know the imminence of her worst imaginings far better than I...Kex, Kex, Kex! I said. If there were a hell, Kex was already toasting at the infernal fire...

My thoughts went down the hill, along the esplanade, to the Vistamare. The bar-restaurant would be alive with gossip, hushed delight. In quarters other than the Dirty Shirt Club Kex's loss would be mourned, and toasts would be offered to the memory of the celebrated *bon vivant*. They would name me an arrogant, angry, unsubtle Yank, with neither perception nor humor; I would be scorned and despised, the man who killed Santa Claus. After the third bottle of wine, the fourth brandy, the reminiscences would begin: the *avant-garde* movie Kex had produced on the beach; his 'Purple Passion' cocktails mixed with potassium permanganate, and their astounding after-effects; the four-day jam session to which he invited a dozen bop and "progressive" musicians, and the resultant 12-inch LP record entitled, 'Kex's Four-Day Wineroo'.

The sentimental *nil nisi bonum mortuis* would not, however, be strictly observed, especially among members of the Dirty Shirt Club. Blaine would be doubtful, Munton vindictive, Oleg analytical, Leibnitz grim, Alma would laugh, Hortense would smile, Countess Margaret would rage. There would be solemn debate: did Clarence Musgrave drop the rock; or did he not? The consensus would express itself in a wise nodding of the heads. "The silly ass made no secret of it — draws the Ace of Spades at a drunken party and then —" with a note of hushed and uncomprehending delight "— he girds up his loins and actually sallies out to kill the man!"

Eyes would covertly watch Blaine, Munton and the others; there would be speculation about criminal conspiracy. Perhaps, in self-defense, but without conviction, Blaine would argue my innocence, and he would quickly be overwhelmed. "For heavens sake, Buster, the man was *seen!*"

The tale of Kex's investigations and the findings of his detectives would seep out; the suicide of Pamela and Hester Ryen would be understood; there would be a drawing away from the others on Kex's list.

Then there were the Dannisters, the austere, unapproachable Dannisters. Kex had included them on his list, but had not laid them bare. There would be speculation, dispassionate malice: "— utterly good authority that Freddy isn't entirely a man — one of those hermaphrodite persons. I'm sure they're all insane; you can see that girl-creature slipping around the mountains at all hours of day and night. A wonder she's not forcibly raped." "Humph, would force be necessary?" "Has anyone ever seen the mother?"

At last I slept, to be awakened not long after dawn by the porter with my breakfast: coffee, half a crusty loaf and a saucer of orange marmalade.

The morning dragged by; I pounded on the door, and when the porter looked in, demanded a telephone, a lawyer, the American ambassador. The porter said politely, "*No capisco, signor,*" and withdrew.

I lay down on the bunk. The morning drifted past; a beam of sunlight entering the cell cut an arc along the floor toward the window, hesitated at its closest point and I knew without looking at my watch that it was noon.

There were footsteps in the corridor: my lunch, I thought, but it was Officer San Marco. He opened the door, beckoned me forth.

I sullenly followed him to the inner office, and here was Lieutenant Piretti, standing by the window, flicking at his boots with an alder withe.

"My friend," he said graciously, "you are free to come and go as you wish. We have proved your innocence beyond all question." And he stood eyeing me with superb insolence, slapping his boots, as if he expected thanks.

"Oh," I said in a throaty and congested voice, "you've proved my innocence."

"Naples is an observant city; your presence there, in the company of a young lady whose name I shall not mention —" here he twisted his eyebrows, and Officer San Marco smirked knowingly "—has been abundantly verified. Beyond all doubt, you cannot be held responsible for the sad event of Monday night; in short, you are free." *Rap, tap*, went the wand against his boots. I thought, if I hit him, I'll be back in that cell. I controlled myself with an effort that brought a pink blur to my eyes.

Lieutenant Piretti watched me a moment with impersonal interest, then turned and stared out the window. Officer San Marco had gone off about his business. I turned, opened the door, crossed the dingy outer room, stepped out into the noon sun.

In the street two young laborers walking past, turned their heads to look at me, watching over their shoulders until a twist in the street blocked their view. They knew who I was, everything about me. News travels fast in Positano.

CHAPTER XXI

NEWS TRAVELS FAST in Positano. I came into the little piazza in front of the post office. As usual a half-dozen loafers lounged on the bench near the gas pump, spitting and smoking and creating staccato Italian sounds. I crossed in front of them; there was a dead stop to the conversation, utter silence, I felt a dull rage mount up; I had the impulse to shout at them to turn their blasted eyes somewhere else. I paused, half-swung around, glared at the owlish array of dark eyes. But it was impossible to stare down the whole gauntlet, undignified to stand glowering. They had no feeling, they watched as they might watch an odd insect.

I swallowed my anger, stalked past. Ahead was the big green convertible. Sudden disgust spilled over from the back of my mind. This was not my car; it belonged to Kex, no matter how I might rationalize to the contrary. The bill of sale meant nothing; Kex had selected, paid for and driven it. It was nothing of mine. Driving it was like wearing Kex's clothes, sleeping with Kex's woman. I reached into my pocket, found the bill of sale. I looked at it, looked at the car, hesitated: only an instant. I might feel sorry later, I might kick myself for a fool. Right now — I crumpled up the bill of sale, tossed it into the front seat. A fine gesture, and I walked on down toward the beach with the truculent sense of not caring two beans for anything. I had gone past embarrassment; I felt free of small restraints. What did I care if a benchful of loafers stared? What did I care for anything? I was a different person, without diffidence, warmth, amiability. The effect of stepping out of the harness of social restraints was to cast loose a load of petty worries. I asked myself in amazement, why hadn't I thought of this long ago?

Clad in this new doctrine of self-sufficiency I strode out into the esplanade. From the tobacconist's shop came the Count Paladini. He saw me, raised his eyebrows in surprise. I said pleasantly, "What are you gaping at, chum?"

He wheeled abruptly, marched off up the street.

I walked into the Vistamare. Giovanni the manager peered at me from his cubicle of an office. At a table beside the door sat Hortense, calmly eating a salad. "Hello," she said. "I see they've turned you loose, ridiculous people."

I had nothing better to do; I sat down beside her. "Well, what's new around town?"

"Just your incarceration."

"I'm out now. They find I have an alibi."

"So I hear."

I looked at her curiously. "You've heard, have you?"

She nodded, a hint of amusement twitching the corners of her mouth.

"What did you hear?"

"That you spent the night in Naples."

"Is that all?"

"No."

"Go on."

"You were with Betty Dannister."

"Where did you hear that?"

"From my maid. She's a cousin of one of the carabinieri. She tells me the lieutenant from Salerno made a thorough investigation." Her eyes flashed with a gleam of amusement or perhaps malice. "I hear he interviewed Miss Dannister early this morning."

"What!"

Hortense shrugged and smiled. "So I hear."

I was up on my feet and out the door; without being aware of the distance in between I found myself entering the office of the carabinieri. The dirty outer office was empty. I tried the inner door. Locked. Trying to calm myself, I rapped.

Officer San Marco opened the door, peered forth. I pushed inside against his automatic pressure. "Where's Piretti?"

The question was rhetorical, for Piretti was sitting at the desk in his shirt sleeves. I went to lean over him, putting both hands on the desk. He glanced up in mild surprise. "What now?"

"I hear you went calling this morning."

"I beg your pardon?"

"You went up to the Dannisters' this morning."

"In accordance with my duties, yes."

"You infernal skunk."

"Mr. Musgrave, you are insulting the dignity of the Italian justice!"

"I'm talking about you — you filthy smug scoundrel. For two cents I'd break every bone in your rotten body."

Lieutenant Piretti rose to his feet, pale and subdued. "I can't understand your anger; are you not free?"

"After you've dragged an innocent person's name into the slime."

"Not at all; I exercised the utmost discretion. I insisted that Mr. Dannister allow me to speak to the young lady in private; I am guilty of nothing."

I was hot and cold together; my fingers were numb where they gripped the table. "What did you tell Dannister?"

Lieutenant Piretti glanced behind me, where I could feel the bulk of the two carabinieri, attentive, interested. Lieutenant Piretti sank back into his chair, and began to reassert his dignity. "You trespass upon official property; you use abusive language; I warn you to beware before you find yourself in trouble."

"You knew at nine o'clock this morning I had nothing to do with Kex's death; you let me rot in that cell until one in the afternoon."

"There was no need for haste; it was necessary that the evidence be carefully reviewed."

I could hardly speak for rage. I finally said in a voice I could hardly recognize, "How'd you like to step outside, Piretti, without your badge on?"

Piretti gestured to his men, spoke in a bland voice. He waved his arm, jerked an insolent thumb; I was seized and ejected. The carabinieri stood looking after me with half-friendly interest, as businessmen might watch the departure of a good customer.

I turned, went slowly down the road to the Vistamare.

Hortense sat where I had left her; she was now sipping coffee. I dropped into the chair beside her, neither of us speaking. She sipped her coffee; I stared heavily into space.

Arturo, the waiter, came politely over; I sent him for a bottle of beer to settle my nerves. Looking meditatively across the rim of her cup, Hortense said, "You're in love with Betty, aren't you?"

"You could put it that way."

"She's a nice girl."

I grunted noncommittally.

"She's all mixed up," said Hortense in her most contemplative voice.

I turned her a sidelong glance. The dimples at the corners of her mouth deepened. "Don't you think so?"

"I don't think there's anything wrong with her a normal kind of life wouldn't fix up."

Hortense smiled at me with a look of knowing mischief. "You mean she wants a man."

The idea seemed overly blunt; my stomach gave a sick twist. I decided that behind Hortense's personable exterior was a mind direct to the point of brutality: her Teutonic origin, perhaps. I picked some careful words. "She's got her normal instincts." I remembered Betty's remark that Hortense had been making advances. "She's fastidious enough to want to stay normal."

Hortense made no pretense at not understanding me. "You're more than a little of a prude, aren't you?"

"What you mean by 'prude' and what I mean are two different things." I drank a hard gulp of beer, to soften the heavy lump on my diaphragm. I hoped Hortense would hold her tongue; I had no interest in her probing, no matter how smoothly she disguised it. She ignored disguise entirely.

"Are you going to marry her?"

"I suppose anything's possible."

"Perhaps she's not interested in marriage."

"Why do you say that?"

Hortense shrugged, teasing like a warm and lazy cat, too comfortable for real ferocity, too perverse for forbearance. "She seems very attached to her family. Somehow," she stressed the word with a delicate nuance, "it doesn't seem quite — healthy."

"That's nonsense," I said in a low voice.

Hortense pursed her lips; a maddening woman. "I wouldn't be too sure. She lives in a peculiar atmosphere."

"She's scared stiff," I said. "She's scared to death. I'd like to get her away before something happens to her."

Hortense raised her eyebrows. "You think she's in danger? Actual danger?"

She was certainly mocking me; I ignored her question. We sat in guarded silence, she smiling faintly. Whether the smile mirrored her frame of mind or whether it was a muscular twitch I never could be quite sure. And peculiarly, the more cordially I disliked Hortense, the more strongly I felt her aura of sheer overpowering *sex*. It annoyed me, adding even another pang to the compound of dull rage and thwarted impulses which were tormenting me.

Sipping her coffee, Hortense smiled even more knowingly. I stared moodily off into space.

A party of American tourists, the men with cameras, the women in gray suits, white blouses and brown oxfords, came into the hotel; how immune and new they were, like romping children. I sat watching them with the weight of ages on my shoulders, and only looked up when Blaine dropped into the chair beside me. "Here he is; it's about time too!"

"All policemen are fools," said Hortense, with the air of delivering an elemental axiom. Blaine accepted it without challenge. "Right. I knew you didn't do it; I told 'em all. Hey, Arturo, let's have a beer!" He sat back, looked at me quizzically.

"How did they do you?"

"Nothing serious; I can't complain."

"You act kinda peaked."

"I've got lots on my mind."

"Who hasn't?" said Blaine fervently. He rubbed his long clown's face, looked doubtfully toward Hortense. "Yes, sir," he reiterated, rather weakly, "I told 'em they were all wet."

Hortense asked quietly, "Who *did* kill Kex?"

Blaine licked his lips, looked all around the room. "Might have been anybody. Man in a dark suit, that's all they got to go by."

"Perhaps they'll never catch him."

I said suddenly, "Blaine, where's the telephone?"

"There's the hotel phone in Giovanni's office. Er, who might you be calling, if it's any of my business?"

Hortense said silkily, "The Dannisters, of course."

Giovanni watched me approach from the corner of his eye. "I'd like to use your telephone," I said. He jumped to life, as if suddenly aware of my existence. "Yes, signor, right here, if you please."

He showed me a little dark nook at the back, and discreetly left me alone. I thumbed through a tattered pamphlet with a tired yellow cover. Positano had only a dozen subscribers; Dannister was one of them. 'Alfredo Dannister, Villa Sirenia…Positano 22.'

I stood looking at the black instrument, full of mingled misgivings and urgency. Slowly I raised the receiver, and at the operator's voice, gave the number: Positano *venti due*. I heard the bell whirring at the other end. If Betty answered, good. If it were anyone else, I told myself, I'd hang up.

The bell whirred. The receiver was lifted. "Hello?" A man's voice — that of Alfred Dannister. In spite of my resolution, I answered. "I'd like to speak to Miss Betty Dannister, please."

"May I ask who is calling?"

"Clarence Musgrave."

There was the pause of half a second; in the background I had heard a question, a voice. He said in a flat voice, "Please don't call again."

I stood looking at the dead receiver, slowly hung up, went back to my seat.

"Any luck?" asked Blaine brightly.

"No."

He stretched his long thin legs, sighed. "This place is wearing me out; I'm getting stale. Time to move on."

"Time to move on," said Hortense softly, looking out the door. "I think so too."

"Where you going, Hortense?" asked Blaine in interest. "Think I'll come along." He winked at me.

"I don't know. I can't stay here any longer. Perhaps Scotland."

"Scotland!" Blaine's voice was an amazed squeak. "Now *that's* a weird idea."

"I suppose I'm a weird person."

"You can say that again."

The door darkened; I recognized Munton's blocky bulk. He peered from table to table, half-reluctantly came to join us. Almost immediately behind him came Oleg, carrying a thick book, his finger marking the place.

Munton settled himself with a grunt, darted a sharp glance in my direction, thereafter ignored me. "Just had a brush with the police; damned detective, insolent sort of chap."

"It'll get worse before it gets better," said Blaine.

Munton growled, "Devilish bit of business; be glad to see the last of it."

"We're talking about moving," said Blaine. "Hortense wants to go to Scotland."

"Well, well, well," said Munton, ponderously arch. "I'll have to come along, show her the sights."

Hortense looked uninterestedly at her fingernails. Blaine said, "I think I'll hit for Majorca myself — or maybe Cyprus." He scratched his chin musingly. "Like to head back to California but that's big trouble." He glanced at Oleg. "How about you, professor?"

Oleg frowned a little. "Yes, I think I'll be happy to leave. But where —" he shook his head.

"Talk about big trouble," said Blaine, "you'd never guess."

"Don't tell me there's more," said Hortense in mock dismay.

"Say it, man, say it!" cried Munton.

Blaine sat back in his chair, grinned thoughtfully. "Countess Margaret's old man came in last night on the Rome bus. He must of got tired of his boy-friend and decided he wanted some domestic life...Man, he's getting it too." Blaine chuckled. "I came down past the Countess' flat, and I could hear 'em from the street. Wedded bliss, ah, me!"

There was a step behind; I half-turned. A tremendous blow on the side of the jaw utterly astounded me. Lights, shadows, faces shattered, jarred. I felt the floor rise up, hit me; there was the dull scrape of chairs, grind of stone on my face, smell of ammonia in my nose. Overhead I heard voices. Blaine's: "— shouldn't do like that; it's not right."

I gathered my wits, looked up. Freddy Dannister stood hulking over me, fists knotted. I had a sudden bewildering sense of return; this was where I came in.

Freddy was saying in a high excited voice, "Get up, you skunk; let me at him."

Blaine protested, "No, no, cut it out, Freddy, you've made a big mistake."

I heard Munton's gruff voice, excited now. "Leave 'em alone, Buster. Good fight does a man good, knock a little sense into both of 'em."

I sat looking up at Freddy, gathering strength, feeling all the frustration and pent rage untie from its big lump, straighten out into a kind of glad fury. I carefully picked myself up, and was ready to dive in, when Blaine jumped between us.

"Now, cut it out; that's enough! I don't want to see any massacres; this thing's gone as far as it's gonna go." He spoke with authority. Freddy began to say, "But he's got it coming, you don't know what he's done!"

I said thickly, "Move out of the way, Buster." I had my fist cocked; I wanted to strike him like an underwater swimmer wants his first gasp of clean air.

"No," said Blaine. "Use your head, Chuck." He had one hand on my chest, the other on Freddy's, pushing both ways. "Don't forget how the land lies!"

I stood panting, my jaw aching, the lump on my diaphragm instantly hard and knotted again. Blaine was right; I could see Freddy's point of view, even respected him for it. Giovanni and Arturo, appearing behind Freddy, took him and finally dragged him politely to the door.

The blood was pounding in my brain, alive, crawling with adrenalin; I needed release. I remembered Munton's grinning eager face in the background, slavering for the thud of blows. I said, "I think I'll take on Munton, while I'm in the mood. That son of a bitch has been asking for it."

Munton's face wiped itself clean. He sat back in his chair. "You'll go up for assault and battery," he cried sharply. "I warn you, stand off."

"Take it easy, Chuck," said Blaine. "Take it easy."

I could have wept from sheer impotence; I could have broken chairs, smashed mirrors, committed a mountain of excesses.

"Go take a cold shower," said Blaine anxiously. "Cool off."

I turned, walked outside. After a moment Blaine came loping after, to make sure I didn't go looking for Freddy, although Freddy was big enough to take care of himself.

I looked back at him; he came to a halt, like an eager dog ordered to go home, then turned back into the hotel.

I went down to the beach, walked along the sand, taking deep breaths. Someone came out on the terrace, whistled shrilly, waved. I paid no heed, wandered morosely down to where the surf thrashed up against the rocks.

Twilight came; I turned back to the hotel. Arturo looked out through the doorway. "Telephone for you, signor, a few minutes ago. I try to call you."

"For me?"

Arturo bowed politely. I pushed through the door.

"Not now," said Arturo. "Fifteen minutes ago."

I walked quickly through the tables to Giovanni's office. "Someone called me on the telephone?"

"Yes, signor. Fifteen minutes ago. A lady," and Giovanni looked knowing.

"Who was it? Did she leave any message?"

"No, signor. I tell her you were not in at the moment."

I stared at the black box, the silent hard plastic. "Did she say she'd call back?"

"No, signor," said Giovanni politely, returning to his work without interest.

I stood irresolutely waiting, then said, "If there's another call —" I changed my mind. "I'll wait in the bar for a while."

"Very well, signor."

I turned away. The telephone rang. I twisted, reached but Giovanni had the phone. "*Si, si?*" politely.

I waited, fuming, boiling inside. "For me?"

Giovanni held the instrument away from him, looked at it. "Just a minute, signorina." He turned deliberately. "For you, signor."

I snatched the phone. "Hello?"

"Chuck?" A soft hushed voice, thick with emotion. "I'm so glad I got you; I tried before…"

"Where are you? What's the matter?"

"Oh, Chuck, I'm scared…I can't stand it any more, I want to get away!"

I could hardly speak. "Can you — what do you —"

"I've got to hurry…" Her voice faded, as if she had turned away from the phone.

"I can't hear you," I said, tense as a clock-spring.

Her voice came back, a rush of words. "Oh, Chuck, I'm frightened! All of a sudden — I want to leave!"

"Meet me out on the road in half an hour."

"I can't!"

"Can't?"

"I don't dare…I don't dare!"

"I'll bring the police."

"No!"

"Then what — where can I meet you?"

During a pause, a second, two seconds, three seconds, I heard the humming of the wires. Then she said in an excited voice, "There's a little beach below our house; it's our private beach. I'll go down the back way and meet you on the beach. You'll have to bring a boat."

"What time?"

"At ten o'clock. No, eleven."

"I'll be there at ten; you come as quick as you can. How will I know the beach?"

"You'll see our house; I'll turn on my bedroom light. Chuck…"

"What?"

"I've got to go." With astonishing suddenness the line was dead.

I looked at my watch. Ten minutes after seven. Three hours. At the table by the door were Blaine, Munton and Oleg. Hortense was gone. At the other tables sat people I did not know, but then I really didn't know any of them; I felt as if I were walking through a tremendous doll house, with artificial figures sitting by artificial food and drink.

I walked past Blaine, Munton and Oleg; they looked pitiful, weak, lost, ineffectual. I nodded, went past, outside, marched up the hill to the green convertible. In the seat, where I had crumpled and thrown it, was Kex's bill of sale. I tenderly smoothed it, tucked it in my wallet.

Kex's car or not, I needed it. Foolish idea in the first place, throwing away a good car.

I went back to the hotel, packed my bag, paid my bill, left the hotel by the rear entrance, locked the bag in the convertible.

Eight o'clock. I sauntered along to the beach. The fishermen were rigging the fishing lights, folding their nets. I picked out a small beamy rowboat, and after considerable sign language, persuaded the two fishermen that two thousand lire in the hand was better than a problematical thousand lire which they might fish out of the sea. The owner of the boat wanted to come with me; this I refused, and as the evening was calm, the water like a satin bedspread, I was allowed to row myself away from the beach.

It was still very early — eight-thirty. Twilight glowed through the overcast; the mountains came down into the sea like animals at a waterhole, one after the other, down the distance, blurring and finally merging with sea and sky. Above was the town, the superimposed square shapes, like a cubist painting.

I rowed quietly, discovering relief in the use of my muscles, in the yield of the water. A psychiatrist gives a neurotic a chunk of clay, lets him knead away his frustrations. Rowing, the swirl of the water under the oars seemed to perform the same service: my breath came slower, the blood in my veins felt less like vinegar.

There was the Villa Sirenia, a gray three-storied jut on a crag, with a curve of white beach a few yards beyond.

The time was nine o'clock. As I watched a light snapped on in one of the upper windows. It flickered, moved, steadied; I rested, looked up at it, projecting a message by telepathy. The light stayed calm. Time went by, the little boat rising and falling gently. The fishermen rowed out on the sea, their lights directed into the depths to charm and bemuse the fish.

Nine-thirty came and went; I began to sidle in to the shore. At quarter of ten I beached the boat; the gravel crunched loud as I pulled the hull up ahead of the tide. The beach was empty, and Villa Sirenia was out of sight, up over the rocks.

Ten o'clock came. I walked back and forth, stopping at each round-trip to listen at the spot where the path came down from the house.

Ten-fifteen, ten-thirty. No sound, no footfall. Overcast swathed the moon, but the night was not entirely dark: a kind of luminous obscurity showed rocks and beach and boat. The black mountain leaned over my shoulder; behind was the sea and the far sprinkling of fishermen's lights.

At ten-forty-five, I paced faster, listened for longer periods, climbed a few steps up the path. At eleven I paced no longer, but stood staring up the path. At eleven-five I climbed a hundred feet toward the house, paused. No sound. Suppose there were another path down to the beach? I hurried back down, scanned the pallid swath of sand. Empty and lifeless. I made a check through the dark to make sure there was no other approach to the house.

My watch said quarter after eleven; she was definitely late. I started up the path once more, step by step, closer and closer, up under the great pale house. The path led under a retaining wall, around to stone steps. Here I paused, wondering what I was doing up here, wondering what I should be doing next. I felt ineffectual and a little foolish.

Perhaps — the thought sidled unpleasantly into my mind — perhaps Betty had changed her mind. Suppose I were discovered lurking here. What could I say? ... But there had been real fear in Betty's voice. Fear of what? Out here in the night, under the dank stones, nothing seemed too melodramatic. After all — people were killed every day, every hour, in circumstances much less extravagant. I stood uncertainly first on one foot, then the other; ashamed to do nothing, afraid to leave, and highly dubious about taking any positive action.

I began to feel sheepish and mean. Suppose she actually were in trouble? Here I stood irresolute, afraid of committing an indiscretion. So I stood biting my lips, clenching my hands, looking up the steps, looking back down the path toward the beach. After five minutes I decided that the very least I could do was make a cautious reconnaissance. Perhaps by luck I might see Betty. I knew the location of her room; it might be possible, by some means or another, to climb up the wall — although if the side of the house were the sheer stone face it appeared to be from the sea, I thought this feat beyond my abilities.

I started up, one stealthy step at a time, came out on a sun-terrace, a flagged area surrounded by a low stone wall, with wrought-iron garden furniture scattered here and there.

Above me was the sheer face of the house, dim light glowing from two or three of the windows. High up on the top floor was Betty's window, absolutely inaccessible. I considered tossing up a rock, and decided not. The French windows giving on the terrace were dark. I cautiously rounded the corner, into a garden; I smelled geraniums, felt grass underfoot. I stood frozen-still. Down from a second floor window came a low voice. I pressed back against the wall.

The sound was not repeated. After a minute or two I took a deep breath and looked up; the window was half-open but quite dark. As I looked a white arm reached out, drew the window shut. Someone perhaps had awakened from a dream.

I crossed the garden, approached the house. A thick yellow bull's eye glowed with light from within. I pressed my face to the glass, moved up and down, trying to locate a clear spot. The glass was old, mottled; striations distorted the view. A vermilion shape, changing and flickering, was a fire. I assumed that I was looking into the big living room. A dark form moved; there was the flicker of a face, a hand. The form drifted across the room, melting and merging with other forms and shapes. There seemed to be someone sitting in a chair; the murmur of conversation drifted through the wall. I listened, but the voices were indistinguishable.

I heard other sounds from up the hill; the soft closing of the gate, the crunch and clack of feet coming down the steps. I shrank back, then stopped. It might be Betty. If it were, I wanted to stop her before she entered the house... No, it couldn't be Betty. Betty was in the house, unable to leave. Freddy? What would Freddy be doing out this time of night?

But it was Freddy. He switched on the colored light, came slowly down the walk. He wore an uneasy, absorbed expression. I watched him from the shadow of the house; he came directly toward me. I could see his lips moving; he was whispering to himself, or he might have been whistling softly.

The corner of the house cut off my view; I heard him put his key in the heavy old lock. The door opened; I stepped quickly forward. Freddy was inside; the door was swinging back. I caught it just before it thudded, just before the latch clicked home.

Now — Freddy might notice the door hadn't closed. I stepped to the corner, waited. No one came out. Back I went to the door, eased it open; slow — slow — half an inch. Voices came down the arched corridor: Dannister's voice, then Freddy's indecisive mutter.

Now I was scared — scared more than I could ever remember. I shoved the door open another foot, looked down the tiled hall. I could see into the end of the living room opposite the fireplace, the ends of the two long tables, two amber sidelights on the wall. To the left was the staircase and a dim alcove below. I told myself that if need be I could duck into the alcove, and gingerly set foot in the house.

I was exposed now. If anyone left the living room I would find myself in a more than embarrassing position — especially since I was hardly a popular person around the Dannister house. But somehow I found myself in the house; the die was cast. I closed the door, the lock clicked; I took a long stride to the alcove, stood listening.

"— bad enough without making it worse," a voice was saying. It was neither Freddy nor Alfred Dannister; it was someone else, and it was a voice full of unctuous mockery, a voice I had never heard before.

"It's trouble which you've made entirely for yourself." This was Dannister.

The stranger spoke with a sinister rising note in his voice. "I wouldn't go quite that far, Alfred."

"I'll take care of him," Freddy pleaded. "I got that other guy good; let me sock Uncle James."

"No," said Dannister dryly, "you've done enough socking."

"I'll shoot him," said Freddy.

"No," said Dannister. "Your Uncle James has us in a position where, for the moment, we don't — quite — want — him — dead..."

I tore my mind away. Now — while I had the chance — where was Betty? Upstairs in her room. This would be up one flight, to the right, the full length of the house. With luck, with desperate daring, I might find her... I started up the stairs, two silent elastic steps at a time.

I peered over the landing. The upper hall was empty. The floor was red tile, covered by a heavy gray runner; the walls were fine dark wainscoting, with white doors leading off to either side. At the end of the hall must be Betty's room.

I listened. There were various sounds in the house. First there was

the murmur from below. Then somewhere nearby a woman was chant-
ing in soft German; it sounded like a nursery rhyme or a nonsense
verse. Someone was sniffling, or snoring softly; and somewhere someone was making a peculiar intermittent clicking noise.

Well, why hesitate? I stalked swiftly down the hall, stopped at the
door I assumed to be Betty's. I put my hand on the knob, turned,
pushed. Locked.

I looked over my shoulder. The German voice had started another
verse. I had been counting on finding the door open, to give me a place
to slip into. I scratched at the panel.

Behind the door I heard startled movement. I scratched again, said
in a husky voice, "It's Chuck; let me in."

Slow steps came to the door. I thought, suppose I've miscalculated; suppose this is somebody else's room? Well, I'd gone past that. I
scratched. "It's Chuck! Let me in."

Betty's voice, full of astonishment and doubt came from behind the
door. "Chuck?"

"Yes. Open up, let me in."

There was a pause, a long second. Then in a low dreary voice, "I
can't. I'm locked in."

I put my face close to the panel. "How can I get you out?"

"I don't know... Chuck — do they know you're here?"

"No." My mind was racing wildly, not doing any particular thinking,
just turning and twisting in mad circles. I blurted, "Can you tie your
sheets together?"

She gave a small laugh. "Two sheets?"

Two sheets would be good for eight feet, when knots were tied.
From her window to the rocks was forty or fifty feet.

"Who's got the key?"

"My father... You'd better get out of here, Chuck... You'd better not
let anyone catch you..."

Long hard steps sounded on the stairs. I jumped away from Betty's
door, tried the first door on the right. But — too late. Freddy stood
stock-still in the hall, staring at me as if I were a gorilla. He opened his
mouth to yell, but his voice was lost and he gave off only a wild gasp. He
started for me, cocking back his fist.

I suppose the honorable thing to do would have been to stand quiet and let Freddy hit me. After all, I was the housebreaker; Freddy was merely protecting his home. But I remembered that Sunday punch. I was angry at being caught; I knew that things couldn't be much worse. I slid along the wall, ducked. Freddy threw a right hook into the wainscoting. I jabbed Freddy in the stomach, pounded him on the cheek; Freddy let out a tremendous bawl.

Dannister's voice came sharply from below. "What's the trouble up there?"

Freddy had no time to talk. He was discouraged, frantic; he swung, connected with the palm of my left hand. My right fist connected with his jaw; he stumbled, ran back in the corridor, fell, lay holding his face.

Dannister's feet sounded heavy. I pulled open a door, ducked through. I was in bad trouble. Dannister had every right and reason to shoot me. I heard Freddy say, "I'll get the gun, I'll get the gun."

I looked around. The room was a pleasant pink and blue bedroom. There had been a clicking noise; it had stopped. A woman sat in a chair. She had been knitting a long formless brown object; I saw she was a very poor knitter.

She was a faded gentle woman — obviously Betty's mother, Mrs. Alfred Dannister. I had seen her face in an old photograph. Since then she had gone a long way downhill. Her eyes were haunted, big, dark, trusting, troubled. Why didn't she scream? Why didn't she draw back, cry?

"James?" she said. "Are you — James?"

Feet were pounding down the hall. I noticed a door half-open into a bathroom; and through the gap I saw another door. With the idea of doubling around my pursuers the way they do in the movies, I ran through. Mrs. Dannister called sadly, urgently after me, "Don't, James! Don't go in there..."

But I was in the bathroom. I glimpsed a peculiar fixture; it looked like a toilet with two seats; then I opened the door, ran into the next room.

I started toward the door; I looked at the bed, halted. Two children sat on the bed. They watched me with wide frightened eyes. They were about twelve, at a guess. On the right was a girl. She was almost pretty, and she looked like Betty. She had Betty's bright eyes, dark blonde hair, but her mouth sagged and glistened. The second child joined her at the waist; they shared a central leg. The second child was misshapen. The head was bald and yellow, the eyelids hung like flaps, and the eyes were far, far apart; a blank smooth patch of skin spread up over the button nose. It had no chin to speak of, and wetness glistened down the front of its neck. It was certainly feeble-minded; the girl-side was rather closer to normal.

The monster-side made a gurgling, sniffling sound; the girl said in a throaty sweet voice, not frightened, "Who are you?"

Behind me Freddy said, "I've got my gun; I'll shoot —"

Dannister said, "*No!* Give me that gun!" I turned slowly. Dannister had the gun — a big .45 automatic. "I'll shoot him myself," said Dannister grimly. He jerked his head. "Out in the hall, Musgrave."

Chapter XXII

I said in a shaky voice, "If you're going to shoot — shoot…Get it over with…"

Dannister looked down at the sick little creature, half-girl, half-monster, then back to me. "Not here, Musgrave."

I turned, walked out the door, half-willing to be shot, sick with life, sick of the pain, the ugliness, the discord, the grinding colors, the sour tastes, the futile hope, the tragic defeats. I saw life from a new blinding perspective, a revelation so sad and terrible that I no longer cared. Birth, agonized contortions to stay alive, death. Dannister felt what was in my mind; it must have provided him sardonic amusement. I think it saved my life.

"Down into the living room, Musgrave. You'll want to meet — James Hilfstone."

I walked slowly down the hall; Dannister came after.

Freddy yelped, "Are you gonna shoot him, father? He hit me, he took Betty out, he broke into our house."

Dannister said in a tight dry voice, "I know all about what he has done." And to me: "To the left, Musgrave."

I came into the living room. James Hilfstone was smoking a fresh cigar, his legs stretched comfortably to the blaze. He did not rise, he did not offer to shake hands. I turned an accusing eye on Dannister, as much as to say, I don't look like this guy! And Dannister nodded, as if to reply, I know you don't.

"So this," said Hilfstone, in a lazy baritone voice, "this is my impersonator! Poor old Kex, what he wouldn't do for a laugh."

I looked sidelong at Dannister. "Just what am I supposed to do?"

Dannister stood spare, gray, drawn. Over his shoulder peered Freddy, excited, breathless, angry. I said, "Before you get any — reckless ideas with that gun — you better listen to my side of the story."

Hilfstone laughed, puffed contentedly on his cigar.

"What are you laughing about?" I asked him, tense and cold inside. Chuckling, Hilfstone turned, looked into the fire with an air of disassociating himself from the proceedings.

I said, "You'll laugh from the other side of your face when Lieutenant Piretti comes to get you."

Hilfstone's chuckle was softer, patently forced. "I have nothing to worry about."

"Except that you were seen dropping the rock on Kex. That's called murder."

Dannister's mouth twitched.

"Murder?" asked Hilfstone. "What's that got to do with me?"

"Acting dumb, eh?" I looked at Dannister. "Do you know that he killed Kex? Dropped a big rock on him?"

Dannister's face moved in the grimmest of smiles. "Do you think I care what he did to Kex?"

I studied Dannister closely and felt no reassurance. The man was already past the end of his rope, he was holding on through sheer habit.

"Personally," I said, "I don't care either. But they're going to catch him."

Hilfstone shook his head. "I don't think so."

"Then you admit it."

Hilfstone gave me a look of limpid inquiry. "What difference does it make?"

"It doesn't make any difference," said Dannister. There was a chilling flavor to his voice. No one got it but me. Hilfstone was too complacent; Freddy too thick. I had heard it before, the night Hester Ryen's voice had come to me through the panels of her door. Dannister sounded light, almost easy, as if a troublesome decision had been made.

"You see," said Hilfstone, "I'm a guest of Alfred's. He'll see that there's a minimum of annoyance."

"In other words — Dannister is hiding you out?"

"If you like to put it that way."

"Well," said Dannister, "I'm afraid you're wrong, James."

"Eh?" asked Hilfstone blinking.

"I'm not hiding you out..."

Hilfstone looked subtly uneasy. "Suit yourself. You know what'll happen."

"You've figured the situation a little too narrowly, James."

"You've got others to consider, Alfred."

"I've considered, James."

Freddy said impatiently, "What are you going to do, Father?"

Dannister smiled, looked from Hilfstone to me, tenderly to Freddy, as if he had a present for him.

There was a pounding at the door — stern, official, uncompromising.

I laughed with sheer relief. "They're here for you, Hilfstone!"

Hilfstone half-rose from his chair. "How could they know —"

"In Positano, everybody knows everything!"

The knocking came again, louder. A hard voice spoke in Italian.

Freddy said eagerly, "Shall I let them in? And they'll arrest him." He pointed to me.

"Yes, Freddy," said Dannister quietly. "Let them in."

Hilfstone said desperately, "You know what that means, Alfred. Everything comes out; I hold nothing back."

Dannister just smiled; I cringed back from the look around his eyes.

Freddy turned away toward the door.

Dannister slowly raised the .45, carefully aimed, pulled the trigger. The back of Freddy's blond head became a grisly sight.

Hilfstone was on his feet, pale, lower lip hanging, trembling. Dannister turned to him. The pounding on the door became a frantic thudding.

Dannister was smiling. "James — you didn't think it would come to this, did you?"

"Don't, Alfred — don't!"

Dannister carefully raised the big automatic, fired.

Hilfstone was dead.

I was next. Dannister turned to me. My knees were like warm mush. I knew how Hilfstone felt. Freddy and even Kex had escaped this. I staggered, half-fell to the side, trying to drop behind the overstuffed chair. The big black hole in the gun followed me; I saw the red flash, felt the passage of the slug; he had missed. I was behind the chair; all Dannister had to do was step forward, turn down the muzzle of the gun.

The door splintered, there was the sound of footsteps. I was alone in the room. I slowly got to my knees. Hilfstone's chest was leaking blood behind me; in front of me lay Freddy as dignified as he had ever looked.

Dannister was climbing the stairs; I knew what he intended. I tottered down the corridor, looked up after him; his long legs were disappearing around the landing. I hesitated, started slowly up.

Behind me the door gave a heart-rending groan as something heavy hit it. Then silence. From upstairs, the sound of a door opening. A muffled girl's voice said, "It's late, Daddy —"

Two shots, then a mutter, a scream. "Alfred —"

Another shot.

I looked over the landing, prepared to duck, if necessary. A stout gray woman looked out into the corridor, jumped back, slammed the door. I heard the bolt click. This would be the German maid.

The front door groaned.

Dannister came out into the hall, walked with steady steps to the end of the corridor. This was Betty's room. He reached in his pocket, pulled out the key. I didn't think of what I was doing; I'm no hero. I climbed up into the corridor, raced on tiptoe at Dannister's back. He heard me at the last minute, turned. I slung an arm around his neck, pulled with an overwhelming surge of power that would have thrown a bull. Dannister hurtled to the floor. I stepped on his wrist, grabbed the gun. He raised up on his elbow, looking at me.

"Give me that gun."

"Humph. Don't be silly." I backed to the door, turned the key, pushed the door open with my rump.

Dannister gained his feet. Behind him the front door at last burst open; the thud of steps sounded loud, heavy.

Dannister took two paces toward me — I backed into Betty's room. She was sitting on the bed.

Dannister's face was long, drawn, white; his hair hung down his forehead. "Give me that gun…"

"You're not talking sense, Dannister."

He turned to Betty, looked at her.

She said in a low voice, "Oh, give him the gun, Chuck."

"And have him shoot me — and you?"

Dannister took another two steps forward; he was going to wrestle with me.

"Give me the gun…I won't shoot you."

Betty said, "Give it to him, Chuck. He wants it for himself."

I hesitated, then shook my head. "I can't…It's just like pointing it at him, pulling the trigger." I went to the window, threw it out.

Footsteps came pounding down the corridor. Dannister strode past me. I saw his grim profile, his mouth tight. He looked neither to right nor left, neither to Betty nor myself. He was gone.

Lieutenant Piretti dashed into the room, automatic ready. "Who went out the window; who was it?"

"That was Alfred Dannister, Lieutenant."

Piretti went to look down into the blackness; I turned to Betty.

She said, "Don't look at me like that."

I was thinking of the scar on Betty's hip.

Chapter XXIII

Mr. Caldecott, of Bray, Medlary, Caldecott, Chivers and Bray, the London solicitors, flew down to arrange the funeral and put the house up for sale.

Lieutenant Piretti took depositions from Betty and me at the Hotel Medaglione in Sorrento, where Betty had taken a room; then announced that so far as he was concerned the case was closed. "There will no doubt be scandal-mongering in the Roman journals," he told us knowingly, "but this is not the official position; we conduct our affairs with all possible discretion. You are free to go." He bowed and departed.

I said to Betty, "Well, what now?"

"I don't know."

"Then I guess I'll have to make the decisions. Jump in the car, we'll head north."

She hung her head, looked away. I took her arm, led her unresisting to the car. I paid the bill; we started north. Five miles passed behind us.

"There's all kinds of things we can do," I said. "We can drive to Paris, to Belgium, to Denmark. We can sell the car in Paris, fly over to Ireland, or Cornwall. Or we can take a slow freighter to Tahiti or Zanzibar or the Andaman Islands…"

She sat looking straight ahead. "Chuck," she said, "do you know what I was going to do that very night?"

"No."

"I was going to hang myself."

"Betty —" words failed me.

She went on, almost with relish. "I had it all planned; I'd loop my belt over the top of the door, where it wouldn't slip."

"You see how wrong that would have been, don't you?"

"I'm not so sure..."

"But look — we've got all our lives ahead of us! You're under a strain, a shock — you're grieving."

She shook her head. "I loved my mother — and Freddy — but I don't miss them."

"Well, you can forget the whole damn business; we'll never see Positano again."

"I don't know what to do."

"When we get to Rome, we'll get married."

"No, Chuck — you don't want to marry me."

"No?"

"No. You know what I am...Half of a monster."

"What happened to the other half?"

"It died."

"Do you remember it?"

She nodded. "I was five. They operated on us in Vienna."

"What I don't understand is why your father was afraid of Hilfstone — or Kex. Having an abnormal child isn't a disgrace."

"Oh — but it is. It *is*!"

"I don't see it."

"You don't know the circumstances."

I was silent. She licked her lips. I knew it was coming; it had been roiling around inside her; here it came up, like vomit, and it would do her good to get rid of it.

"It's a long story," she said hesitantly.

I reached out, took her hand. It was cold and trembling.

"My father was an American. He was born in Richmond, Virginia; his father was American, his mother was English. When my father was seven, his mother, that's my grandmother, took a trip home to England, and the day after she left, my grandfather was killed by a bull. My grandmother found she was pregnant when she arrived in England; she stayed in England, bore her child — this was a girl. A year or two later she married her second husband, Lloyd Powan Hilfstone, and by him she had a third child who was James. So now she had three children — my father, Alfred Dannister, who stayed in

Richmond and grew up there, and the girl, Laura, who took the name Hilfstone — and James."

I said, "Oh," in a rather weak voice.

"Back in Richmond my father grew up. When he was twenty-three he went to England to visit his mother. And now — I'm not quite sure what happened. It was a rather complicated series of events. He went to this little town in Dorset where his mother, now Mrs. Lloyd Hilfstone, lived. But she was in Scotland, or London, I'm not sure where. Anyway, she wasn't expecting him and he didn't know where to find her. But he did meet the vicar of the village and was invited to a garden party. Here he met my mother. Someone introduced them, hastily — or perhaps they weren't introduced. She was nineteen then — and of course — she was Laura Hilfstone. His sister..." She paused, looked up at the sky. "I've read somewhere that people who look alike are attracted to each other... Maybe that's why my father and mother fell in love at first sight. They naturally didn't know who each other was — then. Well, my father was very dashing; he swept poor mother off her feet. They ran off the same night; they were married in Southampton. Now somewhere in here — I've never found out when — they found out the true state of affairs... But they were young, they were in love; they told each other the taboo against brother and sister marrying was meaningless — they'd run away; no one would ever know."

"I admire 'em," I said. "It took guts."

"Yes," she said in an abstracted voice, "I've always thought so... But you know my father; once he made up his mind nothing could stop him. He'd found the woman he wanted, and it didn't make any difference to him that it was his sister... She became pregnant; she had twins. I was one of them. We were stuck together at the hip." Her voice went low, contralto. "I remember my twin very well. It was a little boy — named Paul. But it was — well, it was worse than Edward."

"Edward was the — well, the second one?"

She nodded. "You can imagine how my mother felt. She cried, she was frantic. My father told her it could happen to anyone; my mother said, no, they had sinned; this was their reckoning. She wouldn't let us be operated on. I grew up — until I was five — with Paul." She winced, her face twisted. "I tried to tell you the night in Naples — I couldn't."

"You're telling me now. Doesn't it feel good to get it off your chest?"

She went on. "Two years later they had Freddy. Freddy seemed to be perfectly normal. Of course he grew up a little retarded — but at the time they thought he was normal, and finally my father took me to Vienna. We were operated on — but Paul died… I was glad! Oh how glad I was! Not that I hated Paul — but he was so — so terrible."

"You poor little kid."

"And after a while they had twins again — and this time they were all messed up, with only three legs. They couldn't be separated. I was seven then…We came to Positano when I was eight, and we've lived here ever since. My mother went a little out of her head… My father became very remote and stern… And it got worse as I grew older."

"But how did James Hilfstone come into the picture?"

"When I was twelve he came to Positano — somehow he'd found us. He wasn't doing so well; he wanted to borrow money. What it amounted to," she said bitterly, "he blackmailed father… And that's about how life was until — you came. I went to school in Switzerland — those were the happiest times… I didn't like the house at Positano — it was always so dark and gloomy."

"How did you find out about this — mess?"

"Oh — I always seem to have known it… My mother was always crying, or praying… I don't think Freddy quite understood — but he knew Uncle James was bad, and that's why he went for you."

"I suppose Kex ran the whole thing down pretty fast."

She frowned. "What I still don't understand is why did Uncle James kill Kex?"

"Kex had a cute habit of checking up on everybody. He looked me up. He found I'd been kicked out of West Point… He probably did the same for Hilfstone. He must have found out something pretty bad to make Hilfstone want to bump him off."

We sat silent for awhile, circling the Bay of Naples.

I said, "Well, where is it? Norway, India, Mexico?"

"Chuck, you don't want to marry me — do you?"

"Of course I do."

"Suppose — we have *children*!"

"We *want* children!"

"But suppose —"

"If they're freaks, we'll drown 'em and keep working at it till we manage some normal ones..."

"Oh, Chuck — would you take the chance?"

"Just try me."

She smiled wanly. "I already did." She slowly slid across the seat, rested her head against my shoulder.

"So — where'll it be? Timbuctoo? Moscow? We've got the whole world to honeymoon in..."

"I'll have to think awhile, Chuck..."

Jack Vance was born in 1916 to a well-off California family that, as his childhood ended, fell upon hard times. As a young man he worked at a series of unsatisfying jobs before studying mining engineering, physics, journalism and English at the University of California Berkeley. Leaving school as America was going to war, he found a place as an ordinary seaman in the merchant marine. Later he worked as a rigger, surveyor, ceramicist, and carpenter before his steady production of sf, mystery novels, and short stories established him as a full-time writer.

His output over more than sixty years was prodigious and won him three Hugo Awards, a Nebula Award, a World Fantasy Award for lifetime achievement, as well as an Edgar from the Mystery Writers of America. The Science Fiction and Fantasy Writers of America named him a grandmaster and he was inducted into the Science Fiction Hall of Fame.

His works crossed genre boundaries, from dark fantasies (including the highly influential *Dying Earth* cycle of novels) to interstellar space operas, from heroic fantasy (the *Lyonesse* trilogy) to murder mysteries featuring a sheriff (the Joe Bain novels) in a rural California county. A Vance story often centered on a competent male protagonist thrust into a dangerous, evolving situation on a planet where adventure was his daily fare, or featured a young person setting out on a perilous odyssey over difficult terrain populated by entrenched, scheming enemies.

Late in his life, a world-spanning assemblage of Vance aficionados came together to return his works to their original form, restoring material cut by editors whose chief preoccupation was the page count of a pulp magazine. The result was the complete and authoritative *Vance Integral Edition* in 44 hardcover volumes. Spatterlight Press is now publishing the VIE texts as ebooks, and as print-on-demand paperbacks.

Colophon

This book was printed using Adobe Arno Pro as the primary text font, with NeutraFace used on the cover.

This title was created from the digital archive of the Vance Integral Edition, a series of 44 books produced under the aegis of the author by a worldwide group of his readers. The VIE project gratefully acknowledges the editorial guidance of Norma Vance, as well as the cooperation of the Department of Special Collections at Boston University, whose John Holbrook Vance collection has been an important source of textual evidence.

Special thanks to R.C. Lacovara, Patrick Dusoulier, Koen Vyverman, Paul Rhoads, Chuck King, Gregory Hansen, Suan Yong, and Josh Geller for their invaluable assistance preparing final versions of the source files.

Source: Norma Vance, Harrison Watson, Jr.; Digitize: Richard Chandler, Joel Hedlund, Paul Rhoads, John A. Schwab; Diff: Joe Ormond, Steve Sherman; Tech Proof: Hans van der Veeke; Text Integrity: Patrick Dusoulier, Helmut Hlavacs, Steve Sherman; Implement: John McDonough, Hans van der Veeke; Security: Paul Rhoads; Compose: Andreas Irle; Comp Review: Christian J. Corley, Marcel van Genderen, Paul Rhoads, Robin L. Rouch; Update Verify: Paul Rhoads, Robin L. Rouch; RTF-Diff: Patrick Dusoulier, Charles King; Textport: Patrick Dusoulier; Proofread: Erik Arendse, Angus Campbell-Cann, Patrick Dymond, Marcel van Genderen, Jasper Groen, Evert Jan de Groot, Lori Hanley, Patrick Hudson, Willem Timmer, Hans van der Veeke, Dirk Jan Verlinde, Dave Worden

Artwork (maps based on original drawings by Jack and Norma Vance):

Paul Rhoads, Christopher Wood

Book Composition and Typesetting: Joel Anderson

Art Direction and Cover Design: Howard Kistler

Proofing: Christian J. Corley, Steve Sherman

Jacket Blurb: John Vance

Management: John Vance, Koen Vyverman

www.ingramcontent.com/pod-product-compliance
Lightning Source LLC
Chambersburg PA
CBHW030312200626
46816CB00002BA/870